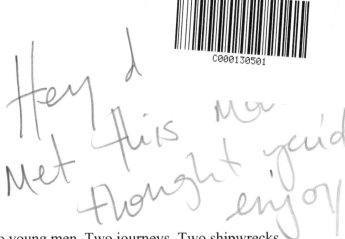

Hey d
Met this Mo-
thought youd enjoy

Two young men. Two journeys. Two shipwrecks.
Over 500 years between them but connected by a
unique object.

Can the discovery of a Saxon sword hilt on an island
off Helsinki really shed light on the Battle of
Hastings?
Stuart Richardson, a museum curator thinks so. But
is his judgement clouded . . . by being bewitched?

Love Mama Ⓧ

To Elian

JACK AND MO

Mark Freeman

Enjoy!

Mark Freeman

W

First published by Wordcarving, 2022

Copyright © Mark Freeman, 2022

All rights reserved

This is a work of fiction. Names, characters, places and incidents are either
the products of the author's imagination or are used fictitiously, and any
resemblance to actual persons, living or dead, institutions, business
establishments, companies, events or places is entirely coincidental.

ISBN 978-1-7396151-0-9

Cover design by Karen Wilks

Wordcarving.org

For Caroline and Ruby

The sun was low on this October morning, the light soft and yellow and it skimmed the rocks below the cliff as if refracted through a jar of honey. Shallow waves lapped the sand a hundred metres out, setting a hypnotic, tranquil rhythm. Deep shadows defined shapes on the surfaces of scattered plates of sandstone that littered the beach, displaced from the strata as the cliff succumbed to successive bites of erosion. A tilted plane of rock bore ripples identical to those ridges on the sand which are changed by the sea with each rise and fall of the tide, but this was created on a single day some ninety million years ago. Why that day? My mind drifted to the event which would have followed the outgoing tide that uncovered this fragile pattern, impressed by the waves into the sand. It surely must have been an inundation, sand and silt from inland suspended in river water rushing to the coast. Trapped in wide estuarine lagoons the particles slowly settled, finely filling each trough and surmounting each peak to produce a layer, subject to such later forces as to turn it into rock. Over how long did successive layers build up? Was the flood annual or rare? What else was trapped? My eyes caught hold of a lump, two feet wide, protruding from the flat surface of another sandstone boulder. Is that the shape of a toe angled to the body of a dinosaur foot? The impression made by one step several aeons ago, filled by silt, compressed into rock and then, as the crumbling cliff allowed it to break free, it fell and turned upside down on to the beach. There it stayed, like a death mask impression, not of a face but of the sole of the creature's foot, and not made in the act of dying, but death may soon have followed with the catastrophe of the flood, capturing that step for all time. The spectre of death stalks the living.

I have always had a fascination with time. Nothing happens. Then something happens. Then nothing happens. Then something happens. The gaps can be minutes, a few generations, or many times the existence of humans on this planet. Sometimes when something happens it leaves a physical trace of that time, that event. This is what drew me into the study of history, the detective work around found objects, the construction of a story.

09.59…Ten o'clock. I turned the iron key in the lock of the heavy oak double doors and swung them open, light flooding in. Nothing happened. There was no queue of people, no flock of birds taking off, no lightning striking amid a wild storm. This was not unusual. Ten or twenty people on an average day may visit the museum, and often the first might not turn up until late morning. A school party sometimes pre-booked for an hour in the day, the anticipation of which was not necessarily to be relished. It took some skill to hold the attention of twenty twelve-year-olds, energised by their release from classroom shackles. A skill I felt I didn't possess.

Christine had doubts about my suitability to be the curator of a provincial museum. A first in history had led me into a postgraduate course, a PhD, and the desire for a future in the academic world. Early Medieval English history was my thing, but universities didn't seem enthused by my smattering of published papers when I applied for junior fellowships. The competition was just too great.

'Look, I think in practical terms you've got to start looking at something else.' Christine tried to raise my spirits after another rejection. There wasn't a lot I was qualified to do. The world of finance didn't appeal, and I had seen too many teachers burnt out by the cruel dictators named protocol and bureaucracy. Then, scanning a newspaper website, an advert popped up. It seemed like a good match. My thesis had been on the aristocracy in pre-conquest southern England, and a museum not far from the site of that conquest needed a new curator.

The interview was a breeze. They seemed as desperate for a curator as I was for a job. Christine was not delighted, but stoically accepted the move down to the south coast. Her job as a teacher was transferable, and she found a post as deputy head at a school not far from the museum.

The museum's collection was diverse. It had been assembled over time from the donations of Victorian philanthropists who had gathered pieces according to what interested them, or what had turned up on their travels, the locals keen to sell. I walked in front of a dark glass cabinet, filled with arrangements of stuffed birds perched above small mammals. The next room had ethnographic exhibits, West African drums and a Hawai'ian Royal cloak made from the bright yellow feathers of a thousand tiny birds, now extinct. All interesting in their own way, but one thing was notably absent. There was not a single relic from the most momentous battle fought on English soil, where the Norman invaders had routed the English defenders. A battle which defined the identity of the English people.

Why was nothing found at the site of the battle? It had had archaeological surveys one after another, trenches dug, metal and bone sought. Other sites of battle in the country had yielded arrowheads, battle-axes, the long bones of horses and bits of armour from the thousands who died in medieval conflagrations. The absence of evidence was a glaring hole in the story of the conquest of England. It raised the question: has the search been in the right place?

These thoughts were fresh when I first arrived at the job. Their energy dissipated over time, and monotony dulled me. But that morning, after opening the doors and nothing happened, something happened. It started a trail that connected the lives of two young men, separated by over five hundred years, Jack and Mo.

Part One

Jack 1

A rope tightened then creaked as the breeze filled the sail. Dusk was falling and a lamp lit on the bow of the barge cast a skein of shadow deep into the empty hull. They were returning home after the last load of the day, timber, destined for the Low Countries, now on its way. Jack hung by one arm as he swung his way back along the rail. His other hand felt in his pouch to check it was still there. A lucky find. The sand had shifted exposing what looked like a piece of metal and he had reached down to pick it up. Turning it over the form took hold, and unmistakably settled as the hilt of a sword. The pommel was heavy to counterbalance a blade which had long disappeared, rusted and powdered away to a stump. Jack let his palm and fingers circle and grip where once a warrior had placed his, swinging this powerful weapon.

His master guided the vessel close to the shore and Jack vaulted onto the beach of the inlet. He made his way up the valley side, his route guided by a vast ancient oak, its complex of limbs, right angled elbows and knees, silhouetted against the darkening sky. Under the oak nestled a tiny one room cottage. He pulled aside the heavy door flap to enter. There was a faint glow from hearth, and the smell of still warm pottage left for him by his mother Ann who was already asleep next to his wheezing father Thomas. Jack filled his stomach, settled down and drew a blanket over his aching body. An owl called close by, tooting for a response. Not the call and response he had sometimes heard rhythmically chanted from the church in the village. No, this call didn't guarantee a response; there was tension in the pause, a future still uncertain. After five moments, or was it fifteen, or even fifty, he heard a return call from a distance. Somehow that gave him hope.

Watery light broke through the darkness as the next day was announced. The cock had been busy with practice crowing for some minutes, but it was this final blasted one that stirred Jack. The cottage sat halfway up the valley side, next to a pond, and from there you could look across the top of a veil of early morning mist obscuring the valley bottom and the tidal waters beneath, towards the woods that covered the side opposite. Oak, ash, beech, birch and thorn. And some hazel. Dense woodland covered this part of southern England, the trees so close together that in places it was said that a horse could not be steered through. Impenetrable, it had been known since ancient times as the waste of Anderida. A place where fugitives could hide from the justice of the courts, and where fairies and pixies could dwell, the bubble of their existence unpunctured by the lancet of church and God. But now Man's appetite was eating into the forest. Trees were felled and turned into beams and planks for export to Flanders and Holland where a good price was paid for building materials. The oak with its great strength combined with its angled limbs was perfect for shipbuilding. Smaller branches were cooked into charcoal, and then smelted with the red earth that underlaid the forest floor to produce a glowing flow which cooled into pigs of iron.

Jack had escaped the forge and foundry, with its noise and smoke and heat. After rising he watched the mist in the valley disperse to be slowly replaced by wisps and trails from the scattered iron workings opposite. A few months working there was enough, and when his father had talked to the barge master, he leapt at the chance to be a ship's boy. He yearned for adventure, and this could be a route away from the suffocating atmosphere of home.

Ann was already awake and mustering a meagre fire from last night's embers. Her normally plump cheeks had been diminished by the privations of midwinter.

'Father's bellows are bad,' she announced. 'Got worse while you were up and down on the water yesterday.'

Thomas was leaning forward, hawking up what phlegm would shift. His heavy working days were behind him, but he could just manage the acre given to him by old Master Yates by way of pension for his long service on the land. Yates also helped at this time of year with supplementing the dwindling stores from last year's harvest.

'I'll have to see what Marion's got for that cough,' Ann added.

'Don't worry, I'll go over there presently,' said Jack.

Widow Marion lived on the other side of the pond, in a wooden lean-to, backed up against a sandstone outcrop. She had been the midwife to the village, and had attended Ann through five labours, five lifeless babies. Then came Jack, crying and squalling to everyone's delight.

Jack slipped out of the cottage and squatted by the pond, first checking there was no one looking. He pushed up on his pouch and out came his treasured find. He swirled it in the water, then with his fingernails picked at the encrustations of sand and ancient mud. The round pommel at the end of the handle showed metal in places as the dirt came off, grey and yellow and then, fixed centrally, an egg shape smooth beneath his fingers, going from brown to deep red. This must be stone not metal. Could it be a precious stone? A ruby?

Why, this must be worth something, he thought. A blackbird's egg size at least. There had been talk in the village, passed down through many lifetimes that a great battle had been fought close by, but nothing had been found and the story had dwindled. This must have come from a knight's sword, or even a king's.

He quickly put it back in his pouch and then inside his tunic as Ann and Thomas emerged from the cottage.

'I'll go over and talk to Marion and see what she's got for father,' he said over his shoulder as he hurried away, concealing his newfound treasure and anxious not to reveal what his face might tell.

On the other side of the pond the path rose slightly as the land along the valley side led up towards the village. Past a rocky outcrop he found Marion tipping out a bucket of slops surrounded by chickens clucking and competing for any titbits. She saw Jack and waved as he approached. Always a favourite, he got his hair ruffled as a greeting. Most villagers thought Marion a wise woman, but some said she was cunning, a worker of spells. Tall and not without admirers, she had never remarried after her much older husband had died soon after they were wed. The small plot of land he left her gave her enough to barter for a reasonable existence. Also, her wisdom had value and she received gifts in payment for her help with confinements and illness. She could see through Jack; he was not quite his steady self.

'Father's ailing today, it's his chest again.' Jack came directly to the point. Not wanting to linger too long he edged from foot to foot.

'He had that cough last winter too, it'll see him off if he's not careful.' She retreated into her cottage. 'I've got some pennyrile here, not fresh mind, not at this time of year. And

10

some thyme, that should help clear his phlegm.' He waited at the threshold while she rummaged in the dim light, then she emerged with two bunches of dried herbs. 'Tell Ann to put these in hot water and your father can breathe the vapour with a cloth over his head. Then he can drink the liquor.'

Marion didn't challenge Jack's awkwardness. He was a youngster not yet of age, but she knew he had something to hide. What boy didn't?

Jack trotted back down the path and, where the woods got dense, he veered off between the trees. A few yards in it was as though the universe had changed. In summer the green filtered light had a quality of being underwater, but this was winter, and irregular squeaks and squeals pierced the air as the tall bare trunks rubbed against one another, rocked by the chill wind. A bird let out an alarm call, detecting his human presence. Jack was nervous, burdened by the responsibility of finding a hiding place for his new possession, somewhere no one else could know about. He looked around to check he hadn't been followed. A squirrel's beady eye met his for a second, then it scurried in a flash up the trunk. What are you up to? He felt questioned. The ground wouldn't do, too easy for someone to stumble across, too hard for him to find again. He saw a large oak tree, three massive branches separating just above head height. He hauled himself up into the tree and crouched in the bowl between the branches. It was filled with twigs and decaying leaves. No one could see this nest from the ground, he thought, as he carefully scraped a hole and placed his precious treasure in it, then covered it over. He jumped down and marked the tree with backward glances as he zigzagged round root and stump back to the path, his step a bit lighter than before.

Jack 2

The barge master looked angry as Jack's rush made him slide onto the jetty.

'Come for the ride, have you? You've missed the loading.' Jack tried to explain about his father's illness, but the master was already casting off, and Jack helped raise the single sail. The westerly wind was behind them, and it wouldn't take long to get to the port. They kept pace with the clouds above as the wooded sides of the valley passed behind. Jack's eyes sought the spot on the shore where he found his treasure; there would be no time for more searching today. The inlet broadened to an estuary, wide and shallow with salt pans to the left, and on the right, as they approached, a town grew in scale. Tower, church and windmill sat atop a hill which was ringed like a crown by the masts of ships moored along the strand. In the distance he could see men straining to hoist barrels of wine from inside the hulls then heaving as they rolled them uphill to be stored in the cellars of wealthy merchants, awaiting onward passage around the kingdom. The timber port was further round, and as they came alongside Jack skipped onto the quay to tie up. A land crew was waiting and helped with unloading the lumber. Job done, the master was keen to get off and snarled irritably at Jack. Everyone knew he had a daytime assignation in the town with a woman of easy virtue. It gave Jack an hour to wander. He walked along the strand looking at faces leathery, tanned by sea, salt and wind. These men had seen foreign lands Jack could only dream of. Snatches of conversation about deals and cargoes, ports just visited and those next to visit, storms that threatened and days becalmed excited him and attracted him to a future away from this grey land. The guttural accent of the Flemish tongue was here and there, brought by ships from Antwerp, a port he had heard was rich from the trade of goods conveyed to and received from all parts of the world. And he had heard that a good price could be paid for a gemstone there.

'What are you staring at?' A man spat on the ground in front of him.

'I think I want to go to Antwerp,' Jack answered hesitantly as he came to from his reverie, not sure whether it was the right thing to say.

'Well Antwerp is a fine place, but not the only fine place you can go to. There's a captain in the Ship Inn looking for a cabin boy. Why don't you go and offer yourself up?'

The inn was three streets away. He passed a line of pilgrims ascending steps from a cellar marked by the sign of the seashell where they had lodged overnight. Embarking on the way of St James, to Santiago de Compostela in Spain, fear was etched on their faces. Today would be their first sea journey.

Inside the inn it was dark and reeked of ale. A little light came round the side of the cloth that covered the doorway, but otherwise only the flame from a single candle played toward the back wall. Faintly illuminated, sitting on a bench behind a rough wooden table, were two men. It was hard to make out their faces at first, but while Jack's eyes were adjusting, he could hear one of them murmuring rhythmically. He was shifting coins from one pile to another.

The other man's eyes lifted to Jack, and he raised a hand indicating, don't make a noise. Jack stood uncomfortably until they reached a climax with a loud "thirty shillings". Jack decided to wait until they were ready to acknowledge him, and that took another minute or two of ale being swilled and congratulatory guffawing. When they settled, the man who had done the counting turned his eyes to Jack, the laughter in them replaced with a stern gaze. He was waiting for Jack to tell him his business.

'I was told down at the quay that the captain of a ship for Antwerp might be in this inn.'

'You're brave for a lad. And what business would you be having in Antwerp?' the captain retorted.

Jack didn't know how to respond to such a direct question. Any answer could lead to suspicion that he was harbouring a secret.

'I'm looking for adventure, and it seemed a good place to start,' he replied a little hesitantly, but he felt pleased he had dodged a sword thrust.

'Oh, we can give you adventure all right.' The captain laughed, winking at his mate. 'But we're not headed directly for Antwerp. Given a fair wind we might make it there, but first we'll be visiting the town of London.'

Jack felt deflated. But they would be going to Antwerp in due course, so maybe this could be the voyage for him.

'We can do with another hand. What experience on the water have you had?' Jack told them he was a boy on the log barges. 'Oh, it'll be a bit more up and down where we're going,' the captain joked. 'We're casting off with the tide in the morn.'

Jack rushed back to the timber port, fearful of what course he may have set himself. He just beat his barge master to the gangplank, and they untied for the return journey upstream along the inlet.

*

14

Jack walked over to Marion's cottage that afternoon. She had known him all his life, and he felt he had to tell someone of his plan. If he told his parents, they would use every trick to dissuade him from leaving, but he knew this was the right thing for him to do. It would be better for him to return rich than spend his life ferrying logs.

Marion was in her garden.

'On the morrow I may be going on a journey.' Jack came directly to the point.

'And where might that be to?' Marion barely raised her head as she continued hoeing.

'I'll be going abroad to foreign lands.'

'Oh.' Marion stopped and looked directly in his eyes. 'And who'll be looking after your elders?'

Jack had already thought of this.

'If I get rich on my travels then I can give them what they deserve in their old age when I return. They are young enough to be safe for the next year or two.' He had decided not to tell Marion of his treasure.

'Well, let's hope they last. You can't stop a young man from his adventures. Don't worry, I'll keep them under my gaze.' Marion turned to look at Jack. Who would have thought that that screaming baby who was such a poor suckler would have turned into this strapping youth with his mop of curly brown hair? He had been slow to speak and remained hesitant. Tongue tied as they said. When he was new-born, she had put her little finger into his mouth to see if she could break the tight chord. But it made no difference. Even though he was approaching manhood she still feared for how he might get on in the wider world. She put the hoe down and clutched him to her chest for one last time, hiding a tear behind his back.

On his return Jack veered off the path into the woods, retracing his steps of the previous evening. He climbed up to the bowl of the oak and was relieved to find the hilt as he had left it. He felt the weight of it, his hand tight around the grip. He slipped it between shirt and woollen tunic and quickened his step back as the light faded, drawn by the curl of smoke rising from his mother's fire.

Jack 3

Jack stood on the sloping deck of the St George, raised above the hubbub of the quayside. His eyes scanned around. On a spar perched a solitary seagull, its yellow ringed eye staring sideways at Jack. A red dot hung from the downturned end of its beak giving the bird a serious expression suggestive of wisdom, but also admonition. Jack couldn't break its gaze which was piercing, interrogatory. How could he have gone from his beloved mother and father leaving with no hint of his intent? What would they feel when he failed to return that evening? He tried to balance his guilt with thoughts of returning with riches but couldn't hold back the tide of emotion he felt, and tears started to well.

'Hoy! Boy! Whatever your name is. Pull that rope in or we'll get snared!' Jack came out of his dream with a jolt. The captain had ordered them to cast off, and the timbers creaked as they felt the strain of the wind fill the unfurling sails. Without a blink the gull opened its wings and allowed the wind to take it effortlessly towards the middle of the estuary.

'You better get a grip boy, we're not carrying you as cargo.' Jack hurried himself round the deck, tidying the ropes as he had learned in the log barge, but this was a bigger ship all together. Its hold had been stacked with butts of Gascony wine to take on to the merchants in London.

There was a generous wind that morning and the ship quickly picked up pace. It wasn't long before they reached the limit of the level waters of the inlet, and suddenly the ship was in the swell of the open sea. Jack had never been so far out, and the motion went straight to the pit of his stomach.

The bow raised up on a wave, peaked, and then the stern tilted up as the ship gathered pace towards the trough. Wave after wave, Jack first lost control of his balance, and then he lost his stomach. Water washed over the deck, clearing away his bile, and he found a small space between the bulwark and the side to wedge his curled body and sore head.

'That new lad's a liability. What made you choose him?' the mate said to the captain.

''Cos he was bold, and that's an asset in life. He'll pick up, just you see,' the captain retorted.

As they turned the Ness, the swell abated and Jack staggered back to the mid-ships, hanging on to the rail as he went.

'Oi, green boy, have some water and some bread.' The mate reached out a jug to Jack, who took it and went below. He'd stowed his bundle between two casks in the hold, and he wanted to check it hadn't been tampered with. He felt through the folded cloth onto the shape of ancient metal he held so precious.

Later Jack went back on deck. Conditions were calmer and a half moon was high in the sky, the setting sun casting a pink light on the underside of scattered grey clouds that were scudding across from the west. His mind touched on what his abandoned mother and father must be feeling, but then he pulled back. Best not to go there. Think about tomorrow.

The morning required careful tacking up the River Thames, and the whole crew was busy with the sails, concentrating on the next order from the captain. By noon, the Tower with its forbidding walls became visible on the right bank, and ahead a forest of masts signalled the Pool of London. Jack had never been so far from home, and excitement vibrated in his chest. From a distance he could see a crowd of people pushing through the narrow middle passage on the great bridge of London, tight against carts coming in the opposite direction. Below, nimble wherries crossed the river carrying passengers, and it took skill and some luck to avoid these as the St George came round under the sterns of bigger ships to take its place by the dock.

While the captain supervised the unloading, the rest of the crew gathered on the quayside. They were eager to sample the delights on offer in the big city.

'I reckon the bishop's got enough pretty duckies for all of us.' The mate led them giggling towards the bridge intent on visiting the stews on the south side of the river. Jack followed as they walked towards the bottleneck where the bridge traffic started. He had never seen so many people pressed together, heaving to get into the narrow lane that ran between the buildings lining both sides of the bridge. Faces came towards him, mouths open emitting foul breath through decaying teeth, unwashed bodies contributing to a community odour. A cartwheel squeaked as it scraped against masonry.

'Keep up lad,' the mate shouted back above the din. Jack managed to weave his slim body through the crowd and caught up.

'What's in that bundle of yours?' asked the mate. 'You've been guarding it as though it's the King's Jewels.' Jack didn't know what to say. 'Let's have a look.' The mate reached over and put his right hand into Jack's shirt. Jack pulled away, and realising he was about to lose his treasure, ducked under the raised arms of two shopkeepers folding a piece of linen between them. He saw a narrow passage between the buildings and darted towards it.

'I knew he was hiding something!' The mate's voice receded as Jack ran down the passage, winding in and out of barrels that had been dumped there. He arrived all too soon at the end, which was blocked by a wooden rail. Jack's momentum carried his upper body curving over it. His head tilted forward, and his eyes looked down to see a torrent of icy water, the flow of the Thames forced through a small gap between the massive stone starlings supporting the bridge. He heard a clatter behind as the barrels were scattered, men's running steps closing in on him. Above him to the right there was a beam within reach. The building was cantilevered with a large overhang over the river to maximise every precious square foot of floor space on the bridge. He reached up and in a second had tucked his body and legs into a cavity behind the beam.

'I reckon old Father Thames has got him now.' The mate and his crew had reached the rail and were looking down. 'I always took him for a thief. Better he chose the easy way than hang.' The crew murmured their agreement as they retreated down the passage.

Jack's face was pressed up against the tarred beam, streaked white by the pigeons. He shifted balance carefully, uncurling one leg then the other. He considered whether to swing back down to the alley, but the risk of his pursuers still being around at the far end was too great. He shimmied slowly, pressing with his feet and wedging his back in the tight space. It was a long way down and he resisted looking; the sound of rushing water was sufficient reminder of the danger he was in. He stretched one arm under the edge to reach up the wall, and with his fingers felt for a handhold. It must be a window ledge. With both hands gripping he let his legs release, so for a moment he was hanging free, swinging gently by his fingertips. The years of handling logs had strengthened his arms so he could easily pull himself up to the window and through, pushing aside the oiled cloth that covered the opening. He was met by a woman's face, mouth open as a scream was developing, then suppressed as shock took over. The room was stacked high on either side with folded white cloth of the best quality. Calmly Jack walked down the aisle and slipped out of the front of the shop with no fuss, joining the press of people passing by. He made his way back to the city end of the bridge, guessing the crew would have carried on with their mission to the stews in the opposite direction.

Jack 4

Jack was back on the quayside. He couldn't risk bumping into that mate and crew of the St George again. What had he got himself into? He felt shaken and alone. Gathering himself he realised he must stick with his mission to find a ship going to Antwerp. The only way he could get rich was by selling his treasure.

There was a crowd around a brazier. A man was roasting and selling chestnuts. The smell was overwhelming in the cold air, a scent of warmth. Jack thought he could see people's bodies steaming, the vapour mixing with the smoke rising from the fire.

'They do look good, don't they?' A young man was standing next to him, his gaze parallel to Jack's as they stared at the cooking nuts. 'Do you want some?' There was something strange about his accent. The words carefully pronounced, but the "w" was struggling not to be a "v".

'Uh, yes,' Jack said, still feeling a bit bruised from his earlier exertions. His stomach registered the offer and told him he really did want some.

The man paid a farthing for a punnet full of warm chestnuts, the pale flesh showing through splits in the burnt skin. He offered them to Jack who peeled and ate them quickly.

'Have you recently arrived on one of these ships?' the man asked.

'Yes, but I don't think it's going where I want to go.'

'Where's that?'

'I want to go to Antwerp.'

'Oh.' The man paused. 'By the way, I am Wilhelm, but you can call me Billy.'

Jack introduced himself, and they settled into a stride walking side by side. Billy was dressed in a green quilted doublet with hose, and a cloak loosely draped over his shoulders. His costume showed him to be a man of some wealth, and Jack felt suddenly conscious of his own coarse woollen tunic, pulled in at the waist by a rope belt.

'We are always in need of strong young men, fresh crew,' Billy said. Jack was starting to work out that Billy may be recruiting him to work on a ship.

'Does your ship go to Antwerp?' inquired Jack.

'We have a few ships. Of course we go to Antwerp, and a lot of other places as well. Look, if you're interested in joining us, I can take you back to the Stalhof, that's the Steelyard in English.'

Jack had heard mention of the Steelyard in the chatter at the quayside in the town near his home. It was an enclave in London where the rich foreign merchants, the Easterlings, lived and traded. For many years there had been tension between the English traders and the foreign merchants who were given special privileges for bringing their business to London. Deals had been done to reduce tax for them, and resentment with the locals grew. In past times the mob had been whipped up and had attacked any foreigner who couldn't pronounce the phrase "bread and cheese" clearly. Jack understood why Billy took such care with his words.

Jack and Billy wound their way past Fishmongers, down Ropery and almost as far as Vintners when they arrived at the entrance to the Steelyard. A burly gatekeeper kept guard at the passage off Thames Street and bowed his head to Billy as they turned in. The sides of the passage were tall, only a narrow slit of sky provided dim illumination to ground level. Jack thought he could make out a building that housed latrines to his left, then the stink confirmed his suspicion. On the right there was a low wooden door and Billy let himself in. Jack felt a blast of warmth on his face, followed by the smell of recent cooking in his nostrils.

'Good day to you young Billy. Been fishing?' asked a stout kitchen servant, looking Jack up and down. Her sleeves were rolled up to the elbows and her pink round face was framed by a sweat drenched head cloth.

'Yes, this is Jack, he could be joining the fleet.'

'You've missed the dinner, but I've got a dish of dripping.'

Billy gestured to Jack to pull up a stool, and they used bread crusts to shovel the warm beef fat into their hungry mouths. Jack took the opportunity to look around, his eyes roving the shelves and counter tops. He had never seen plates stacked up in piles, manufactured to fit on top of one another in contrast to the rough-hewn platters he was familiar with. Heat still radiated from two dying logs in the broad fireplace and from the black ironmongery of the roasting spit over them. He could hear raised voices from a room along the corridor. Men's voices, trying to sort out a problem.

'Uncle is entertaining two gentlemen from the King's court,' Billy explained. 'He has to do this quite regularly I'm afraid. There's been some more trouble with the pirates coming out of the port of Bremen'.

Billy went on to give Jack a summary of the political and economic situation that made trading so difficult. Why he did this for the benefit of someone like Jack, escaped Jack completely. Maybe it made Billy feel good, emphasising his social superiority, and rehearsing the arguments for a more important circumstance. Jack was feeling socially raised just by being in the same building as two of the King's courtiers.

'Uncle has to do many favours for people who have influence with the King. In return they persuade the King to keep the taxes low and that's what makes it possible for us to keep our fine goods coming into England and also allows a good price for English wool to be exported with our mark of quality. When our ships sail, they need to be safe from pirates who can be paid to disrupt trade. Unfortunately, we have many enemies. The Dutch resent our special relationship with your King, so in the past have attacked our ships. You English sometimes want to help us, sometimes you want to attack us. But the city of Bremen is the worst of all. They shelter the pirates, and then take a third of any captured goods. However, they can be bought, and last year we paid them to attack the Dutch ships. But last month they captured one of our ships, and Uncle thinks they may have been turned against us.'

Jack's head was spinning. He had no idea the world could be so complicated. He felt tired and confused by the events of the day. It was getting late and there was little light in the kitchen apart from a faint glow from the fire. Billy indicated a spot on the earth floor near the hearth, and Jack curled up with his bundle under his head.

Jack 5

Crows gathered in Jack's dream. They swirled above the tree that sheltered his parents' cottage, flapping and cawing around the plume of smoke that rose from its chimney. The wind gathered strength until it was a roaring gale, the smoke blown horizontal, the group of crows torn and scattered by the gusts. Then he saw the seagull's yellow eye, with its impenetrable expression, beaded on his own eye. What was it trying to tell him? And now he felt a pain in his back, sharp, again and again.

Billy used his toe to poke Jack who was still fast asleep on the kitchen floor. Jack pulled up from his dream and instantly became aware of the clatter of food preparation around him in the kitchen. Startled, he tried to rise, hand pushing down on the floor to push up his shoulder, but at the same time his bundle started to unwind. Out spilled the sword hilt, his treasure embarrassingly revealed.

'What have we here? That can't have been too comfortable as a pillow.' Billy reached down to pick it up.

Caught unprepared Jack started to attempt an explanation.

'I found it. In the sand. Close to where I live.'

'But it's just a piece of rusty old metal. Oh, I see... It's an old sword handle. Why are you carrying it around with you?'

Jack realised he would have to tell Billy that he thought it was valuable, and that his plan was to get to Antwerp to sell it. He thought Billy was probably rich enough not to have the need to rob him.

'So, you think the red stone could be a ruby? I think we will need to show it to Uncle later, he will be able to tell you.'

Jack felt uncomfortable. This is not how he had wanted things to go.

'In the meantime, let me give you a tour of the Steelyard.'

Jack was beginning to wonder whether Billy lacked companions of his own social station. He was clearly proud of the compound, and Jack provided an audience of one. He followed Billy outside and along the passage.

'On the right here, we have the warehouse where we store all the barrels of Rhenish wine. So much better than the French wine you English seem so fond of.' Jack had never tasted wine, but he had had a mug of ale once.

Billy turned to him. 'Let me ask you a question. Why are the English so rude? I don't mean you personally, you are not rude. But the English in general?'

Jack felt stuck for an answer. Then suddenly one flew into his mind.

'Because we are cut from a coarser cloth?' responded Jack tentatively.

Billy roared with laughter. 'Very good. Very good. I like it.'

Settling down, he continued. 'Now I will show you the finest cloth you will ever have seen.'

They went into a storeroom. Shelves were piled high with fine white linen stacked carefully by the bundle. Billy took a sheet and unfolded it, like a salesman displaying for a grand matron.

'You will not find better material anywhere in the kingdom. See how dense the weave is and how thin the thread, like filaments. And at the corner you will notice our mark of quality, the metal seal stamped with the sign of St Gallen.'

Jack tried to mould his expression into that of discernment, but he thought he probably missed the mark. He murmured some appreciative noises, but Billy was already folding the cloth away and moving on.

They followed the passage to where it opened out on the wharf. There was a small jetty to meet ships for loading and unloading, but none was tied up at present. To the left and downstream was the great bridge of London. Billy looked wistfully in that direction.

'You see that drawbridge between the houses in the middle? Every time a ship comes to us, they must raise it and stop the traffic on the bridge. It is almost as though they want to make us unpopular, and to make it as hard as possible for us to trade.'

Billy looked sad. 'On the other side of that bridge is my home.' He went on to explain that he had been born in a town in the north of Germany but hadn't been back to it for over a year. Jack felt a sudden pang for his own home, but his journey hadn't been more than two days yet. He was starting to realise that Billy, like himself, must be very lonely.

Jack stood at the entrance to the great hall, as instructed by Billy who was hovering nervously behind him. They were waiting for Billy's uncle to emerge from the small room adjoining the other side of the hall, his closet where he conducted his private business. Jack had not been in a place so grand before. Light streamed in from glazed windows illuminating brown tiles on the floor decorated in yellow with curlicues and twisted leafy stems. Rich tapestries hung from the walls displaying exotic creatures unknown to Jack. There were oxen with a single long horn growing up from the tip of their noses, and deer with necks so long their heads were as high as the top of trees. Lions peered out in the gaps between woven fronds, ready to pounce on their prey.

Jack raised his gaze and at the far end of the hall, high in a gallery and behind a crisscross screen, he noted two eyes looking back. As he accommodated to the low light, he could see a young girl, and maybe her mother quietly embroidering behind her.

A shuffling noise came from the closet.

'Billy, what is it?'

A grey-haired man emerged somewhat irritably. Simon Stavoren was a senior merchant of the Hansa and was head of the London Kontor. He was finely dressed in a long black gown tied at the waist and red fox fur trim round the collar. His appearance was topped off by a pillowy black bonnet.

Billy nudged Jack forward. 'This is young Jack sir, he wants to join a ship, and he has something to show you.'

On cue Jack produced from his shirt the sword hilt and proffered it towards the gentleman, who beckoned him to come closer. Simon turned it over in his hand several times, trying to find something of interest in the rusted piece of metal. He looked at Billy in askance.

'Jack thinks there is a ruby set in it.'

'Ah, I see what you are thinking. You think this could be worth trading.'

Jack took a gulp. 'Yes sir, I was hoping to get to Antwerp to sell it and help my poor mother and father with the proceeds.'

'A fine intent, indeed. You must be a good son. But I am afraid I think the red stone is only a garnet, not worth nearly as much as if it were a ruby. I'll tell you what, we'll keep it safe in my chest for the time being. We don't want you losing it in London, do we?'

Jack felt his feet were set in ice as he followed Simon towards his closet. He had now lost control of his one asset, the reason for his journey. But he had no reason not to trust this gentleman, and he thought him so rich that this would seem only a trifle to him.

Simon reached into his gown and pulled out some keys on a chain. He selected one and with a quick turn released the mechanism in his chest to lift the lid. Jack looked away. It would be impolite to look in a man's chest. He glanced around. There was a small table in the room with a cloth on it marked out in columns. Simon had been doing calculations using brass tokens, jetons, and recording the figures in an open book.

The lid now replaced, Simon turned to Jack. 'We have a ship sailing the day after tomorrow. It won't go directly to Antwerp, but it is the best we can do. We need hands like you, you look strong. I will give you your "treasure" back before you leave.' Jack wasn't sure he liked the way he emphasised the word, but he was now bound, tied to a destiny over which he had no control.

Jack 6

The following day Jack followed Billy out of the quiet of the steelyard and into the noise and tumult of crowded Thames Street. Billy spat on the ground in the direction of Vintners Hall, their rivals in the wine trade, and they turned east towards the bridge and tower. They stepped lightly around the filth that had been slopped into the middle of the street. Billy was protective of his fine leather shoes, pointed toes upturned. The smell of Fishmongers on the right preceded its appearance. The cries of street sellers rang out. Billy went over and was acknowledged by a trader, obviously familiar with him.

'You see that stock fish there?' Billy indicated to Jack a tall pile of yellow brown leathery strips of dried fish. 'That comes with our ships from the far north. And those barrels there?' He pointed to some open barrels where a seller was ladling out curled white fillets. 'Those herrings come from the Baltic Sea. None of this would be here without our ships taking the sea crossing. It's all taken for granted by the English. No one seems to care.'

The trader grabbed Billy by the arm and pulled him in. 'We care! We care! You're keeping us in business.' They slapped each other on the back and Billy's mood lifted.

Quickening their step they weaved through the throng at the entrance to the bridge, past Church of St Magnus the Martyr and on towards the wharves by the Pool of London. The Thames was at low tide, and the beach was covered by detritus, with the odd beggar squatting to defecate.

31

'We need to check how the loading of the victuals is going,' Billy said over his shoulder.

Jack was nervous. Surely the St George must have cast off long ago. He didn't want to meet any of the crew.

'This is our ship, the Stadt Elbing.'

Billy and Jack stood amongst barrels and wooden crates piled high, ready to be taken up the gangplank into the ship. Chickens cooped and stacked in wooden cages squawked into Jack's ear. They looked up at the ship. It was of the cog variety, built wide of beam to accommodate lots of cargo, and with the new style modification of a castle fore and aft. A main mast rose from the midships topped by a deep bucket shaped crow's nest.

'Grand, isn't she?' Billy didn't need a reply. Jack was still looking up taking it all in. Stem post and stern post rose vertically out of the water, giving it a square profile. The hull was clinker built of oak with ash couples. Sailors were busy caulking the timbers with moss soaked in pitch to stop the ingress of water through the hull. Wooden crenellations fortified the raised main deck and the foredeck, to provide cover if they were attacked by any passing pirate ships.

Billy was deep in conversation with the captain, who had come over after spotting his arrival. Jack couldn't understand what they were saying and thought they were probably talking in German. He took the opportunity to examine the provisions ready for loading. There were barrels of salted beef and pork, crates of hard tack biscuits, sacks of dried peas, and many giant hogsheads containing beer, water and vinegar for the sea journey ahead.

The captain looked agitated and broke off from Billy in order to supervise the crew doing the loading. Billy turned round and smiled at Jack.

'This is what we will need to get us to our next port. We can load up again there. The captain said that this time we are taking some English archers with us. Look over there at them. I reckon they will each be eating more than a pound of meat a day.' Billy eyed up the barrels.

Jack saw a group of five or six men standing awkwardly on the dockside, their thick necks and massive shoulders indicating they had come into the city from the country. They were wearing leather jerkins, and on the ground next to them were several long wooden cases, no doubt containing their bows and flights. They looked uneasy about going to sea. It was likely this would be their first time. Let's hope they won't be too sick if we must call on them to ward off any pirates, he thought.

Jack volunteered to help move the provisions from the quay up the gangplank onto the main deck and into the belly of the ship. He couldn't believe how wide it was, a full ten yards, and it was already stacked with bales of English woollen cloth, loaded either here the day before or carried from one of the East Anglian ports. He climbed up the ladder from the hold, past the galley tucked under the forecastle and up another ladder onto the foredeck. It was like being up a tower atop a castle, the quayside a long way down visible through the gaps in the crenellation that went all around. Ahead was a small bow mast for a sail to help manoeuvre the ship in port, and to the stern the quarterdeck was visible, similarly fortified. This was to be his home until he was not sure when.

Jack 7

A stall holder by the quayside was shucking oysters. Billy paid for a dozen, and they shared them standing by the counter, downing them with coarse dark bread. After a belch, Billy contemplated how to spend the rest of the day, work now completed.

'I know. Let's pay a visit to the light-tailed housewives of Bankside.'

Jack looked confused.

'The Bagnios! The Stews! We're going to be at sea for a long time starting tomorrow!'

Jack was aware of the stews, famous amongst all travellers who visited London. They were situated outside the boundary of the city, on the south side of the river in the liberty of the Bishop of Winchester.

They moved back towards the bridge and into the crowd going south. Jack felt a shudder pass down his spine as they passed the site of his earlier escape. The shop now looked quiet, and he hoped his presence there had been soon forgotten. People were crushed together to get through a narrow passageway, then emerged again into the light with the large chapel dedicated to St Thomas à Becket on their left. Its stone buttresses rose to small spires pointing the way to heaven. Sombre faced and plainly dressed pilgrims milled about outside this station where they could receive a blessing on their way to Canterbury. Hawkers sold shiny metal pilgrims' badges for those who felt the journey onwards to the place of his martyrdom too onerous, and who could bear the ignominy of a pilgrimage incomplete.

Jack trailed Billy over the drawbridge, and through the stone gate on the southside of the bridge.

'Don't look back. You may see some relatives!' Billy nudged Jack, who turned his head around. Above the arch of the gate crows and a red kite were picking at the heads of executed traitors, held aloft on pikes. Not much remained apart from bare skulls and empty eye sockets. No recent rebellion had supplied fresh heads to renew the display.

The bridge ended and the street broadened as it reached the south bank. Two women with white painted faces and rouged cheeks were leaning through a window high above to their right, and a crowd of young men had gathered below. The women opened their shifts and their bubbies dropped out, dangling and dancing as the crowd cheered. Jack stared. He'd never seen women perform like that. The flow of foot traffic moved them on, then thinned as Billy led the way to a right turn onto Maid Lane, and then another right into a dim passage. A man in a monk's habit slid past in the opposite direction, head down, trying to be invisible under the eyes of God. At the sign of the Cardinal's Hat, Billy rapped on a stout wooden door. A crack appeared and Billy conversed with whoever was inside. He used the guttural tongue which Jack recognised as Flemish, a familiar sound at his home quayside. The door swung open, and they entered.

It took a while to adjust to the dim light from the few candles that cast a faint glow above the counter, and behind that, onto the barrels that lay sideways on a shelf. Billy was in conversation, still in Flemish, with a man of middle years and calm demeanour, who Jack took to be the whoremonger. He heard the name Petronella several times in the discourse, but the rest of the words were unrecognisable to Jack.

'They have a fine selection of wines here.' Billy took a place next to Jack on a bench opposite the counter. 'They have Rhenish, Canary wine, Alicant, Malmsey, Rumney…' Billy shouted across, and the man brought over two pottery mugs, filled to the brim with warm sweet wine. Jack examined the side of the mug which had a jokey decoration of a fat man, eyes shut, coughing spray out of his mouth. He took his first sip, hesitantly, in case he too couldn't stand it.

There was movement behind a curtain covering an opening in the sidewall of the room. A small gap opened, and Jack could make out the head of a woman, eyes down turned, fine features enhanced by the use of colouring, and exposed curls of damp black hair illuminated by the candle she was holding.

Billy rose quickly to his feet and murmured "Petronella". Without looking back, he slipped through the curtain and Jack could hear their two sets of footsteps ascending a staircase.

Jack felt uncomfortable and exposed on his bench without the cover of Billy's presence, and he cradled his mug of wine, raising it to sip frequently.

Two young girls came from a back room carrying steaming jugs of hot water. They wore unbleached linen shifts, and Jack could make out the curves of their body as they moved. One glanced at Jack, but he could read nothing in her dead eyes. They too slipped through the curtain, and silently ascended the to the floor above.

Sometime later Billy came tripping lightly down the stairs. He was merry and grabbed a pinch of Jack's cheek.

'Look at that face! Cockie didn't get to crow?'

Jack reddened but decided to take it in good spirits and was happy just to be leaving now. They stepped out of the

36

door and took a shortcut back to the bridge along Pissing Lane. The light was fading, and rats scattered as their feet approached. Jack knew this was a time and place for cut purses and stayed vigilant while Billy skipped along, pleased with his afternoon activities.

Jack 8

Next morning Jack thought about the walk back across the bridge in the dark the previous night. Every shadow cast a threat; every dark alcove housed a demon. He had slipped into protective mode, looking out for Billy, who was unguarded and carefree. Jack felt sorry for the girls of the stews, who were about his own age. He could see they weren't enjoying what they were being asked to do, and that had dampened any ardour he may have felt.

In the dim passage behind the steelyard kitchen, they loaded a handcart to take to the ship before embarkation. Simon had been true to his word and had shown Jack the sword hilt he had kept safe in his chest. It was now locked up in Billy's chest ready to go. He felt some relief that he knew where it was, but a pang of anxiety told him he was still not in control of it.

On to the handcart went Billy's possessions. His fine clothes were neatly folded, stacked and packed in a trunk, and next to it, wrapped in some brown sack cloth was a long metal pipe. Poking out from the cloth and bent at an angle from the main stem was a polished wooden stock, ornately carved and inlaid with ivory. Jack had never seen anything like it before.

'This I have purchased especially from a Spanish armourer. He wouldn't take less than half a fortune for it. It is a hakenbusche, or in English you may know it as an arque-bus. It is quite the latest thing.'

Jack was none the wiser.

'We put some gunpowder in the barrel, then some shot, and when we light the gunpowder, it blows the shot out of the end. Bye-bye pirates! People say it makes the most incredible noise, like the devil roaring from hell.' Billy enthused. 'I think it will make those archers turn green with envy.'

Jack wasn't sure it would be a good idea to upset the archers but said nothing. Billy promised to give him a demonstration when they were asail.

Billy led the way while Jack pushed the handcart and they weaved through the throng of people towards the dock. The ship was busy with sailors organising crates and ropes, stowing away whatever could roll on a moving deck, while Jack and Billy lifted the trunk into a cabin under the quarterdeck. It slipped in next to a wide shelf where it took up nearly half the space. Billy lifted a wooden flap in the dark timbers high on the wall close to the ceiling to let some light in. Jack could see that the shelf would serve as Billy's bed.

'You can be comfortable sleeping on the trunk,' Billy told Jack. Jack thought it would be better than having to find a corner somewhere on deck.

They went back up top, and Billy sought out the captain. Again they spoke, heads close together, the captain's dark scraggly hair and full beard contrasting with the finely cut golden locks of Billy. The captain looked anxious, no doubt keen to set sail soon in order to catch the tide.

With much shouting fore and aft, the sailors readied the hawsers and stood to for the order to cast off. A rapid movement on the quayside caught Jack's eye as a black cloaked figure pushed through the crowd. His hood up, he dashed for the gangplank just when it was raised. Jack could hear his loud breathing as he gained the deck, and the captain, as he shouted the order to untie, wrapped an arm around the head and shoulders of the boarder and whisked him into the dark interior under the quarter deck. Emerging again a few seconds later, the captain stood tall as if to demonstrate his composure. They pushed away from the side, and under his command manoeuvred into the stream of the river. The main sail was unfurled and with a gentle westerly breeze they proceeded at a stately pace past the white keep of the Tower of London.

Jack wondered who the late passenger was. The archers were in a circle on the foredeck, and they also had noticed the commotion.

'Come over here lad. You look dressed in the English fashion. Not like all these foreigners around.' The eldest looking of the group beckoned over to him.

Jack assessed them. There were six, with upper bodies solid enough to pull a hundred-pound bow string. He could tell they were not yet comfortable on a ship.

'You that German boy's manservant?'

'Boy servant more like,' another chipped in with a sneer. The others suppressed a knowing giggle. This made Jack think about who he really was. He probably was Billy's servant now, even though they had not discussed it, and he was on no retainer, but the difference in their status made it ever thus. He didn't know what to say.

'He calls himself Billy, doesn't he? Wilhelm or something. He put it about that he wanted some archers, and winter doesn't provide much living off the land in our village, so here we are on an adventure, and he pays better than most. He said we should be back for the harvest.' The others nodded, trying to take some reassurance.

Jack sat down beside them.

'I only met him the day before yesterday.' His mind tracked back over the events of the last two days, in which more had happened than in all his life before. Then he felt the pain his parents must be feeling at his disappearance.

'My name's Dick,' the lead archer said, softening his voice as he saw Jack welling up. 'You from the country as well?'

'Yes, from the southern counties. Worked on a log barge.'

Jack relayed his journey so far, omitting the details that could be of interest to anyone who might want to do him harm, or steal his possession.

'Lifting those logs has made you strong in the arm. We could turn you into an archer if you were so inclined.'

Jack liked the thought of that, but he could see a ship was not the ideal place for practice.

Dick went on to introduce his band.

'We're the sons of archers from the French wars. Proud of the tradition. They were great men, unleashing volley after volley of flights that did for those Frenchie Knights in the mud of the battlefield. Then they would finish them off with their bollock daggers, a downward thrust under the helmet.' He looked dreamily, nostalgic for past victories. 'Here look.' He showed Jack his bracer, strapped to the inside of his forearm. Embossed on it, despite the leather being worn and faded, Jack could make out a pattern of lions rampant, and some flowers. 'My father wore this at Agincourt. You can see the emblem of the old King Henry. All the boys have their fathers' bracers. We pay them our respects every week at the butts when we practice.'

The marshes of the Thames estuary spread out flat on either side and the sun poked through a gap in the low clouds illuminating the rushes, colour bleached by the winter weather, gently waving in the wind. The talk in the band now turned to the black clad stranger.

'I reckon he's a Lollard,' one mused. 'I bet his skin is like wax under that hood. He'd go up like a candle in the flames.' The others laughed. There was little love for the Lollards who broke with religious convention and paid the price for it at the stake.

Jack 9

Jack knocked on the door post to Billy's cabin. Through the crack in the door, he had heard a murmured chant of prayers, then the rustle of papers as the occupants became aware of his presence. Inside Billy was sitting opposite the new passenger, whose face was lit from the open outer hatch. He wasn't waxen as Jack had been led to believe, but in fact had a ruddy complexion, and was bald with grey hair hanging in strands round the sides, and wisps of white beard on his chin. His russet-coloured worsted gown was open, and he quickly hid the papers next to his breast. A small Bible remained open on the shelf. Billy made the introductions.

'Ah, Jack. This is Pieter, who is joining us for the voyage.'

'It's Peter, actually,' the stranger said. He looked concerned that they may have been overheard.

'Jack also has some treasure that, like you, he wants to take to the continent,' explained Billy. His lack of concern about keeping the secrets he held caused discomfort to both other parties present. 'Oh, don't look so glum you two. We need to get on together for the trip. It will all be well in the end.'

Peter raised a smile. He must have felt some relief at escaping whatever he had been fleeing from.

'Peter is a scholar from Oxford. He has some important business to conduct in Germany when we land.'

Jack felt his heart sink. Germany was a long way from Antwerp. He realised that he was powerless to exert any control over his destiny. Peter had a kindly face though. Jack hoped they would get on.

'Time to see if this arquebus will do everything the merchant promised.' Billy looked excited. 'If you will excuse us Pieter, we have some powder to mix.'

Peter picked up his Bible and left the cabin nervously, acknowledging Jack with a small nod of his head as he rushed out.

Billy was arranging three bark boxes and had a wooden spoon in his hand.

'Five spoonfuls of saltpetre.' He made a heap of pale pink powder with a depression in the middle. 'And one each of sulphur and charcoal.' He mixed in the yellow powder and then the black. 'And now we have serpentine powder, commonly known as gunpowder. We have to get the proportions right or there will be no bang-bang.' He chuckled.

Billy scraped the powder into a hollow horn with a cork stopper to seal the end.

'Help me get the arquebus out.' Billy was reaching under his sleeping board, and he and Jack manoeuvred the long metal tube. It was heavy and stretched all the way across the cabin as they tried to shift it. Jack could see in detail the beautifully carved stock with its curls of inlaid ivory. Billy pushed the door open with his heel, and they took the weapon out onto the sunlit deck, worked their way to the ladder that went to the forecastle and heaved it up onto the foredeck. The archers were still lolling around there and now could see some entertainment was on its way. They lined up by the rail to give space to Billy and Jack, and the new engine of war.

'I had this special support fitted, so you can aim it all round.' Billy rested the barrel in a simple metal cradle that

44

rotated on a wooden post central on the foredeck. 'Jack, could you get this match lit by the cook?'

Jack took the slow match, a piece of rope frayed at the end and held in a split stick. He went down to the galley below and the cook selected a glowing ember of charcoal and pushed it in the fibres so it could smoulder there. When he returned, Billy was pouring some of his serpentine powder down the barrel, followed by a lead shot, wrapped in cotton cloth. Levelling the arquebus again he made a small mound of powder over the firing hole, not far from where the wooden stock joined the metal.

'Jack, be careful with that match, we don't want it to go off early, do we?' Billy took aim at a group of seagulls, squatting on a sandbank to the port side, beaks into the wind. 'Pass me the match.' Gaze unwavering, the stock nestling in his right shoulder, Billy reached out to his left and slowly brought the smoking end towards the little mound of powder above the firing chamber. It caught, fizzled and released a small cracking sound, barely more than a click. There was a pause, before Billy raised his head, looking nonplussed.

'Christ's wounds, we could have let off thirty flights and won the battle by now,' Dick opined, with murmurs of agreement going round the group of archers. Billy had taken the arquebus off the stand and was peering down the barrel. He shook his head and made a slightly bigger mound of powder to act as the priming charge, then reset the weapon.

This time the charge cracked more certainly when lit. What followed was the loudest noise Jack had ever heard. He was blown backwards onto his rump, his view of the shoreline replaced by sail and sky, then by a cloud of grey smoke, billowing from the discharged gun. It took a few seconds for the smoke to clear, and Jack raised himself to standing. Billy was dancing around the foredeck with great joy. The archers were looking horrified, with their hands over their ears. Jack watched the gulls circling around the mast, their beaks wide as they quarked and squawked, but their sound could not penetrate the high-pitched squeal that filled Jack's ears. Billy was mouthing something to him, close up in front of his face, but Jack only caught the end of the sentence through the ringing in his ears.

'... it works! It's magnificent!'

Jack tried to share Billy's delight and forced a smile. As his hearing slowly returned, he could hear the archers talking loudly, laughing at the improbability that this weapon could somehow make them redundant.

Jack 10

The bench was set up outside the galley under the forecastle overhang. Jack and Billy, with the new passenger, Peter, sat at one end and most of the sailors who weren't required for sail duty or the watch were at the other. The ship yawed awkwardly, making them lean into one another whilst seated. Between the sounds of the sail flapping and ropes tightening, Jack could hear retching coming from above on the foredeck. He had looked up there before the meal service, and saw the archers sprawled on the deck, some with their heads through gaps in the crenellations. The ship had left the flat tidal waters of the estuary and was now in the rising swell of the North Sea. For the archers this was their first taste of life on the waves. They wouldn't have an appetite for their first meal on the ship.

The cook slopped out the grey pease mash into wooden bowls to accompany a piece of boiled bacon and half a loaf of coarse bread each.

'Enjoy this fresh bread while it lasts,' Billy said. 'It might last us all a bit longer if those archers don't get their sea legs.' They knew they would be on hard tack biscuit when the bread ran out.

'Billy, we seem to have turned north. Aren't we going straight across to the continent?' Peter asked anxiously.

'We must pick up another of our ships, coming out of Lynn. Then we can go across in the safety of a convoy.' Lynn was the centre for production of English woollen cloth, so much in demand in the rest of Europe. Billy was being unusually reticent about why a convoy was necessary, maybe thinking not to alarm the ship's company any further about the danger of pirates now they were at sea.

Peter looked across to Jack, hoping to make conversation. He was thinking good company could be thin on this journey.

'You look like a strong lad. Where do you hail from?'

Jack explained he had worked on log barges, in the timber trade on the south coast.

'So, what made you leave home?'

Jack dipped his crust into his bowl to scoop up some mashed pease while he considered his answer. He still felt a pang about leaving his mother and father.

'I suppose I wanted a bit more adventure and a seafaring life.' He weighed up whether to tell this stranger about his sword hilt. Peter looked kindly, and well educated, probably a cleric as well as a scholar. It would seem unlikely that he would steal it. Jack made a decision to trust him. Maybe Peter could help him. He leant towards him so no one else could hear.

'And also I found something that I thought I could sell to make some money to take back to my poor family. But I have to get to the right place where it could fetch a good price.'

'Ah, this would be the treasure that Billy mentioned. What form does it take?'

Jack explained he had found it one morning in the sand of the shore near where he lived. It had been exposed at low tide, the surface of the sand was rippled by the impression of the waves the previous night. He had first seen a shard of rusty metal poking up at an angle. He had kicked it with his toe and it moved a little, with a resistance that suggested it extended deeper into the sand. He reached down and gave it a tug. And up it came. Although blackened with the years it had spent immersed in salt water, it was easy for Jack to identify it as the hilt of a sword, the handle indented for fingers to grip, and a heavy round pommel at the end to counterbalance a blade which had eroded long ago. He had found things while spuddling before, but never such an interesting object. He was excited but didn't have time to examine it in detail so tucked it in his pouch and made for the barge where the captain was already calling for him. It was only the next morning when he had time to clean it in the pond next to his cottage that he realised it may have a precious stone lodged in the pommel.

Peter had listened attentively to Jack relaying his story.

'Maybe you'll let me have a look when Billy opens his chest again. I can tell you what I think of it,' he said as he turned away.

It seemed Peter had had enough of listening to the tale. Jack's jaw dropped. How did he know it was in Billy's chest?

Jack 11

The back of Jack's head hit the beam in Billy's cabin, waking him up suddenly. He had had a fitful night on the lid of the trunk, trying to get comfortable as the ship rocked and rolled. Billy was still snoring on his shelf, a rhythm that matched the movement of the ship. Light was filtering through the sides of the closed hatch, and Jack stood carefully, timing his exit through the door with the shifting angle of the ship. A grey mist hung over the main deck, it being so soon after dawn, but he could make out that the archers were already up and seated at the bench and being served by the cook with yesterday's uneaten pease pudding along with mugs of ale to get the day going.

'Hoy, lad! Come over here and join us.' Jack sat down next to Dick who had spoken to him the day before.

'What do you think of that German lad's cannon?' Two of the archers guffawed, then looked a little sheepish. Jack wasn't sure how to answer, so just reddened. He could be mocked for any response, taken whichever way.

'I reckon it's a lot of fuss about nothing.' Dick softened the tone answering for Jack. 'You'd be overrun before you even got the thing loaded. It makes a good bird-scarer though, and a mighty pretty one.' The archers nodded agreement.

'Billy said he got it from a Spanish merchant.' Jack thought he had better say something, keeping it just factual.

'I bet he did! And he's never been the same since!' The band cracked up laughing at Dick's joke, and Jack smiled through his embarrassment.

'Oh, come on lad, don't take it so seriously. As I said yesterday you could make a fine archer. Forget about all that fancy stuff with bangs, that's just for show. Look at England's victories. It's the archers who win battles, as we have shown time and time again.'

After breakfast Jack joined the archers on the foredeck as they opened the long boxes that contained their bows and arrows. He watched as they looped the bow string on one end then, seemingly without effort, flexed the yew stave against the deck to loop the other end. They moved swiftly and smoothly, their arms and shoulders practised through repetition.

Dick handed a bow to Jack.

'There's not too much tension on that one. See if you can pull it.'

Jack held the bow in his left hand and pulled back on the string with two fingers of his right, as he had seen others do previously. He moved it six inches.

'Come on, put a bit of effort into it.'

Jack straightened his left arm, keeping his elbow extended while he tensed, pulling his right shoulder back, drawing the string until it was nearly at his face. His arms trembled with the force.

'Now, loose!'

Jack released the string, which whipped the inside of his left forearm as its energy was released.

'Good. I think we had better find you a bracer though, otherwise you'll be flayed by the end of the day.'

Jack could see the skin of his forearm reddening. Dick reached into a box to take out an ox horn wrist guard which he attached to Jack with a leather thong. Jack felt much more like an archer now.

'Let's have a look at some arrows. This one is a needle bodkin.' He showed Jack a shaft with an iron head, square in section narrowing to a point. 'This'll get through anything, mail included. It can go through a man and come out the other side.'

Next, he pulled from the box an arrow with a broad V-shaped head, with a sharpened steel cutting edge that glistened.

'This one on the other hand is a barbed broadhead. You won't be getting that one out before someone bleeds to death.'

He reached in again and brought out an arrow with a head that Jack had not seen the like of before. It had two prongs extending forward and curling around one another in a spiral pattern.

'What do you think this is?' Jack looked puzzled. 'Well young Jack, this is a fire arrow. Probably this is most useful one in the box if you were to be fighting another ship. The battle could be all over if you can set light to them, and then you can merrily sail away. You wrap a wad of tow round the prongs and soak it in tallow. You need to make sure it's well alight before shooting, otherwise it'll go out on its journey over to the other ship and become a wasted dud.'

The other archers were limbering up on the foredeck, repeatedly drawing their heavy longbows, holding a pose with chest expanded before releasing.

'It's a pity we don't have a popinjay to shoot at,' Dick said.

'Send the lad up into the crow's nest and get him to hold a clout,' a waggish archer responded.

'It's just as well these arrows cost so much, Jack, we can't go wasting them on you!'

Jack was pleased to be getting on with the group now. Maybe they'll let him have a go with a real arrow if they get the chance to practice near land.

The sun was breaking through in places, lighting up patches of the east Anglian coastline. They passed shingle beach, low cliff and reed bed as they made progress northwards for the rendezvous.

Jack 12

The Stadt Elbing was at anchor near the mouth of the Great Ouse, waiting for the Balder to emerge with its cargo from Lynn. The crew lay idle, and everyone was on deck enjoying a brief spell of winter sunshine now that the wind had dropped. Peter stood close to Jack as they stared across to the thin line of fenland visible on the horizon.

'Do you know why they call it Bishop's Lynn?'

Jack hadn't heard of the town of Lynn before two days previously, so this was taking it to a whole higher level for him.

'Several hundred years ago it was taken by the local bishopric. Think of all the thousands of pounds of silver they make each year from cloth made in that town which sells all over the world. It's the sweat of the local people which fills the coffers of the Church.' Peter looked angry at the injustice. Jack could recognise that this was dangerous talk, especially from an educated man. Ordinary people didn't like ideas that undermined the bedrock of their traditions, their security in a dangerous world.

'The Church in Rome pretends to care for us English, but really they're just interested in getting rich,' continued Peter. He didn't seem to mind that Jack had nothing to add, maybe he thought it was safe venting to an uneducated lad who was unlikely to snitch on him.

'Anyway, maybe that's an argument for another time. Look, those archers are getting restless.'

Jack saw that there was some activity on the foredeck. The tide was ebbing, and the wide bottom of the ship settled on to the sandbank. As the water receded low islands of wet brown sand grew at pace all around, the channels between narrowed and then disappeared as Jack watched.

'This'll give us a chance to practice. Come and join us Jack,' bellowed Dick.

One of the archers shinned down a rope hung over the side of the ship, and Dick threw a post and cloth over the side after him. He let out a yelp of joy as his feet touched the sand, and started running around, terra firma retrieved, while the other archers jeered at him from the side. At about one hundred yards from the ship, he planted the post in the sand and hung the cloth from the top.

'First to hit that clout gets a mug of ale.' Dick challenged his team, hoping the cook would honour his promise. 'Here, Jack, take this bow.'

Some of the archers had now loosed their first arrows and saw them swallowed deep into the mud behind the target, their entry producing hardly a burp.

'Whoa! Stop shooting!' Dick reined his team in. The archer on the sand scraped away in the mud and managed to retrieve a few of the lost arrows, their low trajectory fortunately leaving them close to the surface. Dick was thinking of a different strategy.

'Just use shafts and knock in a bit of cork on the tip, we can't afford to lose our heads.'

He passed some of the modified arrows to Jack, who had been practising pulling the bowstring back and releasing.

'Let's see how you do with these.'

Jack pulled back aiming above the clout and then loosed the arrow. The bowstring released with satisfying force, but which did not transfer coherently to the shaft. The feather flights on the tail seemed to want to overtake the head, as it flopped, settling in the sand not twenty yards from the ship's side.

'Yes lad, that always happens first time,' explained Dick reassuringly. 'Try to get everything lined up. As you pull back the string your thumb should be touching your cheek, your eye looking down the shaft to the tip as you aim for above the target.'

This time Jack's arrow went sailing over the cloth to land on the sand some distance beyond. He felt excited, being able to project so far was something new to him, a power he had not felt before.

'Well done, just keep doing it like that, and you'll get the hang of it in no time.'

The mug of ale was won soon after, and the cook, getting into the spirit of things, had stuffed wet poultry feathers into a pig's bladder and stitched it up. He threw this makeshift ball high over the side, and it landed with a wet plop onto the sand. The archers cheered and made for the rope to follow it down. The first one to it took an almighty kick at it and it went sailing further away towards the post, the only feature on the flat land. The others raced on, competing to get to it first. One picked it up hoping to escape a tackle, but was soon under a pile of bodies, each trying to get a hand on the ball.

Billy stood next to Jack by the rail.

'Why aren't you with them? You English seemed to love a scramble more than anything. What do you call this game? It has no finesse.'

Jack took Billy's advice and followed them down onto the flats to join in the bundle, grabbing the ball when loose, then kicking it high in the air before a well-built archer knocked him over and sent him sprawling across the sand. He had not seen such joy on their faces before, the anxiety of the sea journey swept away.

Turning back to the ship he could see the ship's captain waving his arms frantically in their direction. He fixed on him. He was clearly worried about something, but none of the other archers had noticed. They were splashing around still after the ball, not noticing that the water was rising above their ankles, the tide accelerating inwards, threatening their return.

'Back to the ship!' Jack could just make out the faint call across the sand, through the shouts of the players competing for the ball. He grabbed the nearest one trying to make him pay attention, pointing to the captain gesticulating wildly from the quarter deck.

'Hey, lads, we'd better get back.' It was hard to distract them from the game. Jack got the ball and started running towards the ship, his young legs sprinting faster than the older men's.

'This water's coming up fast,' exclaimed one, sinking in thigh deep as he hit a patch of mud. The others, realising his predicament, pulled on his arms, risking their own legs slipping further down into the mud. He splashed around, his body now tilted forward in the water, head dangerously close to the lapping surface. They pulled him free, and, exhausted, waded the remaining distance back to the ship. One by one they pulled themselves up on the rope and tipped over the rail onto the main deck. Dick had had the foresight to collect up the shafts from the sand and they spilled out of his shirt as he beached on the deck like a stranded whale. The post remained though, and as a group they watched the cloth, attached to the top like a flag on a pole, slowly descend below the rising waters.

On the quarterdeck the captain was agitated, talking loudly in German to Billy, who looked scolded. The archers had had a narrow escape, and the ship couldn't risk losing the security they provided.

Jack 13

Billy paced anxiously, head down and murmuring to himself.

'We nearly lost the archers, and the Balder hasn't yet arrived. We'll have to go up into the crow's nest to look. Come on, two sets of eyes are better than one.'

He beckoned Jack over to the ship's side and put one foot on the rail, swinging the other one round the outside of the net rigging so his back was over the sea. Jack tentatively followed. He'd never been at height on a ship, everything being pretty much on the level in a log barge. As he looked up, Billy's legs were confidently skipping up the net, each foot finding the next rope with ease. He was almost at the point where the rigging narrowed when Jack started his ascent. It took a little while before he could find a rhythm, and even on this still day, he found the slight sway drawing him out over the sea disconcerting. Billy waited for him at the top.

'Put your foot on this ledge, swing the other leg up while pulling up on the side with your shoulders.'

Billy easily slipped into the bucket shaped crow's nest, and then turned round to grab Jack's tunic, helping him over the side. There was just about enough room for the two of them, the top coming almost to chest height. Everything moved, accelerating through the midpoint, then slowing at each extreme before reversing direction. It took a while to get balanced. Jack looked down. He could see small figures moving around the deck which was surprisingly far below. He couldn't have believed it would feel this high when he had looked up from below just a minute or two before.

59

Billy was already scanning the horizon, looking landward.

'I can track the course of the river going inland. Can you see any sails?'

The land was almost completely flat apart from a slight rise far away.

'Is that a church steeple?' Jack pointed. It was really hard to make out, but if it was the town, then there was no sail between it and where they were.

Billy was disappointed. Before leaving London, a message had been sent to Lynn arranging the rendezvous, but maybe it went astray. The Stadt Elbing did have a small rowing boat, but it would be a long journey into Lynn, probably longer than one tide, and you wouldn't want to be rowing against the flow. He had seen how quickly it moved.

When Jack jumped back on the deck, the archers were already tucking into pottage, with a lump of salted beef each. Their exertions on the sands had given them a hearty appetite, and banter was flying around the group.

'Hey, Jack, give us your best throw.' Dick mimicked lobbing a ball to him, which he received in exaggerated fashion. He sat down at the bench next to them, and the cook passed out a bowl for him.

'What did you see from up there?'

'I saw the top of your head, poking through your hair.' Jack was gaining his confidence with them, and a few chuckled at his weak joke. 'No sign of a sail though. Looks as though we've got a bit of a wait here while Billy works out what to do next.'

Their heads went down back over their bowls, momentarily silent. Cook was tidying up the galley and shouted out.

'Do you want a tale about the ocean?'

He took a place at the end of the bench, where a single lantern sat. By now the sun was going down, and the light was dimming.

The cook began. 'I have spent many years sailing these northern waters, ever since the pirates came to my home port of Bergen, killed my whole family, and burnt the town down.' Jack had thought he had a foreign accent but hadn't guessed he had come from so far north. The archers respectfully listened, as this was a man's tale, one who had seen trouble.

'There was no home to go to, so each ship became my home, and in my early years, I saw plenty of different ones. And from these ships I have seen all weathers, and monsters that you could not yet have dreamed of.' The archers murmured, settling down for a chilling story as it got dark.

'It was a calm night, with only the gentlest of breezes that barely rattled the sail. I was on watch, this being the time before my great skills as a cook were recognised.' The archers nodded in agreement. 'There was a half moon in the sky, with a ladder of silver light extending up towards it across the low ocean waves. Our sister ship lay two chains distance to our port side and a little ahead, so I could see a lantern lit above its stern post. All was quiet.

'Then, almost unnoticeable, the ship rose a little in the water. No more than an inch or two, and it settled quickly, but enough to make me think, what was that? Nothing else happened, but my breath quickened. Was I going to pass out? Or have a fit of the vapours? A minute went by, and my mind settled. I must have imagined it. There had been no wave to raise us.

'Suddenly the ship shuddered, and a dreadful low scraping sound came from the deep, right underneath the

61

keel. So low pitched it could have come from hell itself. I grabbed the rail to steady myself and could feel the vibration through the timbers for a good length of time, before it suddenly stopped. It was just as though the ship had scraped its bottom over rocks, but we were miles from land, and there should be no rocks here.

'I thought, should I rouse the captain? Everything was still again, and no one had woken, so he would think me just foolish, a scared young sailor at watch on his own at night. Our slow progress across the ocean continued, and I started singing my favourite childhood song, slowly at first to keep my spirits up.' Cook started a strange low rhythmic murmur in a foreign tongue, which slowly picked up pace. The archers leaned in, entranced.

'I had sung it through three times when, out of the corner of my eye, I noticed a movement in the water, a breach in the surface just beyond the stern post of our sister ship. For a moment it looked just like a rock, capped with white spume, but then suddenly it grew right up into the sky, a sinuous neck uncurling. Water poured from it, and its scales shone in the moonlight, as it raised a head so large it was three times the size of the crow's nest, for it was at the height of the masthead now.' The archers gasped.

'It opened its massive jaws, a red tongue poking through three rows of pointy white teeth. Across the gap between our ships, I watched as the weight of its head toppled over our fellow's main deck, its neck breaking the mast and smashing the timbers as the ship dipped below the waters, only to bob up a moment later on its side showing its keel towards me before it sank slowly into the deep. There was not a sign of any survivors, and all was calm again a minute after, as though the ship had never existed. It was truly a Leviathan, a

Great Orm worthy of slaughter by King Olaf had he been there with his sword.' The archers looked visibly shaken and trembling in the silence that followed the story's end.

Billy had come on deck and approached the group.

'Cook telling you his sea serpent stories, is he? Don't let him put the wind up you, he does it to every newcomer to the sea life.' The archers didn't look reassured. They were fearful enough of putting out to sea as it was. Next day they could be out of sight of land, and in danger of attack by monsters.

Jack 14

Dawn came quickly the following morning, and Jack roused himself from atop the trunk, unfolding his stiff legs from their curled position. Billy's bed was empty. He must be at breakfast already, thought Jack. Then he heard talking outside, and the voices of Peter and Billy approaching. The door opened and light flooded in. Billy stood with Peter behind him.

'Morning Jack, could you move to one side, Peter wants to get his Bible out.'

Billy reached under his sleeping shelf and pulled his chest forward from its position. There was a rattle of keys, and then he lifted the lid. He passed the cloth wrapped holy book to Peter. Jack could see his sword hilt underneath.

'Er, is it possible to get my hilt out to show to Peter?' asked Jack, remembering the previous conversation he had had with Peter, and the trust he showed then. Billy was irritable as the Balder had still not arrived but complied with Jack's request and passed the rusty metal to Peter, who laid it on the shelf next to his Bible.

'Ah, so this is your treasure then Jack.'

Jack observed Peter's face from the side. His eyebrows were white and formed two tufts projecting forward, and from there his forehead rose and continued uninterrupted over the crown of his head. Prominent thread veins populated his cheeks. Peter reached into his gown and produced a strange metal frame which held two bits of polished glass which he proceeded to balance on his nose.

'Yes, definitely a sword handle, it looks as though it has been submerged for a long time. The guards have nearly gone. There is a red stone in the pommel, of some considerable size, held in by a metal ring.'

He scratched at it with his thumbnail.

'That size, it is most likely to be a garnet, but of course Jack you can't rule out it being a ruby, can you?' He looked kindly over to Jack, who wasn't feeling reassured. He would have preferred a more definite opinion.

Peter scratched further round the pommel.

'You know, I think there could be some lettering here.' His nail picked away at the crusted earth stuck to the ring that circuited the stone.

'I can make out a 'D' in a strange angular script. No, it spells out "GOD".' Peter was starting to look excited. 'And there's another word after. That seems to spell "WIN".'

Peter's voice went up a notch.

'I don't believe it! God wins! God always wins! Hallelujah!' Peter was starting to look quite overcome. 'This message has been sent to us in English. Not Latin, or French, but English!' He opened his Bible and started reading verses.

'You see Jack, this Bible is written in English. It's not in Latin, which is just there to confound ordinary folk. Because it's in English anyone who knows their letters can understand it. And the knight who once possessed your sword hilt also understood. God always wins!'

Jack wasn't that interested in letters or the Bible but would have liked to know what Peter thought the stone may have been worth. It was too late to bring him back from his religious ecstasy now. Billy wrapped the hilt in its coarse cloth and placed it back in the chest.

*

Jack went out onto the deck, where the archers were sitting at the bench. They were still subdued after last night's story.

'I reckon that scratching and shuddering was the beastie going under the hull of the ship,' one archer said affirmatively. His colleagues nodded their agreement. 'It was only luck that the cook's ship wasn't overturned as well.'

They looked at one another contemplatively. Then a shout went up from the quarter deck.

'Ship ahoy!'

Jack rushed over to the rail. On the horizon, at the limit of his vision, he could just make out a square sail. Surely this must be the Balder now on its way. Billy had joined him, and was smiling, his mood lifted instantly by the sight. At last they would be able to get on with their voyage. Peter had also followed onto the deck and was now on his knees with arms raised aloft, head thrown back and bellowing: 'God always wins!'

Jack now wondered if his treasure would fetch more as a religious relic.

Jack 15

As the ships drew parallel a great cheer went up from the Stadt Elbing to be answered similarly from the Balder a second later. Billy waved his cap, a broad smile across his face. The voyage could now begin.

While the captain readied the crew to raise the anchor, Billy sat down at the bench. He thought now was the right time to explain to the archers why their presence was necessary, and Jack and Peter sat with them. Billy started, with a serious tone.

'There has been a long history of pirates feeding off the goods we worthy merchants transport from port to port, to benefit the people of England and its allies in the Hansa league. Fifty years ago, the Victual Brothers hounded shipping all across the northern waters and occupied and controlled Gotland itself. Their leader Klaus Stortebeker was reputed to be able to swallow a whole gallon of ale in one pull.' The archers looked at one another and murmured tones of admiration. 'But he had his comeuppance. He was set a trap at Heligoland, and had his head chopped off at Hamburg, with all his henchmen. That was the end for the Victual Brothers, but, soon after, the Likedealers took their place.' The cook rattled his pots, for it was they who had burnt Bergen to the ground. 'Likedealers.' Billy paused for emphasis. 'They professed to give equal shares to all the poor folk in the communities along the coast, a bit like your Robin Hood. But in reality, they just laid waste to all that they found, and extorted money from the poor as well as the rich.

They were not heroes, but villains like the Victual Brotherhood before them.

'And now we have a problem with pirates out of the City of Bremen. The burghers of Bremen let them shelter there in exchange for a share of the goods that they steal, and the ransoms they demand for hostages they take from the ships that they have plundered. But if you are taken hostage, think yourself lucky. Most crews are just thrown overboard and become food for the fishes.' Jack could hear intakes of breath from the archers around, and he guessed none of them could swim.

Billy continued. 'We made a deal through the city of Bremen for the pirates to direct their attention to Dutch shipping rather than us. This held for a while, but, just a month ago, they attacked one of our ships, and took the cargo, going against the agreement we had made. We can't trust the situation now, so that is why we need you, stout archers of England, the finest in the world, to defend us if we are to be attacked.'

The archers raised their heads, puffed out their chests, and with resolute expressions looked willing to take on the task ahead.

'What sort of tactics do these pirates employ?' asked Dick.

'They stalk their prey, like a fox at a chicken coup looking for a weakness, a way to get in. Sometimes like a fox they attack at night. That can give us an advantage if we are prepared sufficiently, as we know the nooks and crannies inside the ship in darkness better than they. However I know of no ship that has successfully repelled pirates once they are onboard, as they are fierce and experienced fighters. The answer is to not let them get from their ship to ours. They will try to gain an anchorage point with grappling hooks from the bows of their ship and haul us together. It is important to be alert, and free up, or cut, any ropes that are thrown across. And they will try to separate us from the Balder, which they will see as being easier prey, not fortified like us.'

All assembled looked over to the Balder, an old-fashioned cog without the castles fore and aft.

'The pirate we need to fear most is called Grosse Gherd, or in English you would call him Big Gerry. He is the one who is the busiest at the moment.' Billy finished his speech. Jack felt a bit confused. He was obviously trying to praise and give confidence to the archers, but at the same time it was worrying when he said no ship had been able to fight off pirates once they were on board. Maybe they hadn't come across English archers before. Let's hope they live up to the reputations of their forefathers.

Jack left the archers talking in low tones, speculating what sort of beard Big Gerry may be sporting, and whether he collected fingers from his victims to add to a string around his neck. He guessed they were trying to big themselves up for the fight ahead.

Jack 16

Peter was now settled from his prayers. Jack had never seen anybody so excited by the act of worship before, when earlier Peter had raised his arms up to the heavens while kneeling on the deck. A long time ago he had heard the slow, low-pitched, rhythmic chanting of priests coming from his village church, but there was something deeply unexciting about that. He was anxious to broach the question again with Peter about the value of his sword hilt, before Peter forgot about it. Maybe now was the right time?

Peter was sitting close to the rail on the deck and Jack sat down next to him.

'Sir, after you had been looking at my treasure, you seemed to think it was something special to do with God.'

'Yes, my son, it does after all have an inscription on it saying, "God wins".'

'Sir, I couldn't help but notice that it stirred something within you.'

'My son, have you never felt the spirit of the Lord Jesus Christ within you?'

Jack wasn't sure what direction this was going in and didn't know how to steer it back to the value of the sword hilt. While he was thinking, Peter continued.

'Put your hands together in prayer my son and close your eyes.'

Jack reluctantly complied. Peter placed the broad palm of his right hand atop Jack's matted brown hair. Peter raised his face to the sky and loudly proclaimed, as God was probably a long way away:

'This child has come to me, O Lord, asking to feel your presence within him. Let your spirit descend to inhabit the body of this lowly sinner, so recently come from innocence, and present him with the light of your soul and raise him up before the Almighty.' Peter dropped his head and brought his own hands together for a loud "Amen".

Jack reddened, conscious of the glances of the archers and the odd giggle coming from the quarterdeck. He wasn't going to be deterred though, otherwise he might miss his moment and not get another chance.

'Thank you, Sir, I feel a lot better.'

'Everyone feels better when they are touched by salvation.'

'It occurred to me, Sir, that my sword hilt may be of value for its religious significance?'

'It is a sin that the Church places value in material objects. It is the spirit that matters. They believe that you can turn bread and wine at the communion table into the actual body and blood of Christ. These are magic tricks, to impress the poor and uneducated, and take them away from the true message of the Lord.'

Jack wasn't quite sure what this had to do with his question, but it seemed very important to Peter. Jack tried to get the conversation back on track. He decided to be more direct.

'I have heard that there are churches that will buy objects related to saints for large sums of money so that pilgrims will come and give big donations to see them.'

'You have heard rightly my son! It is the most abominable practice! Pretending this bit of wood is from the true cross, or this finger bone is from this or that Saint. It is the worship of false idols!' Peter was getting truly worked up now. His jowls were flapping, and spit was chasing the words from his mouth.

Jack realised things weren't going well. He wasn't going to be able to get Peter to give a fair appraisal of his treasure.

'Thank you, Sir. I think I understand a bit better now.' He didn't, but retreat seemed the best option.

He made it up to the quarterdeck leaving Peter to tick down below. The archers smiled at him.

'Feeling a bit cleansed are we now?' Dick chuckled. Jack hoped they hadn't heard too much of the details of his talk with Peter. He didn't want them to know he was carrying some treasure. But they had certainly seen him praying with Peter.

Dick's tone changed. 'That man's a dangerous Lollard. I told you so. Be careful young Jack you don't get sucked in by him.'

Jack 17

The grey line of the English coast thinned and then disappeared as the ship sailed eastwards. Jack was further from home than he had ever been before and wondered when he would return. So much had happened since leaving his parents just a few days before. He felt powerless and obstructed in his desire to get to Antwerp. His thoughts touched on what his mother and father must be feeling, but he pulled back. It was too dark to go there. His heart ached for the loss of all things familiar, the security of his simple job with the log barge. A tremor of fear went through his body as he contemplated the uncertainty of his future. He had lost control of his destiny.

Streaks of spray whipped off the white crested waves as the wind picked up, sending the ship up and down on its course across the North Sea, the rhythm relentless. Jack moved away from the rail and sat at the bench. Cook was swinging his chopper, preparing the next meal.

'You look sad, boy. Homesick already?'

'I don't think I've done the right thing. I felt safe at home, and now I'm scared, what with all this talk of pirates.'

'I remember when I took my first voyage. I spent the first few days curled up, crying for my family. But the first port we stopped in settled all that. There were beautiful women to be had, and sights in the markets I had not even dreamed of. But then we were headed for southerly climes. I can't guarantee you'll get that in the wintery north.'

'Do you know which port we are headed for?'

'I have heard it could be Lübeck. That would make sense as it is the part of Germany that Billy comes from. But first we must get through the Danish straits. You may have to keep your head down when we do, being English.'

'Why is that?'

'The Danes aren't best disposed to your King, not since some English ships attacked Danish vessels in the far north, around Iceland. There's been talk of retaliation ever since.'

'I didn't know the world was so complicated,' replied Jack, feeling bemused.

'Oh yes, things can be complicated if you want to make them so. I just keep on chopping. That works for me. And will do for the pirates if they come for us.' He took another swing, and a large turnip was cleft in two with a satisfying crack.

As the sun dipped behind the stern post and the light began to fade, Jack saw Billy side by side with the captain pointing from the quarterdeck. Billy came down the ladder two rungs at a time and then took another look out to the starboard side.

'You see that ship there.' Jack could just make out the tops of the masts as they crested another wave. The ship must have been well over two miles away. 'That is a three-mast caravel of the southern variety. Just the sort of fast ship favoured by the pirates. It's definitely not a cargo ship. We're going to have to be on our guard tonight.'

The captain gestured over to Billy, beckoning him down to follow into his cabin. They emerged dragging a large chest. Jack went over to grab a handle and helped them scrape it across the main deck towards the galley. The captain raised the lid and Jack could see why it was so heavy. There must have been twenty swords in it. They were of the falchion design with a broad blade which curved towards the tip.

'Can you put a cutting edge on these, Cook? We might be needing them before long.'

Cook reached under his pots and brought out a sharpening stone and set to work honing the edge of each blade. Jack watched the angled sweep of the cook's skilled arm and heard the swish of the stone accelerating along the metal edge. He picked one from the pile already sharpened and for the first time felt the weight of a weapon, the balance lying a little up the blade from the guard. It felt quite different from his rusted hilt, the blade of which was long gone. He examined the metal, visualising the edge cutting through flesh, a man's arm split to the bone. He recoiled from the thought and put the blade down quickly. A surge of adrenaline coursed through his veins, sensing that blood had been spilt by that weapon and may yet do so again, the threat of a fight hanging over them.

'Have you ever handled a sword before?' Cook could see the worried look on Jack's face as he shook his head. 'Well then, you better have a bit of practice.'

Cook stood next to Jack and a bit in front, they both holding a sword.

'This sword is mainly for hacking.' He made a swinging arc with the sword, first from the left downwards and then from the right. "That way you can injure your opponent's sword arm."

Jack tried to mirror his movements, but nearly overbalanced with his first sweep.

'Shift your feet apart more.' Jack found a better posture, and with his strong shoulders found he could gain control of the blade. He slashed at the air.

'We'll make a swordsman of you yet. You had better take that one to sleep with tonight.'

The sailors and the archers each lined up to pick a newly sharpened sword. Sleep was a long time coming for Jack that night.

Jack 18

As dawn broke Jack stretched from his trunk top and went out onto the main deck. Billy was already there.

'That ship has been shadowing us all night. We're keeping the Balder on our port side, as it seems likely she would be their target for an attack, being less well armed. Can you keep watch while I go and talk to the captain?'

Jack took a deep breath and looked at the caravel which was about half a mile to the starboard side and behind them. Its hull disappeared from view each time it troughed between waves. Peter was on the main deck clothed just in his shift despite the cold wind. He was swinging his arms and then twisting at the waist before dipping into a squat. Then he propelled himself forward explosively, right arm extended, thrusting at his imaginary opponent. Jack had never seen him exercise like that before, and was impressed by his lack of self-consciousness. He calculated the caravel would not change course anytime soon, so he turned and stood near Peter who was now breathless.

'God give you good morrow ...young Jack.' He managed in two breaths.

'Are you getting limber in case we have to fight?'

'Oh, yes. I don't fear a fight, but it is always best to be prepared. I have had to fight for the true word of Our Lord on more than one occasion.'

Peter opened his shift and showed Jack a long scar from top of his shoulder down to his left elbow. Jack noticed for the first time that the ends of Peter's thumbs were splayed out like spoons.

'This cut nearly cost me my life, but I was made to wait at heaven's gate on that occasion. I see you have noticed my hands. That was more difficult to bear, but I survived a spell of hard questioning. I was lucky. Those cruel inquisitors had sent many who stayed faithful to the true word to fates worse than mine.'

Jack could see that Peter was likely to be a ferocious ally if it came to a fight. He looked over the rail again and thought he could make out some figures on the caravel. Could they really be pirates? Billy came down the ladder from the quarterdeck, his conversation with the captain over for now.

'They seem to be closing with us. We need to be ready. Can you help me set up the arquebus?'

Jack accompanied Billy to his cabin and dragged out the long gun, swinging it up onto the foredeck before following it there themselves. Billy made himself busy mixing his powder, and then they balanced the barrel in the forked support. The archers were also making themselves ready. Bundles of flights were coming out of the cases and bows were being strung.

'Come up to the crow's nest with me Jack. I want to get a better look at that ship,' said Billy as he darted for the side and swung his leg round the base of the ropes, arms hoisting his body upwards.

They scaled the rigging as fast as the sway of the mast would allow, pausing when the momentum was against them and then squeezing in extra steps on the counter swing. Jack couldn't help but think of the pirates' eyes upon his back as he climbed up. They both plopped into the bucket at the top of the mast together. Billy stood up slowly to peer over the rim, careful not to present too much of a target.

'They're on a course to come alongside us. I thought they would go for the Balder, but it looks as though they think we are juicier prey.' Jack stayed tucked down in the bucket.

'You stay here. I'll send an archer up to join you. They should be able to take a good aim from here.'

Billy swung himself back out of the bucket, heading back down the rigging to the deck. As his foot disappeared, there was a thud on the mast. A crossbow bolt vibrated above Jack's head; its energy compressed right to its tip as it seemed to want to burrow further into the wood. There was no doubt now the caravel had hostile intent. Jack thought for a minute. At least Billy would be down before they had a chance to wind the crossbow back for a second shot. He raised his eyes above the rim and looked down. The caravel was no more than a couple of chain lengths away to the starboard side. He could see the crew moving confidently on its deck, with a discipline which seems lacking on the deck of the Stadt Elbing. One of the archers was readying for the climb up the rigging to meet him up at the top. Billy seemed to be frantically giving him instruction as he organised his bow and quiver across his back. Jack ducked down again, not sure how to warn them about the crossbow. The archer would be a target on his way up.

Jack waited in the bucket. He watched the disc of clouds relay from side to side through the opening above his head. Then a thump on the bucket, followed by Dick the archer's face looking down at him.

'I thought you must have fallen out!' He laughed, as he swung one leg then the other over and nestled down next to Jack, unslinging his bow and quiver. 'It's a good thing they put these bolts in for me to grip hold of. They put another one close to the rim just as I arrived.'

Dick seemed unnaturally calm and in good humour.

'It'll take them forever to get another one wound up and sorted for us. Those crossbows are useless.'

He confidently stood up in the bucket, and Jack more hesitantly followed. Dick was looking for targets on the deck across from them.

'You see that big chap there. I reckon he's the leader of their gang. Oh, and just behind the quarterdeck ladder I can see them winding the crossbow back.'

Dick smoothly notched an arrow on his bowstring and pulled back his elbow while Jack leaned out of the way to make space. It took two seconds for him to adjust for the relative movements of the ships, then he loosed. Jack felt the rush as the bow's energy transferred into the shaft of the arrow, and he followed its track as it sped towards the other ship. The angle of descent carried it toward the group around the crossbow, and Jack could see a commotion, as one man stumbled the shaft embedded in his thigh. Already Dick was setting aim for his second shot, which he released towards the same group. Not so lucky this time, it grazed the deck and bounced off.

'Get your head down, they're setting the crossbow again.' Dick and Jack crouched back down in the bucket. Nothing. Maybe the bolt had missed. Jack darted his head up and could see the caravel was much closer now. The crossbow team was looking up at him. He ducked just in time. The bolt hit the side of the bucket with a splintering sound, the iron tip, square in profile, poking through the wood.

Dick stood up again, and loosed two flights, one towards the crossbowman, and one in the direction of the caravel's captain, who stepped sideways and ushered the arrow as it sped over the side and into the waves.

'I don't like it up here. We're sitting ducks. After the next bolt, let's leg it down the rigging. We should have enough time to get down while they reload.'

They waited until the next thud. Then Jack followed Dick out of the bucket and slid down the rope rigging, keeping his feet away as much as possible so as not to slow down. The deck rose up to him surprisingly quickly, and he landed in a crouch, just happy not to have been picked off. Sailors were running about with their swords, and Jack could see the two hulls approaching one another, almost side by side. A grappling hook had been thrown from the bow of the caravel and was tangled in the ropes of the jib. Three pirates were pulling their end of the rope drawing the two ships' bows together. The archers on the quarterdeck launched their arrows towards the deck of the caravel, and Billy in the middle of them was taking aim with his arquebus.

'This is just the angle I've been waiting for,' he bellowed. The caravel had swung around as their bows met, the two hulls scraping together with a deep tremulous vibration like a roar in a cavern. As the ships bounced apart slightly Billy had a shot lined up across both the foredeck and behind it the quarterdeck of the caravel. The slow match sizzled, and the priming charge snapped followed by a big booming explosion. Small shot swept the length of the caravel. There was silence for a few seconds, then as the smoke cleared, Jack could hear cries of agony as flesh had been stripped from bone.

One of the sailors had slashed away the grappling hook rope, but a pirate had already made it across and was now stranded on the foredeck, separated from his shipmates. Jack watched as the sailors weighed in with their swinging blades, barely a cry from the poor man as his resistance crumpled and, head lowered, he accepted his fate. His macerated body was tipped over the rail into the rising waves.

The caravel now drifted away, and Jack could see men stooping over bodies on the deck. The archers were jeering, lined up against the rail, throwing insults and using the two-finger sign of the undefeated. Look, my fingers can loose another volley at you.

Jack 19

Spirits ran high at the bench that afternoon. The pirates had been seen off with no loss of life from the crew, only the odd cut and graze. The archers quaffed ale, mug after mug, spinning the exploits of the morning as they bounced around the group, tuning the story so it would sound well when told to new audiences at future gatherings. Billy congratulated them on repelling the enemy, confident in the fact that his own contribution had turned the battle when he blasted his gun at them. Jack sat silently. He smiled thinly as the others bathed in their victory, but he couldn't shift the image from his head of that lone pirate being hacked to death on the foredeck. It was the first time he had seen a man die. Hardly a murmur each time steel ripped through flesh. The chilling way his killers set about their task, not a thought for what their victim may have been feeling. He had crouched there passively, head lolling, knowing death was inevitable, awaiting the end, maybe wishing it would end soon. Then the way he was lifted over to drop into the depths, to become food for the fishes. Jack thought of the pirate's family waiting at home for him, maybe a mother and father who loved him, who may never learn what became of him.

'Jack, looking at you, you'd think you'd been taken hostage by those pirates,' Billy laughed. 'Have some ale and join in the fun.' Jack refocused, but he found it hard to share the celebratory mood of the others.

When night came, Jack lay curled on the trunk top, listening to the creaking timbers as the ship rose and fell on the waves.

Billy snored from his shelf bed to a different rhythm, and thin moonlight penetrated around the hatch sides. It took a long time for Jack to fall asleep. He drifted down into the ocean depths, following the dead pirate in his descent, his wide-open eyes staring beyond Jack, seeing a horror that Jack could not yet perceive. Their two bodies became tangled in strands of kelp, the weed winding around their limbs, constraining them and tying them together. Jack examined the green ribbons that wrapped his body, and saw scales that shone, reflecting the silvered moonlight that had penetrated the water. He followed the line of scales to a thinning neck, and then at the end, a snake's head that turned back to face him, its tongue flicking at his face. His breathing quickened, and, as the serpent grew, it was he who was tangled with it, riding it as it breached the surface, now an enormous, terrible Leviathan. He rose on its back high into the air, and looked down to see the ship far below, about to be broken in half by the massive weight of the great worm.

Jack woke with a start, still half immersed in the horror of his nightmare, half reassured by the familiar discomfort of the lumps and ridges of his sleeping place. He looked at the damp wood above his ledge, spiders crawling in and out of the cracks. He turned to try to find a new position he could sleep in, but the ridges on the trunk top poked through the thin layer of coats that served as his mattress. He spent the rest of the night ruminating. By how thin a thread his life hung.

Cook was already up and handed Jack, pale faced and drawn, a bucket and scrubbing brush as he emerged into the gathering light of the dawn.

'We can't have blood stains on the deck. That's not the sort of ship I run.'

Jack got down on his hands and knees and worked at the planks with circular motions trying to lift the browned blood with the bristles. He emptied the bucket over it. However hard he tried he couldn't scour from his memory the images of the day before.

Jack 20

Billy was in a cheerful mood when Jack joined him by the rail.

'I think news will get about that we are not to be meddled with. Those pirates took a hell of a beating.'

Jack nodded but was troubled by the brutal killing and felt detached from the sense of celebration on the ship.

'Look, this fair wind has brought us within sight of Elsinore.' Billy was pointing toward land close to the horizon. 'That's Krogen castle. We are just a few hours from having to navigate through the narrow channel known as the cat's gate before we can enter to Baltic Sea, and I will be home in Lübeck in no time at all. But first we will have to stop at Elsinore and pay our dues to the King of Denmark for using the sound,' continued Billy. 'I want you and the archers to keep below decks while we are moored. The English aren't popular in Denmark, not since you took one of their king's ships on its way to his territory in Iceland.' Jack didn't like his accusatory tone, but when the time came he descended into the hold with the archers. They had to keep their heads down for this part of the passage.

It was dark sitting on the bales of woollen goods. From above they could hear strangers' steps pacing on the deck and chattering in languages Jack couldn't understand. The hatch was lifted and a shaft of light illuminated a square of the cargo directly underneath. The archers and Jack pressed themselves back against the hull so as not to be seen. A head peered in, silhouetted against the light. He muttered something and the hatch went back over.

The archers became restless.

'I don't like this hiding. It goes against my nature,' growled Dick. 'I'd have rather dragged him down and finished him off with my bollock knife.'

'Yes, we're fighting men, not rats hiding from the ship's cat,' another added.

The next face they saw poking through the hatch was Billy's giving them the all-clear to come up. He didn't seem as cheerful as when they had gone down into the hold and had a grim expression as he left to join the captain in close conversation on the afterdeck.

It was late afternoon when Billy spoke to the archers and Jack. They knew something was up from the angry chatter of the crew following the stop at Elsinore, and a subdued mood had descended on the ship. They sat on the benches by the kitchen galley.

'The officials when we stopped told me some bad news. Lübeck had been clear of the plague for twenty years, but in the last few weeks it has returned, and is worse than ever. This makes me sad, not only because my family is at risk there, but also we will not be able to unload the ship. They have stopped all ships docking there. We will have to carry on our journey to another port, so won't be turning back soon.'

The archers looked devastated.

'I don't care about your bloody load. You can dump it in the sea for all I care. We've got to get back to our village for the harvest, or our families will starve next winter,' Dick barked.

Billy tried to lower the temperature. 'Yes, yes I am sure we can get back in time for that. It will only mean a couple of weeks extra on the journey.'

Jack was disheartened. All he had wanted was to travel to Antwerp to sell his treasure. This was going to take him further away still.

Jack 21

There was a gentle plop each time the oars entered the water. Jack watched the rings of ripples expand, each one adding to the trail behind that led back to the Stadt Ebling anchored across the flat moonlit harbour. Peter was pulling on the oars with his hood up, face shadowed in the darkness, and they made steady progress towards the stone quay.

The previous evening Peter had come to Billy's cabin while Jack was there.

'I must disembark at Lübeck. Going further east will just delay my meeting with the printers. God will protect me from whatever pestilence has beset the city.'

Billy looked pensive. 'If we are to take you in, then I will come with you. I need to deliver a message to our office.'

It was assumed Jack would go with them. He was scared.

They tied the rowing boat to an iron ring by the stone steps. Billy went up first and looked right and left. It was after midnight and the watch must have stood down. The massive twin towers of the city gate, giant cylinders topped by cones, loomed black above them to their left. Billy took them right along the outside of the city wall to find a postern gate.

'There's a small passage around here.'

It was dark in the alley way, but they could hear the tip tap scampering of rats scattering ahead of them. The passage, once it had penetrated the curtain wall, opened into a square lined with buildings where a foetid smell of decay hung low over the cobbles. The windows of the houses were all shuttered. Jack noticed a cart left on one side. In the cold light of the moon, he could just make out a form lying on the flatbed. Its head overreached the rear edge, its neck extended, its pale face tilted back, its eyes open in an unseeing stare, presented to the celestial night sky.

'Stay away from those bodies,' Billy warned. 'If we keep a good distance, we should be safe.'

Peter made his farewells.

'I will leave you now. I can walk to the next town where I should be able to find a horse to take me to my friends and allies. You have been good companions and I am grateful for you getting me this far. May God go with you.' He turned and within an instant had disappeared into the shadows of the city.

'I will miss him,' Billy said to Jack. 'I have to take this letter to our house explaining our journey and to where we will be diverted.'

They made their way down a side alley that opened into a smaller square and Billy approached a stone stairway leading up to a grandly carved doorway.

'You crouch down there. They won't be expecting visitors,' he told Jack.

Jack hid in the dark moon shadow of the stairway and could hear the firm knock as Billy struck the door. There was a long wait before the bolt slid back and, in the still of the night, the creak of the door opening seemed unnaturally loud. A man answered and spoke in German, and despite keeping his tone low, showed some recognition of Billy. The conversation lasted some minutes, then the door shut, and Billy came back down the steps. He looked in a bad mood.

'The plague has really taken hold here. We need to move fast as it is spreading along the coast to other ports. In fact Danzig may already be affected.'

They quickened their pace, and as they turned the corner into the main square, they bumped into a figure clad in a black cape with a long beak-like mask. His appearance seemed closer to a giant crow in the semi-darkness. Billy exchanged expletives with the physician, and they passed rapidly, the odour of vinegar trailing behind him as he hurried to his next rich plague victim.

Jack took the oars after Billy had untied their small boat and made for the ship. The moon had set but the sky was already lightening at the first signs of dawn. There was an unnatural silence behind them, an eerie stillness from a sick city which by this time should be starting to awaken. Billy was hunched in the stern of the boat, his spirits low.

'I can't believe I've been to Lübeck and have not been able to see my family. This plague is so cruel. It could be that they might get ill soon, and I may never see them again.'

Jack kept on rowing. He didn't know what he could say to comfort Billy.

Jack 22

The timbers creaked with the rise of the ship on the morning swell. Jack, despite the chill from the night before, had fallen fast asleep on his trunk-top ledge, his eyelids flickering as he dreamt. A group of people approached him, darting forwards, their faces thrust towards his as the flesh fell from them, then they retreated to rattle their bones as they performed a danse macabre, legs swinging then knees knocking. Crows flapped their wings and squawked, causing a commotion around the dancing figures. Their beaks were topped by human eyes, haunted by things they had seen.

Jack woke with a start and sat up. The fear of the plague city had entered him. He checked his arms and legs for marks but there were none. He slipped off the trunk and emerged into the bright light on the deck. Billy was just finishing conversing with the captain.

'We've got a fair breeze behind us. That should put some miles between us and the pestilence. Let's see if we can beat it to Danzig.'

Jack joined the archers who were lolling on the foredeck.

'Don't get too close, I gather you went with his "high almighty" last night into the city.' Dick raised a hand. 'I hope you didn't touch anything.'

'I heard it's spread by bad air,' another added, flapping his hand in front of his face.

'There's plenty of bad air around you. You could infect us all.' They tittered in a subdued fashion.

Jack kept quiet. He knew what mood they were in, and they would twist anything he said to mock him.

'I don't like it; we're going further and further away from home. We should just turn the ship around and sail back,' one grumbled.

'We'd have to take them hostage and make them do it. I haven't got a clue how to sail a ship.' Dick shook his head. 'Anyway, he said it would only be another two weeks. I am missing my Mary though.'

'We're all missing your Mary!' they laughed as Dick took a swipe at the nearest one.

Jack lay on his back and watched the white clouds slowly overtake the ship. He hoped the clouds and blue sky would replace the dream's images. He thought of his parents and how they might be faring, and the way he had left without saying goodbye. Guilt surged. He had planned to return to them with a purse of gold coins after trading his sword hilt in Antwerp, but this ill-fated ship just separated them more. Fatigue and then a dreamless sleep overcame him, lulled by the rocking of the waves.

Billy was leaning over the side, shouting in German, as Jack came to from his slumber. He rose and went to the rail to look over. There was a small fishing boat tied to a pole, and fixed nets stretched towards the coast lying about half a mile back. The fisherman was pulling in his tackle and kept perfect balance as his boat rocked from side to side, alternately head down to heave, then turning his face up to converse with Billy. His face was brown and wrinkled, weathered from years of salt and rain. Billy's expression became increasingly concerned.

'He's saying that Danzig is closed to ships because of the plague. They're not letting any in either because they have got it or don't want it brought in. It's likely that the next port, Konigsberg, will be the same.'

He bade a sad farewell to the fisherman as the breeze carried their ship on its unrelenting course east. Jack watched the little fishing boat get smaller next to the wake of white foam they left behind.

'This is bad news. I was hoping we could unload at Danzig. The only thing for it is to make for Livonia which means turning north. We have an office in Reval, where I am sure we will get a good price for our woollen goods. Then we can load up with furs and wax supplied from our kontor in Novgorod.'

Jack 23

The shaft of the oar squeaked against the sides of the fixed rowlocks as they approached the rocky shore. The Stadt Elbing was anchored in a sheltered bay and Billy had decided to reconnoitre the land route to the city gates of Reval. This was unfamiliar territory to him. He thought if he could get a message to their representative before presenting his ship in harbour, then there would be less risk of something going wrong.

Dusk was falling. Jack pulled hard on the oars to propel the boat the last few yards onto a narrow pebble beach. The hull stopped abruptly with a loud crunch. The forest started just yards away, and they pulled the boat up to conceal it under a tangle of branches hanging over the rocks. It was getting dark now, even more so amongst the trees, and Billy was anxious to find a place they could encamp safely for the next few hours before they took a predawn walk to the city gates. Jack gathered some sticks together and with some dry tinder from his pouch he struck a fire. The temperature was dropping fast, and they crouched together low over the meagre flames to glean what heat they could with a thick blanket draped over their shoulders.

'I can't believe we have ended up here. I so wanted to see my family in Lübeck and now I don't even know if they are alive or dead.'

Jack felt like crying. He couldn't shake his remorse at abandoning his parents. He had never said goodbye.

Billy continued. 'Let's settle down here and move off just before dawn.'

Jack watched the light from the flickering flames play on the nearest trees. Billy seemed to go straight off to sleep, but Jack was disturbed by the creak made by the rubbing of bare trunk against trunk, where they met in a gentle sway far above his head. The still night air was pierced at intervals by noises foreign to him. A distant howl sent him into alert. Was it a wolf, or some sort of strange bird? There was no repeat, and tiredness slowly overcame him as he drifted off to sleep.

His ankle was nudged. It was still dark, and he lifted his head expecting to see Billy about to kick him awake. But Billy was still asleep on the other side of the pile of ashes where the fire had died. There was a snuffling sound. He turned his face and saw a massive dark form, the rump of a great beast, its head rooting around the ground near his feet. He pulled his legs up and away, rose and stealthily circled the fire to rouse Billy, whose stifled scream made the animal turn its head towards them. They could just make out its long pale pointy snout as its jaws opened and let out a body quaking roar. Billy and Jack were sprayed with what soggy flecks remained of the breakfast they had planned. Up they got and fled for safety, zig zagging between the trunks. From a distance they turned and spied the bear checking the rest of their little camp for comestibles before it lolloped off in the opposite direction.

Dawn was breaking as they looked at each other.

'That was a near miss,' breathed Billy. 'but the beast got its timing right. We would have overslept otherwise.'

After gathering what they could of their possessions they took a path a few yards in from the shoreline but still under the canopy of the forest, tracking towards the city walls of Reval.

Jack 24

Jack watched as Billy tried to make the guard at the gate understand through an iron grille. They were tired and footsore after their early start precipitated by the bear, and on arriving at the walls of the city close to the sea they found no path that would take them in. This meant they had an added trek past tower after tower to arrive at the land gate. Billy was using German, but it seemed the guard only had the local tongue.

'He's going to get his captain to talk to us.' Billy looked frustrated, kicking the ground with his shoes, once grand but now worn through in places. 'I hope they let us in so we can find some breakfast.'

The captain arrived and with some negotiation, followed by the passage of a coin or two through the grille, the door swung open. Billy carried on his conversation with the captain while Jack looked up the street. Shops were opening on either side and the merchants were setting out their wares for the coming day's business.

'He has given me directions to the Hansa office. I'm starving. Let's go.'

Jack trailed behind, feeling the cobbles through the thinned soles of his shoes. Too long on the boat, he thought, my feet have gone soft. The streets curved round whitewashed walls, thickly built to keep the chill out in winter. Jack looked up to see red tiled roofs topping the buildings and round conical towers at the corners. Some of the frontages were painted, the designs becoming grander the higher they reached into the city. Billy's pace quickened when he spotted the sign of the Hansa as they rounded a street corner.

It wasn't long before they had their feet warmed by a newly made fire and faced each other over a table spread with bread, cheeses and a mug of mulled beer each.

'I'm truly sick of that ship's cook. Isn't it wonderful to have some fresh food again?' Billy managed to ask between mouthfuls. Jack wasn't going to waste time with words. His cheeks bulged and that said it all.

Some hours later Jack woke. He was lying on fur rugs in front of the fire, and Billy was padding about behind him on the tiled floor.

'Hey, sleepy head, we need to get things sorted out here.'

While Jack had been asleep, Billy had sent a message to the Stadt Elbing to come into dock, and with the unloading underway had accompanied his trunk, pushed in a handcart, up the cobbled streets from the harbour. Its lid was open, and he was rummaging around in the contents.

'Here, this is yours I think.'

He threw the cloth wrapped sword hilt towards Jack, who caught it just before it hit the stone floor. Jack carefully undid the knotted cord that held the cloth in place and, for the first time in weeks, looked at his only possession once more. The size of the red stone in the pommel was as impressive as he remembered, bulging like a small pullet's egg. He looked at the lettering stamped in the metal ring around the stone but couldn't really make out the words "God wins" that had sent Peter into such a frenzy. The blackened metal stump of the blade itself was starting to flake along the sides. He was a long way from Antwerp where he had hoped to get a good price for it. Looking at it now he doubted it had much worth at all in these parts. The sense of loss and distance from home tightened his throat and made him feel choked.

'I have some merchants to meet and business to arrange,' Billy announced. 'You better come with me. And bring that thing with you. You never know. Someone may be interested in it.'

The heavy iron studded door of the Hansa house closed behind them, and they started up the street. Jack looked at the locals' faces and clothes, so different from his home or even London. Most had broad faces with blue eyes and wore fur-lined padded jerkins to keep out the cold.

'What you must remember here, Jack, is that Germans like myself are not always popular with the ordinary people. So, I would be grateful if you could just keep an eye out for my back.' Billy continued. 'This land of Livonia was conquered by Teutonic Knights, and the sword brethren, as they are known, still control the city of Reval. Many of the locals are heathens, worshipping the gods of the forest rather than our true Lord, and they resent being ruled over by the German speaking warrior monks.'

Jack saw two tall men approaching wearing the white scapular over their tunics with the badge of the black cross of the Teutons on the left breast. Their hard eyes scanned the folk in the street, who in turn kept a stave length distance from them as they went past.

While Jack was distracted, Billy had ducked down a narrow curving alley. He just caught up as Billy approached a sunken door down some steps. Billy rapped on it with his knuckles.

He whispered to Jack. 'I have been told that this is a travelling merchant's house, a Hebrew rather than Rus. He may speak a type of German so I should be able to understand him.'

They heard bolts being retracted inside the door, and slowly it swung open. A young man waved them in, and it took a second or two to adjust to the gloom. They were in a corridor draped on either side with thick woven cloth and rugs and passing through the passage they entered a chamber lit by small windows high up on the whitewashed walls. On the floor were piles of animal furs, ordered as to size and colour. Jack could see that most were brown bear skins, but interspersed were piles of paler coloured furs some with exotic markings. Seated amongst the pelts was an elderly man with white beard and hair, his head topped by a black velvet cap.

'Come over, come over.' The old man beckoned to them and directed them to two chairs that formed an arc alongside his own. 'My name is Yacob. Please have some wine, and here are some honey cakes. I am sure you will like them.' The young man proffered them from a tray. 'I hear that you have had a journey rather longer than you were expecting.'

'I am impressed by the accuracy of your information,' Billy responded.

'Well, we always like to keep an eye on what's happening at the docks. Tell me news from England. And I gather that the plague has gathered pace in Germany, your homeland.'

Billy recounted their voyage, repelling the pirates, and the difficulty making landfall because of the plague. As he began to tell of his stymied attempt to land at Lübeck, Jack could see tears starting to well up in Billy's eyes.

'It is always hard to be so far away from family, and not know what is happening to them.' Yacob said, reading Billy's distress. 'We as a people know that as well as anybody.'

100

Billy gathered himself and started to look over the merchandise on the floor.

'Do you travel east for all these furs?' he asked.

'No, not now. I am too old. It is my sons now who do the travelling. But in my earlier days I saw great sights of the east, trekking for weeks over high mountains, to lands where the sun is so powerful people are burnt black. We could do with a bit of that here,' he chuckled. 'But most of these furs are from Russia, whose forests are not so far away. Have a look and see what you may like.'

Billy started sorting through the pelts. Yacob pushed himself up with the aid of a silver topped walking stick, and then used its tip to turn over the pelts.

'As you can see, they are from the finest quality wild bears, none of that rubbish you get from the gypsies, all mangy and worn out after a lifetime of dancing. These will keep you warm through the coldest winter.' Yacob moved to a different pile. 'If those don't interest you, maybe you would like to have a look at the more exotic and rarer species? They are quite the thing as collars and trims on gowns now. I am sure you could lead the fashion if you introduced them to England and Germany. Our buyers from Italy are already taken with them.'

His assistant selected from the pile some ocelot and lynx pelts. Billy inspected them front and back.

'I have something here that is very special. Maybe you have a client who would be interested in something exceptionally rare?' He waved to his assistant who reached behind a pile of bear skins and brought out a leopard skin, grey in colour with smoky spots and its head adorned with yellow eyes and jaws wide open presenting an impressive set of canines. 'This is a leopard that lives only in the snowy

101

mountains and is so rare I have only ever seen one other such pelt in my long life as a merchant.'

Billy and Yacob started to negotiate. Billy knew he could get a fair price for the bear skins, and the lynx and ocelot would sell well in London but was unsure he could find a buyer for the leopard skin, especially at the price Yacob had set. They reached a deal, but without the leopard skin.

'I am disappointed. I thought you would find the leopard an interesting bargain. But I do have something else that may excite you.'

Yacob reached into a small casket that his assistant had opened on the table next to him. He undid a velvet pouch and gently cast the contents onto a polished tray. The stones that rolled out were of different colours: green, red, white and blue, the bigger ones rounded, and some smaller ones faceted. The polished planes of the tray on which they sat cleverly reflected light at an angle up and through them, adding to their allure.

'These precious stones have been brought all the way from the Isle of Serendib. I might be able to do a special deal for you?'

Billy's eyes widened.

'Maybe you have someone to whom you would like to give a gift like this?' Yacob, registering Billy's interest, picked out a green one. 'Do you like this emerald? It could bring you luck and you could meet a green-eyed girl.' Jack wondered whether Billy's girl in London, Petronella, had green eyes.

Billy picked up and examined several of the stones. He settled on the emerald and a sapphire, of deepest blue, its internal planes bouncing the light back through its surface. The price for two was whittled down.

'You drive a hard bargain,' the old man winced. 'But I will agree to that.' They touch hands.

Billy paused. 'My young friend here has something he would like to show you.' It caught Jack off guard. Jack reddened and at Billy's encouragement, he loosened his jerkin and lifted the cloth wrapped package through the opening under his chin. He laid it on the table and carefully undid the cord to reveal the sword hilt.

'What is this? You think I am a dealer in scrap metal?' The old man looked severely at Billy.

'No, no, no! Look at it carefully.'

Yacob picked it up gingerly, black particles from the metal marking his clean fingertips.

'Ah, I see, you think there may be some value in the stone.'

Jack watched him scrape at the dull red stone with his thumbnail.

'I can see it is quite large, but size is not everything. And I think it is a garnet rather than a ruby.'

For a second Jack could feel his face being examined by the old man's penetrating eyes, measuring him up, weighing his power.

'You look like a nice boy. I am feeling generous. I will give you this flawless ruby in exchange for it.'

Yacob nudged with his finger a bright red stone on the tray to separate it from the others. It was the size of a small split pea. Jack's face betrayed his disappointment at the disparity.

'I can see you do not understand. This ruby is worth more than your garnet, however large it is. It has been damaged by earth and water and will have to be recut again if anybody is to be interested in buying it from me.' Jack looked confused.

Yacob's voice was rising. 'I was a fool to offer the ruby to you. I withdraw it.'

He swept up the stones off the tray and funnelled them into their pouch.

Billy tried to repair the situation.

'He is only a poor cabin boy who knows nothing. Please forgive us.'

Yacob was now standing, and his demeanour was calming down after his sudden outburst. Billy joined him at a side table where he began writing out a bill of sale. Jack bundled up his sword hilt and tucked it into his clothing once more.

'We have done good business today. I won't let it be spoiled,' Yacob intoned as they left by the passage.

Jack 25

Jack blinked as he came back into the alleyway.

'Well, I did try for you young Jack,' Billy said. 'I think you might be stuck with that piece of old metal for some time yet.'

Jack was confused as to exactly what had gone on. He felt he was being offered something less than the worth of his treasure, but maybe its worth was not what he thought it was? Anyway, his luck might change for the better next time.

Light was fading as they regained the main thoroughfare, and some hostelries had lit flaming torches on either side of their entrances. From lower down the street, bouncing off the cobbles, they could hear raised English voices.

'I gave the archers an instalment of their wages before leaving the ship. I don't think they're going to hang onto their money for long here.' Billy looked down the hill.

Jack could make out Dick and the archers rolling up towards them in the gloom.

'Good to be on dry land again isn't it, Jack?' bellowed Dick, his voice unmodulated, the effects of alcohol showing already.

'Not so dry though in these parts!' another chipped in, slightly worse for wear.

'Come on Jack. We've got a tip for some pretty duckies up here.' Dick leaned in and whispered loudly in Jack's ear.

Billy peeled off when they passed the Hansa house, claiming fatigue, and left Jack with his compatriots. A man standing in the street directed them down the steps into a cellar lit by candles. They weren't the first of the ship's crew there. In the murk the captain was sitting in state with a girl on each arm. They nodded acknowledgment in his direction, but he was too preoccupied to notice. The archers shuffled past to a set of stools arranged around a table with a single candle on it, half burnt down. A fire was well established in the grate, and a serving girl fed it with fresh logs when they sat down, then added what looked like a large bunch of dried herbs on the top. It flamed purple and red and spat a volley of embers on to the floor, followed by curls of violet coloured smoke that wound through the darkness that surrounded them. Jack drank from the clay mug placed in front of him.

'Careful young lad,' warned Dick. 'They make it here with strong stuff from the forest.'

It tasted of honey, but with also a bitterness that Jack could not identify. As the liquor hit his throat a soothing calm entered his body, and he began to feel strangely separated from the chatter and noise of the hostelry around him. He quaffed more of the liquid, each successive gulp making the next more appealing. For a few moments he could focus and bring himself back into the room, but then, irresistibly, the allure of the spirit won again and took over. The people around the table seemed to come and go, their words indecipherable to him. One would leave, and another take his place, then the first one would be back. The chattering noise of the group reached a crescendo, then abated as he gave himself to the calm once more, the cycle repeated itself over and over, until the ripples of his resistance dissipated. A smooth softness touched his skin, his face nestling between two pillowy breasts, firm hips grinding above his pelvis, moist and elastic. A mouth was over his, its warm tongue searching. Was this a dream? He didn't care, the effect of the drink left him powerfully unconcerned.

Reality poked through Jack's subconscious with an urgency that woke him suddenly. He was on a soft mattress, lying on sheep skins, in a room which, as the noise was coming from below, he knew was directly above the tavern. His shirt was open, and his package was gone. At the door a dark-haired girl was exiting, her shift lifted by her speed. Jack scanned the floor in case it had fallen, and then he leapt after her, realising she must have it. She was already around a bend in the corridor, and he could hear her rapid steps descending wooden stairs. A door slammed shut at the bottom, and when Jack arrived there a second later he wrestled with the latch, not knowing which way to push or pull in the darkness. Eventually it freed, and he was through into a narrow back alley, the white form of the girl rounding a corner past the privies some twenty yards ahead. Jack pursued her and entered a courtyard where half a dozen horses were stabled, their dozy heads visible above the half doors. He tried to see into each stall but in the dark it was useless. The mud and straw slipped under his feet, and in anger he kicked the wooden board, causing a horse to nay. He stood silently for a while, hoping the thief might break cover, but then decided she could have disappeared anywhere in the vicinity.

Jack slowly made his way back along the alley, grieving for his lost treasure and rueing his decision to reject the merchant's offer. As he neared the street, he heard shouting and Dick's unmistakable voice.

'I'll knock that fucking Teuton tits block off!'

The archers were being manhandled out of the tavern and into the street, where they were being beaten with staves by the Teuton guards who received them there. A rope was called for, and their wrists and forearms, now pinned behind their backs, were lashed together. It didn't take long to subdue them in a manner which would have been impossible were it not for their drunken incapacity.

'All my men here have been robbed of their money. Every single coin has been taken by the women in there,' Dick implored, his voice slurred.

The guards were uncomprehending and unconcerned of the pleas that came in a language they didn't understand.

Jack 26

A drop of cold water detached from the ceiling and landed on the back of Jack's neck. He looked up and glimpsed the snout of a rat poking through an iron grate way above head height, the only source of light from the outside world for their damp dungeon. The rat scuttled away to enjoy the freedom Jack now lacked. Hours had passed since they had been shackled to iron rings in the wall, their wrists now aching in the manacles behind their backs.

'I reckon, if we could shift that grate up there, then Jack could wriggle through it.' Ever the optimist, Dick was devising strategies for escape. In reality they were securely held and the rest of the band, with their heads held low, didn't even grace the remark with a response. They were feeling sore from the beating, and also from being fleeced of their money.

Footsteps sounded from way up the corridor, resonating along the stone walls louder than their true distance, but unmistakably getting closer. Two sets. The unseen figures paused on the other side of the stout iron-clad cell door and a key rattled into the lock and turned. The gaoler entered first and then Billy.

'If I had any sense, I would leave you all here to rot,' Billy started. 'It would be a lot cheaper for me, and I wouldn't have to pay you any more money that you just throw away at the first opportunity.' The archers sat silently, tilted forward by their chains, examining the floor. 'But instead, like the idiot that I am, I have paid a ransom more suitable for a king than for you wretches. You'll find it missing from your final wages, if they ever come due.' Billy turned and left while the gaoler went round unchaining each of them. The archers stood up in turn, flexing their sore shoulders and extending their backs. Jack was the last to be released. He wanted to catch Billy to explain that his sword hilt had been stolen. As they filed up the twisting corridor, he saw Billy sitting in the gaoler's office.

'I can't believe you English. As soon as you get the chance you get into trouble.' Billy was ticking. 'I don't know why you joined them. They're just a bunch of losers.'

Jack looked suitably admonished. He tried to find the words to explain.

'I think they used a potion in the drink to make us lose our senses. There is a lot I can't remember about last night. But when I came to, a girl was running away from me, and my package was missing.'

'You mean you have lost your sword hilt?' Billy paused then laughed. 'That is going to save a lot of trouble for you in the future. You won't have to worry about guarding a piece of old rusty metal no one else wants.' His mood lifted temporarily with his amusement at the situation. Then his expression became serious again when he saw Jack's lack of bonhomie. 'Yes, I suppose there is a fairly large red stone in it that could be of value.'

The gaoler came into the room and sat down opposite Billy, satisfied with the night's bag of reprobates, converted into hard currency. He shifted his substantial paunch to one side and raised his feet onto a stool.

'Just one more thing,' Billy said to the gaoler. 'This young friend of mine had a very important package stolen from him last night at the tavern. Do you think there is a way of retrieving it?'

The gaoler turned to Jack. Billy translated Jack's statement of how he saw the white clad figure of the girl running from the room and then disappearing down the alleys. Billy listened to the gaoler's response, then relayed it to Jack.

'He says it is a Kratt. They are very common around here. They are often built out of straw and are in the control of an evil person who employs them to go out and steal. The chance of finding your piece of metal is very low indeed.'

Jack looked disconsolate. He felt certain it was a real girl who was there, not one made of straw.

'But I felt her body. She wasn't made of straw.'

'Ah, that is a trick the magic plays on you. He says all the controller needs is three drops of blood, and then the machine is made flesh. And think how quickly it disappeared. If it were a real girl, you would easily have caught her.' The gaoler thought the conversation over and made to get up.

'Do they go back to straw?'

'Sometimes they do, and sometimes they ignite and disappear amongst the flames.'

Jack had an idea. He last saw the girl near the stables. Once the gaoler had seen them out, he explained to Billy.

'She ran towards the stables behind the back of the tavern. There is lots of straw there. Maybe that's where she has hidden it.'

'You go on your own adventure if you like. I can't spend my time searching with you. I have business to get on with.' Billy walked with a confident stride down the hill to the docks while Jack turned and made his way back to the scene of his misadventure at the tavern.

Jack 27

Jack was nervous approaching the tavern. He had already been in trouble there once and had been locked up for it. Why risk going back there again? But he felt compelled to check the stables.

The alley by the side of the tavern looked different in daylight. It had high brick sides, and he proceeded with caution, past the stink of the latrines, and round the corner. He could see there was no possible way the girl could have escaped but via the courtyard at the end. The alley opened on to a cobbled area around which stables formed two sides of a square. The doors were open, the horses out working their tasks for the day. Jack kicked at the straw on the ground in the empty stalls, turning it over but found nothing apart from lumps of manure. Above and behind him there was a rustling up in the hay loft, and Jack turned. He thought he saw a pair of eyes looking down on him, but the light was dim up there. He climbed a wooden upright and swung his body onto the platform above the stalls. He started checking behind the hay bales, but then heard a thump as something hit the floor below. Rushing to the edge he looked down and glimpsed a figure running out across the yard making for the alley. Was it the girl? He couldn't tell from his angle of view. He thought for a second. Should I run after her? He would never catch her before the street. He hesitated. Best to carry on checking up here and make sure the sword hilt is not hidden here. But not for too long, he thought. I'm trapped and if she gets help, I may not get out of the alley.

Jack assured himself that there was nothing hidden under the straw. He dropped down onto the floor and braced himself for a possible confrontation as he walked tall from the yard to the street along the alley.

With some relief he emerged into the open street. Billy was coming up from the docks.

'Any luck?'

'I think I may have seen the girl running away when I checked the stables just now.'

'Well, we need to make haste. The captain wants to sail this evening. We're already late in the season and the storms won't be too far away.'

Jack looked down. Billy carried on.

'Look Jack. I can call in a favour from one of the Teutonic Knights who hails from near my hometown. He won't fear putting some pressure on the tavern keeper to see if we can get hold of your bit of treasure.'

An hour later Jack was standing in the back room of the inn with Billy translating his story to Jurgen, the Teuton. He in turn was standing over the owner of the tavern, who was cowering in his stained apron. His head was turned away as Jurgen had a grip on his black greasy hair. Jurgen casually grated his swelling face against the cold stone wall.

'Don't give me that Kratt nonsense. Imps and pixies!' he bellowed at the crouched man, who whimpered. 'I'll beat you into a pulp until you tell me the real story.'

The man gathered himself as if to speak, but first spat a gobbet of blood onto the floor.

'Go to the gaoler. He knows what's going on.'

Jurgen then kicked him hard on the rear and sent him sprawling across the room.

'Ah, I see, you've got a nice little business operating here. You drug and rob the sailors who come to your tavern, and the gaoler locks them up when they make a fuss and complain. Let's see what he has to say about it shall we?'

Billy and Jack trailed after Jurgen as he strode forcefully towards the town gaol. By the third knock the heavy wooden door swung open, and the gaoler, on seeing the angry face of the knight rearranged his own normally surly expression into one of extreme obsequiousness.

'Oh, honourable sir, is there a prisoner you have a special interest in?' His eyes roamed to Billy and Jack as he tried to keep his expression steady and resist it descending into desperation. Jurgen grabbed a handful of his dirty shirt below his chin and thrust back, the gaoler's head pitching against the wall.

'I am interested in the profitable arrangement between you and the tavern keeper. He seems to think you may know something about this boy's possession from which he was separated last night.'

'Ah, yes, I remember. If you would kindly allow a little air for me to breathe.' Jurgen released his grip, and the gaoler straightened his collar and cleared his throat. 'He explained to me earlier today a small matter of a Kratt, common around these parts, which clearly ran off with something he said he owned.' The sentence was terminated abruptly by Jurgen's swinging hand connecting with the gaoler's right cheek.

'Enough of your heathen lies! I am not so stupid to be taken in by your stealing fairies!'

Jurgen grabbed the gaoler by the shirt and slapped him again.

The gaoler recovered from the vicious blow and looked sheepishly at Jurgen. He calculated it might be better now to change tack. 'We do keep some items of lost property that mariners may have dropped in the town. I could check the special closet to see if something has been handed in.' Jurgen frog marched him down the corridor and around the corner. Jack and Billy followed. The gaoler's hand shook as he fumbled his large ring of keys and found one to insert into the hole in a small iron door in the wall. The door swung open, and Jack immediately recognised the cloth of his package and pointed to it.

'Well, we must be in luck, it does seem to have been picked up somewhere.' The gaoler tried to maintain the pretence, but Jurgen gave him a further swipe around the top of the head.

'I'll take that key,' Jurgen said as the gaoler quickly shut the door and locked it before any further examination of the contents of the closet could take place. 'I'll be back later, and we can go through everything in there that "the Kratt" may have brought to you.'

Outside the gaol, with the sword hilt safely tucked in his jerkin, Jack stood as Billy thanked Jurgen. Jurgen spoke of his family in Germany that he had not seen in many years and Billy promised to find them when he is next in his homeland.

'Your very lucky still to have it,' Billy addressed Jack. 'It's caused no end of trouble, and nobody but you really thinks it has any value.'

Jack thought the gaoler must have realised its value but thought best not to say so. They trudged back down the hill towards the gate and harbour.

Jack 28

The wind filled the sails as Jack looked back to the town of Reval, its pale walls connecting tower after tower, each capped by a cone of red tiles. The ship heaved and yawed on the swell. Dick was standing next to him at the rail.

'You had a lucky escape there young lad. Mixing with all those witches an' all that. If there's one thing I've learnt in life, it's best to keep well away from magic and all that stuff. You never know where it might lead.'

Jack thought Dick must have heard the story about the Kratt but decided not to elaborate on how he had got his sword hilt back. He was keeping it firmly inside his jerkin from now on. Dick was used to Jack's reticence, and, undeterred by his silence, let his thoughts turn to home.

'I can't wait to see my Mary again. She must be wondering where I have got to. She'll make me a fine feast on my return. Anyway, with this fair breeze it should only be a few weeks now.'

Jack felt stung. His mother and father would probably have given him up for dead by now, but he could be back with them in time. If only he could realise the value in his treasure and turn it into hard currency. It hadn't worked out so far, but maybe he could get to Antwerp on the way back.

The following wind was strong, and the sky was high and blue. A spirit of optimism suffused the ship as it made good progress. They were homeward bound. The crew worked hard managing the sails, not letting them rip with the power of the wind, racing up the rigging to unfurl them or take them

116

in when the captain ordered. The bow cut through the waves, slicing the spuming white water into two great folds on each side of the ship as it surged forward. And then, quite suddenly, the wind dropped.

No one noticed at first. Or at least Jack and Dick didn't, still standing looking out at the sea. For a while the waves rolled the ship forward, but minute by minute their power diminished, and, where before there had been the sound of water slapping the prow and wind cracking the sails, a silence descended. The captain strode the quarter deck, and the eyes of the crew collectively followed him, waiting for the next order, but there was none to give. The sails sagged flaccidly.

Billy came up on deck and stood next to the captain viewing what was now a grey flat sea. Jack could see a frown on his face, reflecting the anxious look the captain had adopted. He turned and looked towards the horizon, following the direction of their gaze. The sun was still two or three hours from setting and blazed in their eyes. Below it the horizon was obscured by a blurry dark streak that stretched from one side of the sea to the other.

Some of the crew tried to break the menacing silence and hang on to the spirit that had maintained them for the last few hours. They cracked feeble jokes and told of how they would give their loved ones such a surprise after months at sea. But the bond to that happy moment weakened and frayed and then fractured as the grey streak grew, changing from the colour of pigeon feather to a shade of dark purple, coating the billowing underside of the approaching bank of clouds a menacing aubergine, while the tops remained white and fluffy, hanging on to the last light of the descending sun. And then the sun was gone.

Anxiety gripped the ship. Jack could feel the wind pick up, but this time it was in his face, the reverse direction to before. The captain bellowed orders and the crew raced up the rigging to take the sails in. The hull skewed and sheared as new waves struck the prow at angles, swinging it from side to side. The timbers groaned with the strain, piercing the sound of the gathering wind.

Jack clung on to the side as a wave crashed over the foredeck, white water sweeping across the planks from port to starboard. The bow dipped precipitously, tilting so far down that the next wave appeared as a sheer wall of water, its top invisible. The captain tried to turn the rudder to face it square on and Jack braced himself. The spine of the ship shuddered as it struck the face of the wave, and then followed sheets of icy water thrown up and over to cover Jack and whoever else was brave enough still to be on deck. So it went on, wave after wave, the fading of the day providing no respite as the ship was pushed backwards from its path. Jack chose a brief moment to make the dash from his handhold to the hatch, and dropped, or rather was washed through it, with a flood of bubbling frothy water. He joined a huddled mass of bodies wedged up against a bulkhead. In the darkness the whispered prayers of these frightened souls took on a rhythm, an offbeat that followed the regular crash of wave against the hull. Sometimes the murmured paternosters rose in volume, trying desperately to summon a spiritual response when the fearsome uncontrollable sea threatened to overwhelm them. Then the hum would settle lower, a tone watchful, not pitched to tempt fate but relieved to fill the few seconds between cataclysmic rupturing jolts. Jack looked around now that his eyes had accommodated to the gloom. All were soaked through. He couldn't distinguish between archers or crew, young or old. Their heads were down, their individual identities subsumed to a frightened mass of humanity, a melding together of people faced with such an existential threat.

They raised their heads as one when an awful crack, followed by a rending, ripping screech shook them from hips to neck. 'That'll be the mast going.' Jack wasn't sure if this was said out loud or just sensed all as one. The prayers rose in response. The hull yawed as the captain, after such a valiant action to keep the ship straight against the storm, was overwhelmed, either by a rush of water or by the tragedy of a broken mast. Now sideways on to the storm, the ship keeled over as it rose, the wedge of the wave driving below, steadily, relentlessly forcing them up, the collective stomach left down there and always behind on the rise. Up they all went, thinking when will it stop and reach its peak. A level was found, but their stomachs overshot as the drop began, a delayed pull down on the long descent into the trough. If there was anything left to vomit, up it came, but the loss of scanty bile did nothing to improve their outlook. Wave after wave crashed into the side of the hull, driving it back way beyond its starting point just hours before.

The hull scratched in a down trough, the souls all registering the vibration however brief it was. They waited as one for the ship's next descent, and now, to their certainty, it dragged and ground against a hard surface before being lifted off and up, up again. Heads turned to one another, shoulders moved for the first time in hours and spines stiffened. The hull peaked on its wave and then dropped, but now sideways forcing body to fall onto body. The trough this time was not a smooth transition, but an abrupt stop as the clinkered timbers were stove in, the entry of a massive black rock into their

119

sacred space chased closely by jets of spuming water. Jack was at the top of the pile bodies, being the last one in, and those figures whose identities he could not make out when he had joined the praying mass now separated as the sea flooded in. Below the surface he saw Dick's face imploring him, eyes wide but bathed in saline. And there was Billy, expression even, as though he knew this was always going to happen. The rising wave carried Jack up and away from the tangled bodies, and towards the rent in the ship's side as it rolled over. He felt his package, too heavy to stay inside his jerkin, loosen and slip, knocking on thigh, knee and foot before sinking slowly into the depths. He felt its loss, the cause of so much trouble, but it had been his talisman and his imagined route from poverty. The wave separated him from it, but he couldn't swim against the force however much he wanted to do so. Passively he rose with the wave and at its peak was gently placed face down on smooth rounded granite, the water dragging back to gather itself for the next wave. He scrambled up the rock and turned to look back at the timbers of the ship, once so grand but now so feeble, being crushed and torn apart by the horrible force of nature. There was not a sign of any other survivor. He shivered and groaned and then tilted his head back and yelled into the darkness 'Mother!'

Part Two

Mo 1

The electric motor started up. It whirred as Mohammad's scrawny arms swung the floor polisher from side to side. Not Mohammad. It's Mo now. That's easier. Mo glanced up and saw the tops of the trees where the birch forest started. The thin watery light lost its battle at the window. How could light be so dark?

He worked his way backwards, down the corridor. The harsh ceiling light bounced back off his polished floor. His mind drifted, to golden splinters of sun reflected from the surface of the river near his village. Sounds of splashing as he played with his friends in the water. Those were happy times. But then men with guns started visiting the village in their trucks. Give us your boys, they said, and we will turn them into men. One of his friends went with them the first time they visited, but no one heard what happened to him. By the third time they visited, Mo was wondering what sort of man he was. He knew he didn't want to be a man with a gun. But could he stay in the village? Times were changing. His uncle had some savings and offered to lend him money to make the long journey. Then he could get rich and give the money back.

The asylum lawyer was kind. She had let him Skype his uncle on her computer. At least his mother knew he was safe now. The lawyer had said, if you work for a year then you get something called a "credit rating" and then you can get a contract for a cell phone. She had got him this job cleaning at the hospital. You could eat at the canteen before going back to the hostel.

Cre-dit...swing to the left. Ray-ting....swing to the right.

He looked back along the corridor, light glinting on his handiwork, the blue floor rising. A wall of water rose in his subconscious, breaking through, white cresting. There was no horizon to see from the boat, their bodies flexing together as they willed themselves over the next wave. Cold salt spray stung their faces. A pool of water grew in the middle of the boat, and anxiety turned to panic. He didn't really know most of those who hadn't made it. Best not to. Block it out.

Three hours until mealtime. There were pretty girls there, blond with broad pale faces. He sometimes caught their soft blue eyes on his face, his wispy beard and black hair, but they turned their eyes away. Would they take him home to meet their families? He couldn't take the risk. All his risk was used up. What sort of man was he?

Mo 2

It was raining on Mo's walk back to the hostel. He felt like skipping and splashing in the puddles, water from the heavens should be a cause to celebrate, but here it just didn't seem like the right thing to do. Men and women, their hooded heads bowed, quickened their steps in the grey twilight. Up the slope, he used his shoulder to push through the swing doors of the hostel. Dripping, he went past the lounge, lit by the television. When he first arrived, a few months before, he would sit and watch the news. Sometimes an item would come up about his home country. Why did they always get it wrong? So often a group he knew was bad were presented as saviours, that a militia leader who had tortured people was now a hero. He felt betrayed. The truth didn't seem solid and so he stopped trusting the word of the TV journalists.

He shut the door and lay on his bed. Snakes slithered and wriggled into his semiconsciousness. His mother had said she found a snake next to him when he was sleeping as an infant. As he got bigger, he became the great snake hunter of his village. Neighbours would call for him to help if they found one by the well or in the laundry. He felt confident that he knew how to handle them, dispatching the dangerous ones, relocating the innocent. But on his journey there had been different species of snake, camouflaged in ways he didn't understand. One bite could send him home.

'Are you travelling alone or in a group? Do you have any dependents?' He looked at the official. He hoped his eyes didn't betray the raw fear he felt inside. What is the right answer? Which answer could he give that would not trigger the unravelling, the uncoiling of his journey so far? He re-lived question after question as he lay on his bed, sweat forming on his brow. The official compiled his form, head down, expressionless, no hint of a clue as to how he was doing. Had the snake emerged from the grass and bitten him yet? Was he going home? More questions came. His answers weaved a thread of credibility, in and out between truth and his imagined truth, the one that would make his journey stick. Later he caught a glimpse of this form at his asylum lawyer's office. It had a scale of unreliability versus reliability. His score was a solid six. He was getting to know the local snakes.

He felt momentarily ashamed that his mother might not approve of his unsteady relationship with the truth. But times were changing. He had seen big men on TV. Even the president of the USA. The truth can be anything that gets you what you want, what you need.

Mo 3

Mo descended the stairs and walked past the lounge. Unusually for morning there were two fellow refugees sitting in the lounge facing one another over a table. Their heads were down, and they didn't see Mo's feeble raised hand greeting. One rolled the dice. His counter was near the top of the board, and he had a lot to lose. The only game the hostel had was snakes and ladders. Mo's cheeks tightened; his mouth stretched into a thin grin. It seemed somehow appropriate, lessons they all had to learn.

On Saturday mornings there was a community project to get young people in the city to interact with refugees who had recently arrived. Mo stood on the pavement not far from the hostel, waiting for the minibus. Weak sunlight was trying to pierce the misty cloud that seemed to hover just above the rooftops. The street was still wet from yesterday's rain, and cars going past hissed as their tyres cut through the shallow puddles. The minibus pulled up and the doors folded back allowing him to hop up the stairs and swing down the aisle to his favoured back seat. There weren't many people on it yet, but it would fill up as it toured the city. The window was misted up and he gave it a quick wipe with his sleeve. They drove past massive grey granite buildings with decorated columns between the windows. The shops underneath were starting to open. This city was rich. It must have taken a lot of money to create all this. The bus stopped at traffic lights outside the railway station. A tram rattled by. Two giant men sculpted in stone, each holding a faintly illuminated globe of light, stood guard on either side of the entrance to the station.

Dwarfed between them another man, much more mobile, raised his head and let out a cry, mouth wide open. The sound didn't penetrate the glass of the bus, but Mo could hear it in his head, just from the look in the man's eyes. He started to swing his arms round, windmilling. The stream of pedestrians separated to give him space, like the flow of a river round a rock. Nobody broke step or looked at him. Mo had heard it said that the Northern winter can do this to you.

The bus was starting to fill up. The youngsters, mainly blond but some black, had their heads down, their faces illuminated by screens, their portals to another world. The tin roof of the bus, and the people passively facing the same way, reminded Mo of a cattle shed that a friend Abdul had told him about. On his journey Mo had walked alongside Abdul and had enjoyed his perspective on the world. Abdul had told him that cell phones were a way of farming people.

'The farmer tempts the people into the cattle shed with lovely rich food, and they all line up with their heads in their own individual trough. They like this so much that they don't worry about the farmer attaching his milking machine to the other end. Everyone is happy. Then the farmer buys a new additive for their feed. It's called like some sort of biscuit...no, "cookies". Everybody loves cookies. What's not to like? The cattle don't mind because the feed tastes even better than ever. The milk that the farmer sells is getting richer and richer. And the farmer is making so much money he doesn't know what to do with it. But if you take too much creamy milk out of a cow, in such large amounts, it will get weak and start to waste away. Maybe that's what is starting to happen to people.'

Mo chuckled remembering clever Abdul. His mind drifted back to the cattle that were part of his village. They weren't in sheds, they could roam free, but they only had scrubby grass to eat, when they could find it. And if you tried to milk them, and they didn't like it, they would give you a kick. But he felt sure they would like to have artificial feed just like the rest of the world.

Mo came out of his reverie when a girl sat next to him.

Mo 4

Mo tensed when the girl's shoulder pushed against him as the minibus rounded a corner. He was looking straight ahead but could just catch in his peripheral vision the form of her fair hair and straight nose. They were too close together for him to turn and say something in the way of a formal introduction. He felt awkward as they said nothing.

The bus pulled up at a low building set in parkland with bare birch trees draping their twiggy limbs over the pavement approach. The bus emptied from the front, and the girl stood up. Mo could see she was wearing a beige parka, her hair nestling in the fur lined hood which was pushed back. He rose to follow and joined the group spilling out onto the pavement. At the front someone who he could not see led them through the glass doors of the building to a room filled with plastic chairs arranged in concentric arcs in front of a projector screen. There were far more chairs than people, but he placed himself near the back, one seat away from the girl on the bus.

The presentation started. A middle-aged man with a large belly and his hair in a ponytail began speaking in Finnish. Mo was not yet able to understand more than a few words and was relieved when the speaker swapped to English after a sentence or two.

'We welcome you here to the Suomi friends' fellowship, where we can help our new visitors and introduce them to the ways and traditions of our country.'

Mo watched while slides flicked over on the screen, of reindeer, traditional costume, and saunas. He noticed the girl shifting on her chair. They were hard, and the lecture was boring. The speaker's monotonous voice didn't compete well for Mo's attention and his gaze strayed to the sunlit grass and trees framed through the window. The cloud was lifting and starting to break up. Chair legs scratched on the hard floor as people stood up and stretched, the talk now over. Mo rose quickly and looked around. The girl was also standing and looked straight at him.

'Hey, I'm Isla.' She held her hand out to him. He reached and touched it momentarily.

'I work at the hospital.' It was the first thing that came into his head. Isla looked confused. 'My name's Mohammad, but please call me Mo.'

'So, you're Mo and you work at the hospital.' She repeated slowly, as though trying to take in the information.

'Yes.'

'OK. Anything else I should know about you? You haven't killed anyone have you?' Isla briefly smiled, but then thought that may have been inappropriate. Who knows what these refugees may have seen? After a pause she nodded towards a trestle table at the side of the room where the others were picking up coffee cups neatly arranged next to a large thermos jug. Mo followed her over.

'I like the salt in Finnish coffee, but it's not as thick as we make it at my home.' Mo said as he took a sip.

This seemed like safer territory. Isla thought about asking about Mo's home but held back. She had been told not to dwell on where people had come from. The idea was to integrate them, and that meant keeping them in the here and now.

Mo took a glance at Isla's face. She had a long straight nose and a strong jaw line with grey eyes and a pale

131

complexion. There was a streak of blue in her dark blonde hair, and she had a nose ring.

The doors had opened, and some people were drifting to the area outside. Mo was pleased to be in the open air even with the chill that it brought. He stood beside Isla as they looked up the hill.

'I do this on Saturdays just to break the boredom. I work in a shop through the week and also do a bit of studying.' Isla explained.

'Oh, what do you study?'

'I would like to be a social worker. Are you a doctor?'

'No. I just clean at the hospital.'

They started walking on a path that curved around bushes up the hill.

'Are you going to do the beach cleaning next weekend?' Isla asked.

Mo wasn't sure what she meant. He didn't think his job at the hospital was linked to cleaning the beaches, and why would anyone want to go to a beach when it was so cold.

Isla sensed his confusion. 'You know, the beach clear up. He explained it in the presentation. There's a group going to the islands to clear up all the plastic that gets washed up. I don't think you were listening very closely.'

Isla gave him a mock reproving look, then broke into a smile. Her eyes lit up when she smiled. Mo smiled back and for the first time they connected.

'Yes, I would like to go if I am not working. Of course, it would mean on my day off from cleaning the hospital, I would be cleaning the beach.'

They both grinned.

'Hey, you can see the islands from the top of this hill.' Isla broke into a run and Mo chased. They arrived at the top a bit short of breath. In front of them lay the harbour, and beyond the steel grey of the sea which was dotted with many small islands. Some had a cluster of low pine trees, some with the odd wooden cabin.

Isla pointed. 'I think we will probably be going to that one.'

It had a red roofed hut on it, but he really couldn't see much beach. It was mainly rocks.

'There is a beach on the other side.' Isla said. 'It's quite popular in the summer so it needs a good clear up.'

Mo noticed a sculpture not far away on the hilltop, where several paths met. It looked old, made of blackened bronze now pitted by the weather. They walked over towards it. A man held a limp child over his shoulder as he reached up, searching for rescue. A lifeless woman lay curled up below his legs, spuming waves cast in metal swirled around her. They paused to take in the image.

Isla could see Mo was affected by it.

'I think it must be about a shipwreck,' she said.

'Yes. I can feel what they feel,' Mo replied.

Mo 5

The following week passed very slowly. Mo thought a lot about Isla. It was the first time he had spoken to anyone of his own age apart from in the hostel. She seemed nice and sympathetic, but he wasn't sure she could understand the experiences he had been through, and he thought that explaining them might not be a good idea. He looked in the mirror as he brushed his teeth. His face was framed by a crust of old toothpaste splatter. He smiled and for the first time in a long time he saw the old Mohammad returning.

The minibus stopped in the same place as the previous week. He climbed in and the aisle felt springy as walked to the back to find his seat. He counted off the stops until the one he remembered Isla had got on. The minibus drew to a halt. Mo strained to see through the window, but all he could see was a boy getting on. His heart dropped. It was she who had suggested going in the first place.

The bus rattled over the tramlines and came to a halt by the harbour. Mo was the last to get out. There were some kiosks and signs pointing towards the small ferry boats. He followed as the queue moved slowly. How could she have let him down like that? He felt betrayed.

The man who had given the presentation the previous week stood counting by the gangplank as Mo followed the others onto the boat. Inside the rail he was faced with a choice. He could go forward and stay outside, or else go down into the cabin. He went forward. He didn't really want to talk, and the cabin looked busy. There were just a handful of people who were braving the outside. He found a perch facing forward and could see the islands they were headed to across the harbour. He put his hood up and sunk his neck down.

The engine started. For a moment he felt he was back in the refugee boat, and he shut his eyes to reign back the sudden rush of anxiety he felt. The tone of the engine was different though, much deeper with a low vibration, not like an outboard motor at all. He opened his eyes. Seagulls were sitting on the rail, drawn by the free ride. The closest one returned his gaze, its perfect eye fixed on him. The boat moved quite suddenly, a small jolt as the last rope was cast off.

The buildings to his left seemed to be moving backward and, with a steady chug, the boat gained pace.

'Mo, I've been looking for you.' He turned and saw Isla coming up the steps from the inside cabin. 'Hey, where have you been?' she asked.

'I... I thought you weren't on the boat. You weren't on the bus.'

'That's because I had to help get the equipment we need.' He noticed she was pulling up a black bag behind her.

She sat down next to him. He looked at her again for the first time in a week. He knew he liked her face, but he couldn't get any feeling as to whether she liked him as well. He felt foolish for feeling so down when she hadn't appeared on the bus. He felt restored now.

'So, are you enjoying the boat trip?'

'I had a bad time on a boat once.'

'Oh. Do you want to tell me what happened?'

'I've never told anyone before. I paid a lot of money to the people who owned the boat. Most of the money my uncle had given me to get to Europe. It was one of those rubber inflatable boats, but quite big. I had enough for a life vest as well, but lots of people didn't. There must have been about two hundred of us. I was lucky, I could sit on the side, but there were so many in the middle you couldn't see the bottom of the boat. The first few kilometres were fine, and the mood was good. Everybody was happy to be escaping. I remember enjoying the cold spray of salt water in my face. Then when the coast behind was just a thin strip the waves got bigger, and we started slamming into them. People were trying to make the driver go slower, but he wasn't interested. I could hang onto a rope that went round the sides, but the ones in the middle just got thrown about. Some of the waves came into the boat, and it didn't take long for it to start to fill up. That's when the driver did slow down, and he handed out buckets to scoop the water out of the middle, but it was impossible. Nobody could get their balance with the big waves. You couldn't stand up in the middle to fill the bucket, and besides you were too far away from the sides to throw the water out. I saw people drown while they were still in the boat. The driver cut the engine then. He couldn't make the boat go forward when it was full of water. So, we waited. The waves were frightening. It got dark and everyone was tired and scared. Being on the side probably saved my life. I tried to help keep people's heads above the water, but they were thrown about with every big wave, and some gave up because it took too much effort to stay alive. It was towards the end of the next day before a ship spotted us and slowed down to rescue us.'

'Wow. You have been through something there.' She looked sad and concerned.

'Yes, it felt strange getting on this boat. The first time I've been on water since.'

'There's the island. We will go round it to land on the other side.'

Did Mo feel better for talking about it? He wasn't sure. Isla had listened, but what could she say?

Mo 6

A broad-backed crewman tied the rope to a post as the boat came alongside the wooden jetty that jutted from the sandy beach. The sun was breaking through between dark clouds and Mo could feel his mood lifting. He was pleased he had had the opportunity to tell Isla something of his journey and the dangers he had endured, even if her acknowledgement was cursory. Maybe she was concentrating on what they had to do next.

When the gangway was secure, the line of volunteers was led onto the beach by the middle-aged man with the ponytail who had presented to them the previous week. Mo and Isla followed at the rear, Isla carrying the bag of equipment.

'Starting at this end of the beach, we must pick up all the plastic that is embedded in the sand. As I told you, it breaks down into smaller bits very slowly, and they can stick in the guts of the marine wildlife that lives around here,' he droned on.

Isla opened her bag and started handing out litter picker sticks, with a trigger handle at one end that worked jaws at the other. The volunteers each took one together with a black plastic bag for the plastic harvest. Mo practised making the jaws work on his picker.

'Come on. Let's get going.'

Mo tracked between Isla and the gently lapping waves on the sandy shore. The beach was bounded by grey humps of granite, worn smooth by the weight of ice that in past millennia had formed a thick cap here. Now the sun shone on them, reflecting a spray of glitter from the shards of mica embedded in the rock. A sense of freedom came over Mo. He felt free from the city, it's darkness so unfamiliar to him. And he felt lifted of the burden of his story, somehow lighter for being told to Isla.

'Think Mo, you're missing bits!' Isla shouted across to him. He got his head down and scanned the rippled sand. There wasn't really that much to find. He picked up a bit of old fishing float, faded blue by the water. He looked over to Isla who already seemed to be dragging her bag, as it was filling up. He felt he could not be outdone. His movements got quicker as he tried to cover a bigger area. Then he found a plastic rose and not far from it a broken sandal, it's long stiletto heel intact. He looked at the rose. Its washed-out colour retaining just a little pink in the swell of the bud, but not the bright red it once would have been. The knobbly thin stem still had hints of green in places. This must hide a story he thought. Was it lost from a boat at the same time as the shoe?

'What have you got there?' asked Isla, her eyes twinkling with curiosity.

'It's a flower.'

'Oh, you shouldn't have. I didn't know you cared.' Flirtatiously, Isla took the plastic flower from him and pretended to sniff its scent. Mo felt his cheeks blush, lost for words in the moment.

'I would have given you a real one if I had known you like them so much.'

'I'll take that as a promise then.'

Isla scampered off back to the tide line, where there were much richer pickings of flotsam. The group of other volunteers were moving ahead on the beach and had turned the corner round a granite hump.

'Let's have a rest.' She beckoned over to Mo and started walking up the beach to the round rocks. He followed her to a sheltered crevice. They sat close, forced together by the dipping slope of the rocks. Mo was conscious that their thighs were touching.

'It's hot here in the sun.' Isla reached up with both arms to lift her sweatshirt over her head. As she twisted her body Mo felt, through her tee shirt, the outside of her breast brush his upper arm. He felt awkward and aroused at the same time, and shifted his legs, pressing down in the sand with his right foot. It first met resistance, but then gave way as the sand shifted under it. He looked down into the depression his foot had made.

'It looks like a bit of metal,' Mo said, not sure if he welcomed the distraction or not.

They both stood up and Mo crouched down to scratch with his fingers. With some effort he managed to get down the sides of the metal which was firmly lodged in the cleft between the two rocks. It could move up and down but not side to side. He gently eased it backward and forwards, breaking bonds formed over centuries of contact. It seemed to have a handle which aided his grip and then as he pulled, it came free.

'Wow...' Isla said. 'That looks as though it could be quite something.'

Mo looked at it. There was a lump that seemed heavy at the end of the handle and that stuck out beyond his hand. The other end was longer and tapered to a jagged point. He let go of the handle and looked at it, holding it between the fingertips of both hands. The whole was blackened by years of water, salt and sand.

'I know, let's wash it in the sea.'

They both hurried down to the water's edge. Mo let the low waves wash over it. There seemed to be some fibres of cloth that floated from it. The grit that coated it fell away and its shape took on greater definition. Mo could see it had been finely crafted. He scratched at the black with his fingernail and made a streak of yellow which soon faded to grey.

'What do you think it is?'

'It looks like a knife, or a sword which has been broken off.'

'How do you think it got here? Nobody's lived on this island for centuries.'

A shout reached them from further along the beach. 'Hey, what are you two doing!'

It was the man with the ponytail, trotting back towards them.

Mo couldn't understand the conversation between Isla and the man, but he did know that Isla had slipped the piece of metal into a separate bag she was carrying before the man reached them. Isla was looking despondent as they walked along the beach to join the rest of the group.

'That man is so annoying. He's just told me off for hanging back with you. He said it's not safe, and he is responsible for me, so I must keep up.'

'What are we going to do with it?'

'If I can get it back to my house, I'll keep it safe for you. It was you that found it after all.'

Mo wondered if it was worth anything. It looked like just a bit of scrap metal at first glance, but if it actually was a handle to a sword, there might be a collector or someone who would pay money for it. That way he might be able to get a cell phone.

Isla gathered the black bags and the litter pickers as the man gave his final address to the group before they reboarded the boat.

'Well done. It looks as though we have about twenty bags of plastic rubbish, which is a very good effort. The marine life around these islands will thank you, and it will stop plastic getting into the food chain that ultimately ends up in our bodies too after we have eaten the sea creatures.' He paused, and Mo sensed Isla flinching slightly. 'When we do this again, I want everybody to work together as a group. That means everyone, and I mean everyone, should be able to see me, and so I can see them at all times.' His eyes settled on Isla to check the message had been received, but she lowered her head.

The motor chugged, pushing the bow through the smooth plates of near freezing water. It looked so calm now, but Mo knew that the sea could be wild and dangerous. Isla had been stowing the rubbish bags and equipment, and now joined him on deck taking the seat next to him. She was still sulking.

'That man treats me like a school child. He is so supercilious. All that pompous stuff about plastic. We probably picked up a millionth of what is around us now.'

Mo considered the thought that the man might be concerned that Isla was out of sight with an unverified foreigner, and that informed his attitude, but decided against voicing it to Isla.

'Where did you put that piece of metal we found?'

'It's down with the rubbish, but don't worry, when we unload I'll find a way of getting it home.'

Mo thought, what will happen to it then?

After a pause Isla added, 'Maybe you could come round to dinner with my family. I am sure they would like to meet you. And then we could have a proper look at it in my room.'

'Thank you. That would be nice.' Mo felt both honoured to be asked, but also terrified.

The minibus was already waiting at the quayside as the boat was tied up. As they parted, Isla slipped a piece of paper into his hand and whispered in his ear, 'Next Saturday at 5 o'clock.'

Mo 8

Mo unfolded the paper in his room at the hostel. It had an address written on it. He folded it up again and put it back in his pocket. The room was warm and lying back on his bed he looked at the swirls made in the plaster on the ceiling. There were shapes there that formed overlapping semicircles, and if he let his mind drift, he could add colour to the drab pattern and see dense vegetation, deep greens with some brown and red, creating something of home. For a few minutes he could take a walk through forest and sense animals nearby, the chatter of birds, and the drip of water from leaf onto ground. His feet crunched over dried twigs as he came to a clearing. There were some houses there. A woman was coming out of a doorway. He braced himself. Was he trespassing? What would they think he, a stranger, was doing there? Then he recognised his mother's face. She did not look happy. In fact she looked angry.

He sat up. A thin red curtain hung limply over the window that could not be opened. It was the only colour in the room. He had felt anxious all week. He wished they hadn't found the sword handle. He liked Isla but this is just going to complicate things. She's going to come up with some scheme to sell it and that could get them both into trouble. He had a lot to lose. His asylum status could be jeopardised if they were found out and he would be sent back.

Maybe he could just not turn up to dinner at Isla's. He rehearsed the ordeal in his mind. He, stammering, is introduced to her mother and father who are very grand. Do you shake hands? He could see in their eyes a look of disdain as they appraised him. Skin dark, but not too dark? He doesn't look very tall or strong, Isla? Is his English good enough? Will they speak English? Is all the food placed on the table at once? Will he be expected to eat first as the guest? Will everyone watch to see how well he uses a knife and fork?

He was sweating. A few months ago, he wouldn't have given a second thought about entering a new experience. That was before the trauma and difficulties of his journey. But, he told himself, this could be an opportunity to regain some dignity and self-esteem. He must push through it.

Mo 9

Mo examined the city street map in the foyer of the hostel. It was maybe the fifth time that week he had done so, double checking the address. He had it fixed now in his mind, his route through the city to Isla's apartment. He opened the carrier bag in his hand and checked again the box of chocolates for her parents, and the red rose he had bought for Isla herself.

Out through the swing door and down the steps, into the shocking chill of the Nordic air. Mo lifted his collar. The daylight was all but gone now, and deep shadow filled most of the street between the tall lights. He set off down the pavement at a brisk pace and crossed the road to cut through the square. There were a few people about, not as many as might take a stroll in the summer months when the early evenings could be almost warm. Now winter was on its way, and the darkness seemed especially dense amongst the tall shrubs to the sides of his path. He turned down a shopping street, the glow from the store windows illuminating the sidewalk. So much to buy, but so few people to buy it. He mentally rehearsed his greeting, over and over, but never quite getting it right. He slowed his pace, best not get there too early, before they are expecting him. He paused to look in a window. Holidays were being advertised, a video running of pale blue sea lapping against white sand with a backdrop of deep green coconut palms. It looked not too different to the coast near to his home. He smiled at the irony of the reverse journey to his. Then he looked at the price. It was far cheaper.

Down some smaller streets, and then up a hill along a narrow road with massive dark buildings on either side. He felt tiny as he crept his way up this deep manmade canyon. A left turn at the top, and there was the entrance to Isla's building. It was flanked by a column on either side and a square carriage light above cast a faint glow onto a vertical panel of about a dozen apartment numbers. He carefully selected the right one and pressed the buzzer.

'Just push the door.' He recognised Isla's voice, even when electronically processed through the speaker. The hall had a table to one side and mirrors lining the opposite wall. Mo took a glance at himself. Be brave now.

Isla was coming down the stairs to meet him.

'Hello, you look cold. Come on up.' Before she could turn, Mo whipped out the rose from his bag, relieved that he could present it to her before meeting her parents. Her face lit up.

'Oh, a real one! Much better than second-hand plastic!' She pecked him on the cheek and sped up the stairs. Mo followed feeling a bit better and becoming emboldened.

'This is Inge and Jaakob.' Isla's parents stood just inside the threshold of their apartment.

'Welcome Mo. We have heard so much about you.' Inge reached out her hand and clasped Mo's. He felt the warmth of her grip, matched by the warmth in her pale blue eyes. Mo relaxed a bit.

'Thank you for inviting me.' He fumbled in the bag and brought out the chocolate box. Jaacob grabbed it and then caught Mo's arm in a friendly clasp, pulling him into the apartment.

'You had better slip that thick jacket off. You'll bake in no time here.'

The table was laid, and food was placed along its centre line. Mo took a place as Inge indicated. Isla sat next to him, and Isla's younger brother Kevin sat opposite.

'Mo, we have some creamy salmon soup. You can eat it with some bread.' Inge ladled out a bowl full of steamy hot broth. The smell was wonderful.

'This is delicious,' Mo said as he lifted the lumps of pink salmon and dill flavoured potato up to his mouth with a spoon. It was nice but lacked the flavour of food from home.

'Isla has been telling us that you were rescued from a boat in the sea? It must have been very frightening,' Jacob inquired.

'Yes. I am afraid I was a survivor. Lots of people didn't make it,' Mo explained. 'Then after a while they sent me here.' The sound of spoon scraping against bowl reverberated around the table.

'I want you to know we fully understand why you wish to come to our country to make a better life.' Jacob reached out reassuringly. Mo smiled.

'Thank you. You are very generous.' As Mo said this Kevin opposite him pulled a face, unseen by the others. He stuck his lips out and crossed his eyes. Was he trying to make a face like a monkey? Mo would like to have explained to them that the decision to leave his home was not taken lightly, and really was not about his destination. He had been faced with a choice of either to be killed, or to become a killer himself. But the dinner table didn't seem the right setting for that.

Kevin made another face, and this time was spotted by his father, who reached across and with a stern look pretended to smack him on the back of the head. There followed raised words that Mo didn't understand, then a silence. Isla raced to finish her bowl and turned to Mo, so the others could overhear.

'We need to finish some work for the beach cleaning project. Come on Mo.'

Mo 10

Isla's room was quite different to the rest of the apartment. They entered from the clean monochrome lines of Scandinavian designer chic through a portal of orange and green drapes, into a cave of scattered cushions, and vibrantly coloured gauze nets hanging from the ceiling. Isla patted the bed for Mo to sit next to her.

'I wanted to thank you for the rose.' She leant towards him and kissed him full on the lips. Her tongue penetrated his mouth and swirled slowly with his. He was twisted awkwardly towards her, and they fell back lying next to one another across the bed.

'We can't do it here. Not with Mum and Dad in the flat.' Isla sat up again, and then flipped over to reach under the bed. Mo watched her hips and buttocks rise in her patterned leggings as she rooted around, shifting boxes aside to get to the black bag from the beach. She placed it on the bed and as she pulled the sword hilt from it, damp fragments of corroded black metal flaked from the stump of the blade.

'It looks a bit of a mess,' Mo said, as he put his fingers and palm around the grip.

'I want to show you something.' Isla took the sword hilt back and carefully arranged the bag across her lap to catch the drips. Then with her thumbnail, she scraped the lump at the end of the handle and, beneath the slime and incrustation from years in the sea, she made a line of red appear.

She scraped a little further, and a bigger area was revealed. 'What do you think it is?'

'It looks as though it could be a weight to balance the sword. When the blade had been full length it needed something heavy at the other end to make it feel right into the hand. But this one look as though as well as the lump of metal to make it heavy there might be a red stone in it.' Mo looked close at it. Then he put it down in Isla's lap. 'I don't really like this. It doesn't belong to us. We should have just handed it in at the beach.'

'I know we can't keep it. But I know someone who might take it from us and maybe give enough money to get you a cell phone.'

Mo tried to suppress his reservations. His life would be easier if he had a phone. And it would get rid of the sword handle at the same time. 'Ok then.'

Isla was already messaging on her phone. Mo took the time to look around her bedroom. Childhood cuddly toys mixed with death metal masks and piles of loose clothes strewn across the floor.

'He says he can meet us now. Come on, let's go.'

Isla was already up and had opened the door. Kevin, startled just outside, retreated rapidly from the corridor to his own room as she snarled something at him that Mo didn't understand. She flung her coat on as Mo reached for his.

'Mum! We're going to the shop!'

Mo 11

'Who is it we are going to meet?' Mo was panting as they reached the street, trailing behind Isla as she marched rapidly holding the bag with the sword hilt in it.

'Oh, he's just someone I buy weed from occasionally,' Isla answered casually over her shoulder.

Mo didn't feel reassured. They cut down a narrow street, dark and silent apart from their echoing footsteps. His mind started along its own trail, down an alley he had tried to forget. At the end of the long walk to complete the first part of his journey, he and his companion Abdul had reached the coast. They could smell the sea before they could see it. It had been after dark, but it was still hot. The narrow dusty path was bound on either side by high wire fencing, separating it from the shadows of large buildings. Up ahead there were voices raised, shouting. They joined the back of a line of other anxious young men, all committed to a journey that they realised could end prematurely at this point. The fences channelled them as they inched forward, and others joined the line behind. Mo had felt panicked at being hemmed in and it was Abdul who had helped calm him. 'This is what it is all about. It is our route to escape. OK, it may feel a bit uncomfortable but let's just get through it.' The fenced path led to the entrance of a building, and they could see into the lit interior. Through the doorway there were three men in what looked like army camouflage fatigues. A man before them was being taunted, and one took a stick and hit him on the side of the head. 'It's not enough! The price is five thousand dollars!' Mo had felt the bulge of paper money that sat inside his belt. His uncle had counted it out in front of him, before he had left the village. Adrenaline coursed through his veins. Is he going to get beaten as well if he or his uncle had made a mistake? The man ahead was on his knees now and was dragged out of sight as the next person stepped into the light.

Isla was leading at a brisk pace and took a right turn down some steps. Mo was sweating inside his jacket, despite the cold night air. Thick metal grills protected shop windows on either side of the narrow passage, which opened into a small courtyard, loose rubbish overflowing from overstuffed dumpster bins. Isla halted. She made a little call and from a dark corner there was a low-pitched response. A conversation ensued that Mo didn't understand. He couldn't make out the figure, it was too dark.

'He's got this cell phone we can have in exchange for the sword handle.' Isla had a box in her hand now and with the light from her own phone put the SIM card in and handed the new phone to Mo. Some light fell on a hooded figure by the bins. He was unwrapping the sword handle from the black plastic bag and examining it with his phone torch. Mo felt his heart thumping.

'What is this piece of shit! You said you had a sword!' The figure stepped from the shadow, his torch shining directly into Mo's eyes. It went off then flashed on again, dazzling Mo. 'And who's this guy you're with?' Mo felt a thump in the chest as the man grabbed the front of his jacket. He was being pulled forward but couldn't see a thing. Isla had taken hold of the man's arm and was pulling it back. Mo pushed forward as the man fell to the ground.

'Run Mo!' Isla screamed.

Mo stumbled as his feet caught the man's leg but then jumped clear and ran up the steps, his vision still saturated with yellow light. At the top he turned right and went full pelt down the hill. His trainers slapped loudly on the pavement, the sound echoing back off the buildings on either side. He wished it would be quiet, but that was impossible if he was to maintain his speed. He turned his head back but still couldn't see clearly enough to check if he was being followed. As he approached the main road, he slowed his pace so as not to draw attention. His eyes were readjusting from the flash now, and he crossed through the thin stream of traffic, and on the other side walked briskly in the direction of his hostel.

Mo 12

The phone rang for the third time in an hour. Mo was lying on his bed, gazing up at the ceiling. He guessed it was Isla. She probably had the number from the SIM card wrapper. How did he get into this scrape? He let it ring and after a minute or two it went silent again.

He felt shaken by the incident. What was he doing in a darkened alley, possibly stealing a mobile phone, when he had been so careful to keep everything straight and above board while his asylum application went through? Isla seems to be bad news. She led him into this trouble. But at least they have got rid of that rusty piece of scrap metal.

The phone made a plopping sound. He looked at it. Three missed calls and now a message from the same number.

'I'm sorry Mo. Should never have got you into this. Please forgive me. Ixx'

Mo looked at the ceiling again. He was angry with her. He had a lot to lose. He looked at the phone. He was missing home badly now. They would probably be eating there now. Some spicy food, heat to match the sunshine. He missed his mother's stew. He could use this phone to send a message to his uncle. Then maybe he could have a video call with his mother. That would be nice. But he wondered if it would be unlucky to use this phone which had not come into his possession by legitimate means.

'Hello Mohammad... oh you look so well!' His mother squealed as the connection opened two hours later. Her face wobbled from side to side on the screen as his uncle tried to find a perch for the phone at their end.

'Hello Mama!' He didn't know what to say. He just looked at her, and the walls and furniture of the house he had left six months before. What could he say? So much had happened, it was impossible to summarise it in a few sentences.

'It's quite cold here.'

'That must be nice.'

'Yes, I am very well. I have a job working at the hospital.'

'So, you're a doctor already! Are you eating enough? You look thin.'

'The food is very bland here. Not enough spice.'

'I am so pleased your journey went well.'

Mo paused. His mother was beaming through the camera. He couldn't take away that big smile by telling the truth.

'Yes, it went very smoothly. Thanks to Uncle, who made it possible.'

Mo's uncle dipped his head into shot and smiled and waved.

Mo laid back on the bed when the call was over. He felt so happy to see his mother. She will now tell all her friends that he is a very important person in his new home and will be starting to send money back in the very near future.

Mo 13

Mo's day was going well. He had polished the floor on three corridors at the hospital and his supervisor had praised his work. Having the phone had given him extra confidence. Now he could connect with the world using the free wi-fi at his hostel.

He lined up in the canteen and filled his plate with as much stew as he could. His mother said he looked thin, so he had better make up some ground. He took his usual place at the end of a table and squeezed the sauce bottle over his plate. After two mouthfuls he looked up and saw his supervisor on the other side of the canteen near the entrance. She was pointing towards him. With her was his asylum lawyer. His heart rate accelerated. The only time she had come to hospital was when she brought him at the start of his job. Maybe she is back to give him some encouragement. His supervisor said he is doing so well after all. He watched her face as she made her way over towards him weaving in and out of the tables. It gave nothing away.

'Hello Mohammad. Don't get up. How are you doing?' she inquired breezily and pulled out a chair opposite.

'I am being very good.' Mo replied nervously, aware of the clumsiness of the phrase.

'That's nice to hear. Your supervisor tells me you're doing excellent work. Well done.'

She drew some papers out of her briefcase and took her spectacles from their case. She paused and gave him a smile before putting them on.

'Well, I thought I would just update you on how your application is going.' She said head down, slowly turning several pages of paper over to make a second pile. 'How are you finding the hostel? And I gather you went on the beach cleaning trip?'

'It was very nice thank you.' Mo's throat felt dry. He knew he wasn't answering her questions properly. He took a sip of water.

She looked up. 'Oh, I'm so sorry Mo. Please carry on eating your dinner. It was very rude of me to interrupt. Don't let it get cold.'

Mo picked away at it taking a couple of forkfuls to his mouth while she read silently from her documents opposite. Chewing and swallowing was taking a much greater effort than before. She seemed to be waiting for him to finish, but he was getting slower and slower.

'It's ok, I can finish it later.' It seemed to be the only way he could break the tension.

'Well, the application with the immigration service is progressing up the queue. I did warn you it may take a long time. As you know it may depend on how they perceive your risk at home. We just need to be clear. There was armed conflict in the area in which you live, and you were being coerced into taking up arms, and were under threat of death if you didn't?'

'Yes, that's correct.'

'I hope you don't mind but it would be helpful if we could just go through the dates and times again, and what was said and by whom?'

Mo braced himself but felt able to restate all the information that he had told the border official on his arrival in the country several months before. He felt more robust now, and on retelling his story he didn't get the same gut wrenching feeling that he had then.

'Great. That's really helpful Mo. I am sorry I had to take you through it again.' She smiled one more, this time faintly. 'There is just one more thing. It's possibly nothing, but I had a call from the city police this morning. Bizarrely, they told me they had arrested a man yesterday who had a photo on his phone of someone who looked like you. They must have passed it through their facial recognition programme, and it came up with you as a match. But we all know that technology can be very unreliable.'

Mo 14

Mo was not looking his best in the photo that the policeman slid across the table. He looked really scared and his face was off centre.

'Do you agree this is you?'

Mo's asylum lawyer answered for him. 'It doesn't look like him to me.'

'I think your client is capable of recognising himself in a picture, don't you?'

Mo didn't think it was so easy. He had never seen himself in a photograph before looking quite like that. Some doubt could remain.

'Well let's try a different approach. Do you think there is any way a man could have taken a picture of you,' the policeman glanced down to look at his paperwork, 'at 19.53 last Saturday?'

'I know. I am just remembering. I was walking back from having dinner, and someone shone their phone torch in my eyes. Maybe they took a photo at the same time.'

'And you didn't stop or speak to them?'

'No. They sort of bumped into me and then carried on walking.'

'Where had you been to dinner?'

'A girl from the Suomi fellowship had invited me round.'

'Ah, a romantic evening then? But you left early.' The policeman softened his tone. 'What is her name?'

'Her name is Isla.'

'I think my client has been very helpful to you,' the asylum lawyer interjected. 'He has been truthful and honest.'

'I would be grateful if you could give me the contact details for the Suomi fellowship so that we can get in touch with Isla and ask her a few questions. We will see if she can confirm your client's story.'

Mo looked at the phone. He was back in his room now, having been dropped off by his lawyer. Should he call Isla to warn her?

'Mo, I've been really worried about you. Why didn't you answer my calls?'

'I am sorry Isla. I felt confused and didn't know what to do with the phone. I think we had better meet up though. I had to see the police.'

'Oh. I can see you by the waterfront in half an hour.'

Isla's eyes looked sad when he joined her on a bench facing the sea. The wind was getting up, and the grey sea was rolling in beneath them. Mo settled down in his copious jacket, hood up.

'Is it a problem with your asylum application?' asked Isla flatly, the two of them staring ahead.

'I don't know. It could be. My asylum lawyer took me to the police station today because the police found a photo of me on the phone of someone they arrested.'

'What?'

'I think it could be that thug you took me to see. He must have taken a photo when he shone his phone in my eyes.'

'Oh no. I hope I haven't got you into trouble. Mo, believe me, I was only trying to help.' Isla's voicing was cracking.

'Anyway, they asked where I had been, and who I was with, so they are probably going to get in touch with you.'

'Ok, let's think. We need to get our stories to match up.'

'I told them I was just walking along the street when a man shone his light in my eyes.'

'That's good. We could have been just walking to the shop as I told my parents on the way out. There's nothing to it really. I don't think he will tell them about the cell phone. Why would he? It'll just get him into more trouble.' Isla perked up. 'We can get through this, Mo. Trust me.'

Mo 15

Mo followed his asylum lawyer through the double doors at the entrance to the police station. Her stilettoed footsteps on the shiny black and white chequered tiled floor echoed across the lobby. To the left, sitting on a low bench against the wall, were Isla, her father and the man with the ponytail. Mo glanced over quickly. Isla's head was tilted towards the floor, avoiding eye contact. Her father was looking straight ahead, strain showing in his face. The man with the ponytail looked directly at Mo, his expression hostile and angry. Mo looked away and then saw his lawyer being ushered down the corridor by a man in a leather jacket. He quickened his step to follow.

'Do you recognise this?' The detective slid a photo across the table towards him. Mo looked at the blurry image of what looked like a shard of corroded metal attached to a dirty handle.

'I can't see what it is.' Mo answered honestly.

'Yes, I agree, it is not the best shot.' The detective reached under the table and lifted onto the top a plastic bag, the sort they store evidence in. 'Does this help at all?'

Mo looked at the bag, and, through the dirt that stained the inside, and the bits that were coming away, could make out the form of the sword hilt.

'I am not sure. Am I supposed to recognise it?' Mo responded.

'Well, interestingly, this first photo was taken just thirty seconds before the photo of you.' The detective had both photos on the tabletop now.

'Oh.'

'Can you explain that?'

Mo's lawyer shifted uneasily in her seat. Mo didn't say anything. He looked blankly ahead. He wondered if his lawyer would step in, but the detective continued.

'Maybe I can help. When we arrested our suspect, he had in his possession this…' He paused, not quite sure what to call it, '…piece of an old sword. I know it doesn't look much, but we rang the museum and sent them a photo, slightly better than this one. They say it could be nearly a thousand years old. I wonder why our suspect had it?'

Mo's jaw tightened. His lawyer said. 'What are you accusing my client of exactly?'

'Well, as you know, trafficking in antiquities is a very serious offence.'

Mo had some experience related to the trafficking of people, and the organisations doing it seemed to get away with it without the police getting much involved. But were they suggesting he was a scrap metal trafficker?

'This is ridiculous. That man could have found it anywhere. There's nothing to implicate my client.'

'I beg your pardon. We need to interview his friend Isla next. I am sure she will be able to corroborate your client's story.'

Mo 16

The lawyer came back with two paper cups of brown liquid from the machine in the corner. She handed one to Mo. He took a tentative sip, but the coffee was still too hot to drink.

'I can wait a little longer, but they have been in there thirty minutes already, so we may have to defer to tomorrow if they don't come out soon.' She looked stressed.

Mo had watched Isla file in between her father and the man with the ponytail, all following the detective, after he had taken his place on a bench on the opposite side of the lobby. It was an unhappy procession, as though each member carried a burden with them. Mo had felt both scared and guilty at the same time.

His lawyer fidgeted next to him. She took her phone out of her bag for the third time in five minutes and checked it for messages. She glanced up and saw the detective beckoning towards them from across the room.

'Come on Mo. We're wanted again.'

They got up and followed the detective down the corridor. Mo hadn't seen Isla or the others leave. Maybe they had gone out through another exit.

'Sit down again. Please finish your coffee,' the detective said. 'Well, I had an interesting conversation with Isla. She told me about the trip you had made beach cleaning with the Suomi fellowship. Very worthy work. I like to take my family there in the summer. Some people are just pigs leaving plastic around.'

The detective let that settle between them, not in a hurry to move on. Mo looked ahead with no expression.

'Anyway,' he continued, 'she told me that you had found this sword handle buried between two rocks. You must have been very thorough with your beach scouring technique.' He raised a thin smile. 'Do you remember it now?'

'Ah, yes. It looks different in the bag. I really didn't look at it closely then. I just handed it to Isla thinking it was just a piece of rusty metal and she put it with the other rubbish, so I thought nothing of it.'

'Yes, I agree it doesn't look much.' He glanced at it on the table. 'But Isla thought enough of it to take it to the dealer she gets her weed from.'

The detective's eyes were tight on Mo's face. Mo tried not to make eye contact but found it impossible not to look back.

'I really don't know what you are talking about,' said Mo. 'We just went out for a walk after dinner to go to the shops. I saw she was carrying something in a bag, and she did stop at one point and told me to wait on the street while she went behind some bins. It was just after that that the man with the phone torch bumped into me. It didn't seem like a big incident at the time.'

'Thank you, Mo, that's very helpful. It is pretty much what Isla told us. What she is doing out at night with that sort I just don't know. I think her father is very disappointed in her.'

Mo tried not to relax too much but couldn't resist a sense of relief coming over him.

'Just one thing, Mo. Could I just take down your cell phone number in case we need to get in touch with you again?'

As Mo reeled off the number, his lawyer tried to suppress a look of surprise.

Mo 17

There was some problem in the kitchen. Mo waited to one side while his order of double cheeseburger was assembled by the stressed girl with the cap on her head, wrapped and placed on his tray. He turned around to see the line of young people extending from the counter towards the door. They were chatting and relaxed today, more so than usual. He made his way between them to where Isla had found a place by the window.

'We did it, Mo! We fucking smashed it!' She took a long draw on her milkshake, eyes fixed on Mo with a satisfied look of victory. She was determined for the two of them to have a celebratory burger.

Mo smiled back. 'Yes, I hope so.'

'You seem not so convinced.'

'I let something slip at the end. The detective asked for my cell phone number, and I gave it to him without thinking. My lawyer knew that I didn't have a phone before, but she didn't say anything. She was a bit cold to me when we left the police station, as though she was disappointed with me. I need her to sort out my application. I don't want her to lose trust with me.'

'You're making too much of it Mo. Nobody is going to let on about the phone.' She took a bite of her burger. 'Anyway, today is a special day here. I think you're going to enjoy it.' She chewed and swallowed. 'All the kids who have just graduated high school really let their hair down after months of studying and exams. They get on these big trucks and parade around the city in a convoy, drinking and throwing buckets of sweets to all the spectators lined up on the pavement. I did it last year. It's crazy!'

They got up and pushed past the line of waiting customers to get through the door. The streets were filling with excited onlookers as they made their way down towards the harbour.

'The best spot to watch is at the top of the square looking down towards the sea.' Isla shouted to make herself heard. She led Mo through the crowd until she was satisfied they were in a good position. The square had patches of lawn divided by beds of shrubs which, with winter approaching, had now lost all their leaves. In the middle was a glass pavilion with a fine black metal superstructure, built in the art nouveau style.

The approaching column of trucks was heralded by a rising cacophony of horns and claxons. A police car at the bottom of the square which had been parked across two lanes reversed and let the first truck through. It drove slowly as the students, balancing inside the panels of the truck's sides, waved and screamed at the onlookers. It was followed by another, and another, until there was a trail of about ten trucks making their way up the side of the square. As they got closer Mo could see the kids were dressed up with scary makeup and some had brightly coloured wigs on. They were throwing handfuls of wrapped sweets from buckets on the truck. People were scrambling to pick them up out of the gutter. The first truck passed, and then the second. Isla was pointing towards some students she knew, and they spotted her in the crowd and tried to shout between cupped hands, but it was impossible to hear. A shower of sweets hit Isla and Mo.

Mo got caught up in the noise. He hadn't been in a crowd like this since arriving. His brain was invaded by the sound and smell of the massive diesel engines as they passed, black tyres turning just feet from his head, and the whirr of the rapidly rotating differentials. But maybe it was the sweets that took him back. He started sweating and his heart thumped irregularly. Suddenly he was in his home village. The column of army trucks could be seen from a distance by the dust the wheels threw up, but they slowed down as they rumbled down main street. Fierce looking men, rifles slung across their backs, stood on the flatbeds of the vehicles, trying to smile benignly as they distributed sweets and other goodies to the teenage boys lined up below to watch the spectacle. The column would halt, and the men jumped off to assess the youths, chatting to them and see if they could be robust enough to carry arms. Often they had a list of names acquired form previous visits, and they would ask the assembled boys, where is so and so today, why isn't he here? The boys would point out the house where he lived and the men might knock on the door, and, when there was no answer, take a look round the back.

'Mo, are you all right?' Isla's voice penetrated his bad dream. 'You look really ill.'

Mo was sitting on the ground surrounded by strangers' legs. Isla leant over him and then squatted down.

'You're really breathing fast. Do you have any pain anywhere?' Isla asked.

Mo felt tight in his chest. He tried to get up, but his legs wouldn't let him, so he stumbled back onto the pavement. Isla looked into his eyes and could see he wasn't focussing properly.

'I'm calling an ambulance, Mo. It looks as though you're having a heart attack.'

Mo 18

The doctor at the emergency department was gone for a long time. Isla sat inside the curtains next to Mo who was propped up lying on a gurney.

'Well at least they didn't find anything on the ECG, Mo.'

Mo didn't respond. He had done enough talking to the doctor as he had taken the history. It had been embarrassing to be stretchered to the ambulance, people on either side looking down on him with concern on their faces. He couldn't remember too much of the journey to the hospital, apart from being swung side to side as the vehicle took the corners at high speed.

The curtains twitched, and then opened slightly as a nurse poked her face through the gap.

'It won't be much longer. Everybody ok?' Isla and Mo nodded. The curtains were closed again, but the rattle of trolleys being wheeled past on the hard floor penetrated loudly and jarred.

'Isla, there is no need for you to stay. I am sure they will just send me home in a minute,' Mo said, and then added. 'Thank you though. You have been very good to me.'

'I'll stay for a bit longer. I want to make sure you're ok.'

Mo had told the doctor that he had seen men with guns on the lorries and that had scared him. The doctor has asked whether he was often frightened by people who might be trying to harm him. Yes, who wouldn't be? Does he hear their voices, and what do they say? They say you must come with us, or we will kill you. Do they say anything else? We want you to take this gun so you can fight for what is right.

Mo could see Isla was shocked. He had tried to explain that that was what it was like in his home village, but he was not sure he had been heard, and was now wondering if he should have said anything at all. The doctor had asked if it was ok for him to talk to Isla. Yes, it was. They had stood outside the curtain and although whispering, Mo could hear them. The doctor asked Isla how long she had known him. A few weeks. Does he have any access to weapons that she knows of? No but he lives in a hostel, so she didn't know what he had there. Has he ever expressed any intention to hurt anyone? Absolutely not. He seems like a very gentle person.

The doctor finally returned.

'Mo. I am a little concerned about your mental state. You clearly have been under some stress lately. I have been trying to get hold of one of my colleagues who deals with psychological issues, but unfortunately they are not available to see you here straight away. We have a choice. You could either go home and you can have an appointment in the clinic tomorrow, or you can stay in the hospital tonight and be checked over in the morning.'

'I don't think there is any need for me to stay here. I feel fine now,' Mo said weakly.

'Well, we are concerned for your safety, and I think it would be better if you stayed.'

Mo thought about it.

Isla chipped in. 'It would only be for one night, Mo.'

Mo 19

It felt strange being pushed in a wheelchair. Nobody had asked if he could walk. It was only when they had left the emergency department that Mo realised he was in the hospital where he worked.

'I polish these floors.' He tried to throw his voice up and back to the unseen force propelling him forwards along the corridor. All that came back was a grunt. He wasn't sure whether it was of acknowledgement or incomprehension. Another loony going from emergency room to acute psychiatric ward. They took a left turn and paused at the entrance desk. Mo could see his name on the white board behind the desk, in the column "expected". Next to it was written, in black marker pen, "acute paranoid schizophrenia". He wasn't quite sure what that meant, but he thought it probably wasn't good.

The nurse took the notes and his bag of possessions from the porter and laughed as they exchanged some words that Mo didn't understand. The nurse settled down to read the first page. Mo sat silently, looking forward. Eventually she got up and looked at him.

'Hello Mohammad. I am sure you don't need this wheelchair. Would you like to stand up slowly?' She held onto his arm as his feet tried to find the floor past the footrests. 'I expect you're a bit hungry now? We are just serving up in the dayroom over there.'

Mo walked slowly with the nurse still holding his arm. She found a place for him at a table where a man was already eating.

'Just sit down there and I'll get you a plate of food. Anything you don't eat?' Mo shook his head.

Mo felt uncomfortable. His table companion was tucking in and chewing voraciously. He looked around and there were several other tables with one or two patients at each. No one was talking.

'What are you in for?' The man next to him took him by surprise. He had finished his dinner, put his plate to the side and was now addressing Mo.

'I don't really know,' Mo said. 'I think there may have been some sort of mistake.'

The man giggled a bit, then was possessed by uncontrollable laughter. He seemed unaware that the whole room was turned towards them now, faces blank but staring. Mo's discomfort multiplied a hundred times.

'That's ...' he drew a big breath, and almost choked. '... that's what they all say!' The man was able to extract a bellow between waves of guffaws.

'Come on, come on everyone, let's make Mohammad welcome,' the nurse interceded. The man next to Mo was still chuckling and mumbling to himself. The others turned back to their own plates. Mo stared at the plate now placed in front of him and decided he really didn't want it.

After another five minutes the nurse came over. 'I see you're not too hungry. I expect you've had a busy day. Maybe you would like something a little later on? In the meantime I'll take you to your room.'

Mo was relieved to get up and follow her down the corridor. There was a neatly made bed with a light fitted just above it, and a table and a chair to one side.

'There's a towel on the bed and the washroom is just opposite. When we've cleared away the dinner things, we'll turn the TV on in the day room. I think there's a champion's league match on tonight.'

Mo lay on the bed and stared at the ceiling. He would have liked to have his phone, but it was in the bag of possessions that was still sitting behind the nurses' station. He thought about getting up and asking for it but decided against. Maybe patients weren't allowed phones on the ward. It felt just too much of a risk to have his request refused. It would be another knock back on a very confusing day. He listened to the cheers and chants of the football fans coming through the TV in the dayroom, and he couldn't have felt more alone.

Mo 20

'And when did you last see your mother?' The psychiatrist asked. Sitting slightly behind him were a medical student and a social worker. They were in a room next to the nurses' station. Mo had been able to have a wash after a troubled night's sleep.

'It was two days ago.'

'And you said you have been here for four months now?' The psychiatrist was looking down at his notes.

'Yes.'

'And your mother is in Africa?' He was looking up from his notes now.

'Yes.'

'Where did you see her?'

'In my room.'

The psychiatrist was busy scribbling some notes now. Mo was weighing up whether it would be better to tell the psychiatrist he had a phone, or just let this bit of the interview pass over. After all, the psychiatrist hadn't asked him if he had had a phone.

'Moving on now, can you tell me what happened yesterday.'

I was watching some trucks with people on them go round and round a square. They were throwing sweets. It was all very strange.'

The psychiatrist turned round to his companions. 'These local traditions can be very confusing to foreigners.' They all laughed politely, apart from Mo. He turned back to Mo. 'In what way did you find it strange?'

'Well, normally the trucks have men on them with guns. So, I felt scared at seeing them.'

'And what do the men do?'

'They search for you and get you to join them, and if you won't, they threaten you with the guns.'

'Has this happened to you?'

Mo paused and thought how he should answer this. 'It could have happened to me.'

'"It could have happened to me",' the psychiatrist repeated it back slowly, emphasising each word. Mo was worried. This psychiatrist seemed very important. What if he told the immigration service it had never actually happened to Mo? He had felt threatened by the armed men. Is that the same as actually being threatened?

'Just a few routine things to go through now. Have you ever been in trouble with the police?'

Mo paused. He hadn't been "in trouble" with them. 'No.' He felt sure this was the right thing to say. If he had to explain that he had found an old sword handle it would confuse this old man even more.

'Mohammad, I am sure you won't mind while I discuss your diagnosis with my companions here.' The psychiatrist had stopped scribbling and turned away from Mo. He addressed the medical student.

'This patient was admitted last night with a provisional diagnosis of acute paranoid schizophrenia having been brought into the emergency room having claimed to have seen armed men at the student celebration yesterday. Why would you think that could be the diagnosis?'

'If he had been having delusions and hallucinations, then it might have been the right diagnosis.' The medical student responded.

'So, what is your formulation regarding the diagnosis? What do you think the diagnosis is?'

'Well, given the extreme events Mohammad will have experienced both before and on his journey from Africa, he is likely to be suffering from post-traumatic stress disorder. In its severe form it could lead to mild psychosis with intrusive thoughts and paranoid ideation. I think yesterday he suffered from intrusive thoughts about his past experience of being threatened by armed men which were triggered by the truck parade and probably led to a panic attack thus precipitating his admission.'

'Bravo! Bravo!' The psychiatrist clapped his hands. He turned back to Mo. 'I am sorry for all that technical language. What it means is that the upsetting events you have suffered in your life have led to a situation where they come back to you at odd times and alter your mood and your actions. I think we can discharge you, but you will need to attend some appointments to decide what form of therapy might help you.'

Mo wondered if he was expected to thank him. The man was smiling at him.

'Thank you. I didn't know what it was called before.'

'That's all right, Mohammad. I think our social worker would like a chat with you before you go.'

Mo 21

His phone had rung three times. It now said three missed calls. They were from a number he didn't recognise. He lay on his bed at the hostel and contemplated who it could be. It wasn't Isla's number, and anyway she would have followed up with a message. It could have been the detective, wanting to see him again. He should never have given him his number. He looked at the phone. His mother's voice sounded in his head. Nothing good ever comes from ill-gotten gains.

The phone ploinked. *Mohammad. I would like to talk to you about the ancient sword hilt.*

Mo's heart skipped a beat. Who would send a message like that? They hadn't even signed off with a name. He had almost forgotten about the sword hilt, and this didn't seem likely to bring good news. It could be that thug that supplied weed to Isla. He tried to put it out of his mind.

There was a knock on his door. That never happened. He thought about pretending not to be in, but someone would have seen him on the way up. He opened the door by just an inch.

'There's a person downstairs who wants to see you. It's a woman.' The guy moved off quickly, message successfully delivered.

Mo made his way slowly down the stairs, legs feeling heavy, unsure as to what he may find, and turned the corner into the lobby. His asylum lawyer was standing by the reception desk.

'Mo, how are you? I was so worried when I got the message from the social worker at the hospital.'

Mo smiled, relieved it was at least a familiar face. But what news was she about to bring?

'Shall we sit down?' she said, moving towards a pair of low chairs, facing one another over a coffee table.

'I gather you spent a night in hospital after collapsing at the parade. That must have felt very strange.'

'Yes, unfortunately the parade brought back some very bad memories for me.'

'Well, it is good that you have now seen the right people to help, and they will organise some appointments to help you work through those memories.'

Mo thought that might not be such a good idea. Wouldn't it be best to try and forget what had happened in the past rather than be reminded of it? But it might be rude to say that. They were only trying to help after all.

His lawyer continued. 'Well, in every cloud, there is a silver lining.'

Mo hadn't heard that phrase before but liked it.

'Because you now have a mental health condition recognised, we can add the diagnosis of PTSD, post-traumatic stress disorder, to your asylum application. It will really help. They might well speed up the process, and it would make it much harder for them to send you back. It would be seen as cruelty when you had been so traumatised there.'

Mo looked back blankly. His mind had drifted back to the message about the sword hilt.

'Mo, are you all right? You do agree this is good news, don't you?'

'Oh, yes. Thank you.'

'I can see you are worried about something, Mo. Is it still about what happened in the police station?'

179

'Yes, it wasn't very nice being accused like that.'

'Well Mo, they didn't actually accuse you of anything. In fact, there is not likely to be anything else that comes of it. If they can't find anything to charge you with a crime, then there is nothing that needs to be mentioned about it on your application.'

Mo felt partially relieved. But it still didn't account for the phone, which his lawyer had decided not to mention. Maybe she had forgotten about it. He thought that unlikely. And now he was getting messages on the phone from someone he didn't know.

Mo 22

Mo looked at the ceiling. Although it hadn't felt like it straight away, he decided it was good news. It might mean he is able to move on with his life. The phone vibrated. This time it was Isla.

'Why didn't you tell me you were back from the hospital?' She didn't sound happy.

'I'm sorry Isla, it was all so confusing. I needed time to think.'

'How are you feeling now?'

'Better, actually.'

'That's good. I am sorry I took you to the parade. Maybe it wasn't very sensitive of me.'

'It's not your fault. You couldn't have known.'

'Did you get that message from the museum?'

'What message?'

'They said they would get in touch with you. I gave them your number. They want to see us about the sword handle. It seems the police have passed it on to them for safekeeping or something, and they asked if it would be ok if they could talk to us about it.'

Mo thought, that's what the message was about. 'I don't think I want anything to do with it. It hasn't brought us any luck so far, has it?'

'Oh, come on Mo. It could be fun. I think you need to get out and it will take your mind off other things.'

Mo trailed behind Isla as they went up the steps to the door of the museum.

'We have an appointment with Dr Heikkinen?' asked Isla at the ticket desk, her voice trailing up, uncertain whether this was the right place.

'Just wait here. I'll buzz her.'

They stood around in the reception area watching visitors taking their big coats off and placing them in lockers. Dr Heikkinen, the curator of the museum, emerged from a side door and approached them.

'Isla and Mohammad? Very nice to meet you.'

She was a dark-haired small woman with serious looking glasses. But she showed them a wide smile.

'Would you like to come through here?'

They followed her through the same door and twisted and turned through a series of corridors before arriving at what looked like a laboratory. A harsh light shone down from ceiling strips onto the wooden worktops that capped white storage cupboards.

'I thought you might like to see the sword hilt again. I can take you through what we think about it. You found it on the island?'

'Yes, actually it was Mo who found it between two rocks there.'

'OK. That's interesting Mo.'

She looked at Mo and waited for a response. Mo wasn't quite sure why he was there. He really wasn't interested in the sword hilt. He didn't want to get more involved. It could only mean trouble. He smiled thinly but didn't say anything.

'Well, let's take a look at it.' She reached under the countertop and pulled out a plastic box and raised the top. It was packed with jellified tissue. 'We try to keep it damp, in conditions similar to those it has been in for however long it was there.'

She pushed back the tissues and lifted it out. Somehow Mo thought that it would all have been cleaned up and polished by now, but it looked just as dirty as when he had found it.

'What we have here looks as though it is a Saxon sword hilt. That means it is the handle part of the sword, created somewhere either in Germany or England. As you can see the blade has been broken off.'

Isla was following closely. Mo looked around the room, seeing what else there was of interest.

'The guard is the part that protects the hand holding the sword. It is quite short and curves slightly in the direction of the blade.'

She paused and looked to see whether they were following. Mo brought his eyes back to attention on the counter.

'This is where it gets interesting.' Mo suppressed a yawn. 'At the end of the grip, which is the part you hold with your hand, there is a big lump called a pommel. It is there to balance the weight of the blade.' Mo elbowed Isla in the ribs as if to say, told you so.

'This pommel is a bit special. You probably noticed that it has a red stone in it. That is quite unusual and suggests this sword must have belonged to a high-status individual. We haven't yet run the tests to identify the nature of the stone, but it is likely to be a garnet, which is a type of semi-precious stone that was mined in central Europe.'

Mo showed a bit more interest.

'But the most unusual thing about it is that there is some writing on the metal ring that goes round the red stone.' She lifted it up so they could see it.

'It says "God wins."

'That's in English, isn't it?' Isla said.

'Yes.'

'What's it doing here?'

'We have no idea.' Dr Heikkinen leant back, as though there was nothing more to say.

Isla felt compelled to fill the silence. 'I had my DNA tested a few months ago.' She smiled, preparing the curator and Mo for something exciting. 'The result came back as 99% that was Finnish, and 1% matched people who live in England. My dad said, "that bit must have blown here on the wind"!'

Isla was disappointed by the lack of response from her audience of two.

'Well, the sword got here, so anything is possible I suppose,' said the curator, dourly. 'Anyway, because it is such a special object, the museum would like to issue a press release, and one of the reasons I invited you here today would be to see if you would be interested in doing some filming on the island where you found it. The television news would love a story like this.'

Isla started jumping up and down and grabbed Mo to join her. 'Mo, we're going to be famous!'

Mo 23

The therapist came to the corridor to fetch Mo. His supervisor had said it would be ok to take an hour off for his session.

'Mo I would like you to tell me what happened the other day before you were taken to hospital.'

He still felt bewildered by the events of the last few days. He really didn't want to talk about it.

'From the notes I have, it would seem that you feared the trucks in the parade, and that you felt you couldn't breathe and couldn't stand up properly. Is that correct?'

Mo nodded. She's trying to be helpful, he thought.

'Can you just tell me, briefly, what you were thinking about before you felt like that.'

Mo gathered himself. 'In my home village, trucks come carrying armed men and they try to make you go with them. It happens every few months.' He was prepared to go on and tell his story in more detail, but the therapist lifted her head from the notes she was taking.

'Are there other things that make you scared?' enquired the therapist.

Mo immediately thought of what was making him most scared at that moment. Someone might discover he had an illegally acquired phone. That would be a disaster. He can't talk about that.

'Well things happened on my journey that were very bad.'

'How about we make a little list?'

'I saw people being beaten by men when they didn't have enough money to get on the boat.'

The therapist had her head down and was scribbling fast. 'And...?'

'The boat sank, and I watched people drown.'

She lifted her head and looked at Mo. He was starting to sweat.

'Would you like to tell me a little more about that.'

'They ...' Mo hesitated. 'They were in the middle of the boat as it filled with water, and because the boat was moving so much with the big waves, they couldn't stand up. It took hours before they were so exhausted that they just gave up. I watched from the side of the boat but couldn't help them because I was hanging onto the rope. If I had gone to help them, I wouldn't have been able to get back and would have died as well.'

'How are you feeling now, telling me this, Mo?'

Mo felt his chest tighten and his breathing quicken.

'Is it like you felt before you were taken to hospital?'

'Yes.'

'Mo, I think we can develop a plan to help you cope better with what has happened to you. I am going to give you a task. You can think of it as homework. I would like you to write something down about what you have just told me. But I want you to do it in a specific place. It is a public place. The reason for that is that I want you to be able to deal with the feelings that come on when you think of the bad things that have happened, and to still be able to carry on doing what you were doing, wherever it may be. Do you have someone who could be with you while you do it?'

Isla and Mo stood in the park and looked up at the front of the city library.

'I love this place. It's so wild and quirky!'

Mo thought it was the strangest building he had ever seen. The glass frontage rippled and undulated before them. Long and slithering, it extended to the limits of their view on both sides. The surface didn't allow focus. It was as though it was made from a material that wasn't truly of this world, one that reflected images that it had absorbed and then transformed them, projecting them into something new. It made Mo feel a bit sick.

They pushed through the rotating doors and entered a universe not entirely presaged by the tranquil exterior. People were pressing to get to the reception desk and groups were going to the cafes that dotted the ground floor. It was crowded. Mo thought, oh no.

'Well, it always is a bit busy on Saturday mornings.' Isla said. 'I love coming here to study, and the second floor has the most amazing resources. Chill out rooms, 3-D printers, all sorts of things.'

They moved to the escalators. 'I think we ought to head for the reading room on the top floor. It will blow your mind.' That was not what Mo thought he needed at that moment.

He trailed behind Isla, and they ascended. Up one floor, swap escalators and then up to the top.

The reading room extended on either side to cover the full floor area of the building. Getting off the escalator, they entered a maze of white bookshelves, chest height so it was easy to see over. Isla made for the windows on the opposite side.

'Look, you can see down to where we were standing,' Isla said.

Mo looked side to side. The room was full of curves. Those curves included cut outs in the floor, allowing sunken areas for more intimate study, but they also involved the floor surface itself. It wasn't flat.

They made their way up towards one end of the room. The gradient started quite shallowly, and they passed some single people, some in pairs, reading or quietly conversing at little round tables, or sitting in designer chairs. As they reached the end of the building, the floor steepened, and it required some effort to make the final few metres. They were nearly at a vanishing point. The walls had narrowed and the floor curved upwards to meet the slightly shallower curve of the ceiling. They took the last table of feasible habitation.

'This is my favourite spot,' Isla said. 'You can't see the whole way from here because the ceiling comes down. It's like being in a special place.'

Mo looked back. It didn't really feel safe up here. He had felt his trainers slipping on the polished floor in the final few steps. He could see the lower half of figures down the slope, but the ceiling obscured the view otherwise.

'You said the therapist wanted you to do some writing.' Isla was rooting around in her bag. 'I know you wouldn't bring anything, so I've got a pen and some paper here.'

Mo sat with the paper in front of him. Isla was slightly turned away reading a book. He tried to reach into his memory, as the therapist had suggested. He shut his eyes. He opened them again. This is a strange place. He shut his eyes again. He felt himself sliding down the slope. The face of a wave curved up before him, blue and white crested. It grew, and grew, until he felt spray hit his face. There was fear in the eyes of everyone around him. The boat tilted, rising, rising up the wall, accelerating as though controlled by a force taking them to their deaths. He felt powerless, so small against this overwhelming force of nature. They were beyond any hope of help. When they were near vertical, the wave broke, and water entered the boat. The faces opposite him looked pleadingly into his eyes as they were impelled forward, the weight of water dislodging them from their flimsy hand holds. They fell in a jumbled mess, into the churning pool forming in the soft middle of the boat. Limbs thrust out grabbed by hands, heads surfaced then submerged, the energy of chaos recharged as each successive wave destroyed each and any tiny step towards safety for those poor souls. And he watched all this.

There was nothing on the paper. There didn't need to be. Mo was now in full blown panic. Isla was standing behind him, bent forward, her arms stretched around him, feeling the rapid rise and fall of his chest, smelling the sweat of fear as her face buried into his neck, moved by the flickering pulse shaking his whole body. They stayed like that for some minutes. Isla could feel Mo's breathing slowly subside, his heart start to calm, the comfort she was giving him working its way into his soul. She released him. They sat side by side for a while in silence.

'Shall we go and find a place to get a drink?' Isla said softly.

In the cafe on the ground floor, Mo smiled at Isla. 'Thank you.'

They each had a coffee in front of them and had found a niche under a staircase, the curved ceiling coming down to create a cave that felt secure from the people moving around a few yards away.

'I always knew this building was special,' remarked Isla. 'Let's hope it's the first stage of healing for you.'

Mo 24

Mo watched the drone hover. Four sets of copter blades kept it above the waves about ten metres from the shore. It tilted and then skittered to a new location a little higher and further out. Someone came up from behind Mo and took from his shoulders the big puffer jacket that was keeping him warm.

The director shouted, 'Three...two...one...and walk!'

Isla grabbed his hand and they set off at a steady pace walking along the beach, parallel to the track the drone was taking over the water. Mo found it much harder than normal to walk when he was being filmed. It was as though every part of every step needed thinking about.

'And... cut!'

The journey to the harbour had been a little different this time. The limousine had pulled up outside his hostel. It had blacked out windows. He hoped some of the other residents were looking from their windows above when he pulled open the door and stepped inside. Isla was already sitting on the back seat, beaming at him.

'Isn't this incredible? I have never been in a car as big as this before.'

Mo settled back, determined to enjoy the journey. Grand shops, their windows lit, flashed past. Maybe if things go well, I could even buy some of the things in there, he thought.

At the harbour a motor launch was waiting. It was gleaming white with a fast-looking profile. Some men were loading camera equipment into the cabin. Mo and Isla waited on the stone quayside before the director, who was supervising the loading, turned to them.

'Welcome, our stars for the day! You must be Isla, and you are Mohammad?' he asked, grabbing him by the arm. 'Step right in I've heard a lot about you two.'

He led them around the big boxes in the cabin.

'Here is our reporter, Greta.'

'Hello,' she said, shaking them each by the hand. She was sitting on a curved padded bench beneath the windows at the front of the cabin. 'I think we are going to have a great day.'

Greta took them through what she and the director had planned.

'Do you think you can locate the spot where you found it? We would like just to recreate the moment it came out of the ground. We have a sort of reproduction sword handle so we can bury it again. It should be fun. Now, Mohammad, can I just make a few notes. You arrived in the country just a few months ago, is that correct?'

'Yes.' Mo hesitated. He wasn't sure how much he should reveal.

'How was your journey?'

Mo thought he shouldn't reveal too much. 'Er, it was sort of normal under the circumstances.'

'For a refugee you mean?'

'Well, yes.'

'And what made you decide to come here.'

'It was getting quite dangerous to be at home.'

The boat's motor fired up, sending vibration through the cabin.

'Is there anything else you would like to tell us.'

'I am really enjoying being here, working at the hospital and living in the city.'

'And Isla, how did you meet Mohammad?'

'It was at the Suomi Fellowship. He looked like the most interesting person there. But he did take some persuading to go on the beach cleaning trip because he cleans at the hospital. He didn't want to take up his day off doing the same thing!'

'Ah, that's a gem, Isla, I am sure we can use that.'

The ship took no time to reach the island and it swung around to the far side where they had discovered the sword hilt. Isla and Mo had not seen the beach from the sea before. The weather was different this time, not the sparkling sunshine of their last trip, but a grey lowering sky with the odd flake of snow falling. The director had the boat slow right down so they could take some footage of the beach from a distance, before mooring up and unloading.

'Can we go back to starting positions please?' the director yelled at them from further down the beach. This was the third time they had walked along the shore. It didn't seem to be getting any easier. The drone operator was in a heated discussion with the director which Mo didn't understand.

'Now, I would like you to do the same walk again, but this time turn up the beach to sit on the rock like you did when you found it.' He looked and sounded angry.

Isla was giggling holding Mo's hand on the walk. They very deliberately put one foot in front of the other, in an exaggerated movement. 'We're getting quite good at this now.'

'It takes practice.' Mo, catching Isla's mood, felt it was starting to be fun.

'I'm looking forward to this bit coming up,' Isla said. 'It was the first time we were close together.'

They approached the rocks, each taking a seat on the down slope on either side of the groove. They slid down and fell in a heap laughing as they crashed together.

'Oh, no. Oh, no. This won't do.' The director was turning red. 'Can we just get you sitting next to one another now and we'll take it from there.'

Greta positioned herself five metres in front of them, with her back to them but facing the camera. She nervously fiddled with the microphone, shook her hair and made exaggerated throat clearing noises.

'Three, two, one...' the director made a broad chopping motion with his hand and Greta was off. She talked rapidly to camera while the director wheeled round to the side and waved at Isla and Mo. He then did a mime of digging a hole with a spade. Isla nudged Mo. 'You're on'. Mo leant forward and started scrambling with both hands in the sand. He couldn't find it.

'Is this the right place?' he whispered to Isla.

'Try a bit to the right. I saw them bury it.'

The director was rotating his arms at Greta, and she took a glance in his direction, but without a pause she managed to keep up her rapid-fire discourse to camera.

'Ah, I've got it.' Mo levered up the replica sword handle and held it aloft so the camera could see behind Greta's shoulder. Isla leaned in and hugged him.

'You're a star!' she whispered in his ear.

'And, cut.'

Mo 25

Mo stretched his toes up under Isla's feet, so he had complete contact with her soles. His shins touched her calves, his thighs pressed against her bottom and his chest weighed against her back. He buried his nose in her hair. The blue streak didn't smell of blue, he thought. More like raspberry shampoo. He looked down at her skin. Translucent white like alabaster, so different from his. She had been fascinated by the tight curls on his chest. Now she was asleep.

They had watched the YouTube clip of the news report four or five times that evening. Isla couldn't believe she had been on TV.

'Look Mo, she carried on talking all the time you couldn't find it. It's hilarious!' Mo could only just understand the odd word the reporter was saying but was reassured by Isla she just kept saying the same thing over again, each time in a slightly different way.

'I think the director was so fed up by then he couldn't be bothered to shoot it again,' said Isla. 'Anyway, I am sure you are the most famous person in Finland right now.' She cupped his cheeks and kissed him on the lips. 'I am so proud of you.'

Mo couldn't think of a time he had felt so valued. He beamed at Isla and felt genuinely happy. It was so special spending time with her. She had called him earlier that day to say her parents and Kevin had taken a trip to see an aunt upcountry.

'Let's chill. I can cook something.'

It didn't take him long to stride up the hill, so confident of his step compared to the last time he made the journey to her apartment. She was stir-frying, and they settled down on the couch and shovelled the hot food into their mouths.

'I think I'm getting better, Isla. And it is all down to you. When the reporter was asking me something about my journey, I felt nothing. I managed to control my emotions. That wouldn't have happened before.'

Isla's eyes gave a prolonged smile, her mouth occupied with chewing and swallowing.

'But Isla there is something I want to tell you. It's important to me because I have been carrying a burden for a long time now, and I haven't told anyone else. But you have made me strong enough to say it so now is the right time.' Mo took a gulp of water.

'On my long walk I walked with a friend called Abdul. He was a clever man and a good companion. He was strong when I was feeling weak and pulled me through when it seemed I couldn't go on. It was he who managed to get us on the boat. He was next to me when we hit the big waves and people were struggling to stand up in the middle of the boat. They were sliding and going under before our eyes. While I was hanging on to the rope that went around the inflatable's edge, Abdul let go and went to try to help those people in the middle. I watched Abdul drown. I didn't go and help him.' Mo's head was down, and tears slid down his cheeks.

Isla kissed him and tasted the salty tears. They made love and for a brief time Mo felt like a man again. Restored.

Part Three

Stu 1

06.29... Six-thirty. The alarm chirruped. I rolled over and reached to turn it off. Another working week. Monday morning blues.

The weekend hadn't started too well. Christine was having one of her low moments.

'Why are we even down here, Stu? You sit in your office at a job going nowhere, in a museum that gets twenty punters on a good day, searching the internet looking for inspiration, and I...' Christine's voice sobbed. 'I have to put up with all that shit at that crumby school. They may have given me the deputy headship, but I am still doing a full-time teacher's job as well. It's cut back after cutback. We can never replace teachers who leave, and my, if they do get a new one, they don't stick around too long. The bloody kids around here, they're so unmotivated. No aspiration to achieve anything.'

I looked out of the window. Christine wasn't expecting a response from me. I had heard it all before. It had been her idea to move to Hastings in the first place but going over that again wouldn't help one bit. Before me was a good reason for being here.

'Look Christine. The yachts are out. They must be having a regatta at the sailing club today.' I thought Christine would bite my head off at this childish distraction technique, but instead she joined me at the window. 'Where could we afford a view like this anywhere else. We can watch the weather coming in up the channel. It's never the same two days running.'

It hadn't taken long to make the decision to buy the flat we were in. From a gravel drive there was a sweeping stone staircase that curved up to the front door. It was set in a mock Scottish style castle, on a miniature scale with tiny corbelled round towers at the corners, all built out of burnt yellow sandstone. Ok, the rain may have weathered the edges, and taken the odd chunk out in the last one hundred and fifty years, but it still looked pretty grand. Those Victorians certainly knew how to put on a bit of a display. The streets around were lined by large foursquare villas built in the 19th century for wealthy London families when St Leonards-on-Sea, this adjunct to Hastings, was the holiday playground, the St Tropez of its time. Below our sea view we could look down on a tiny park, with dark pathways shaded by overgrown trees whose leaves are now turning orange and pink as autumn sets in.

'I'm sorry Stu, I know you've grown to like it here. But I'm under crazy pressure at school.'

'Well, let's enjoy today. It's Saturday after all and you need a day off. You know it's Hastings day? The anniversary of the Battle of Hastings? There'll be a bonfire and fireworks in town this evening.'

'Yes, we could go to it. That'll be fun. But don't forget Matt and Bianca are coming down. Will you cook that famous moussaka of yours? You know they like it.'

I gave Christine a hug and kissed her cheek.

'I'll get the shopping.'

Stu 2

I put the roof up on my ancient Triumph Herald in the car park underneath the supermarket and reached for the carrier bags on the back seat. Friends mocked me for it, but I loved the car's two-tone styling of cream and pale blue, its lines defined by strips of chrome, once gleaming but now pitted by age. Grabbing a trolley, I joined the stationary ascent on the moving walkway up to the shopping floor. Before me was a Hastings arse. Wide, and encased in a brown velour trackie bottom, it was my enforced companion for the fifteen second journey. Out at the top and into the aisles.

'No fucking aubergines.' I couldn't keep it totally inaudible, my mind losing control of my lips. A woman glanced at me and moved away, sensing anger. I rushed through the vegetables, onion, peppers, garlic, potatoes. On to passata, cheese and minced meat. And Italian wine? Two bottles of valpolicella to go with my moussaka. Rome washing down Greece. How very classical.

The self-checkout was having an off day. *Please place item in bagging area.* I just have. *An assistant will be with you shortly.* No, she won't. Half the beacons above the checkouts were signalling red. No fucking hope.

It was a relief to drive out into the daylight. Now, where am I going to find an aubergine, or preferably two?

The Iranian shop on the corner had its fruit and veg out. I scanned it as I slowed for the junction. Yes! Beautiful shiny black aubergines, stacked so neatly it was almost a work of art. Just need somewhere to park now. Ah. Loading only. Perfect.

I dashed out of the car and selected the firmest, smoothest perfect black fruit. Two of them. Thank you very much. One pound fifty-eight. Beautifully suspended in a crisp brown paper bag, I carried them back round the corner. A parking attendant was paying a bit too much attention to my car.

'This is a loading bay, sir.'

'Yes, I am just going to load up and then I'll be on my way.'

He looked at the brown paper bag in my hand, then looked back up to my face.

'It's for loading and unloading.'

'Yes.'

'It looks as though you have just been shopping.'

'Yes.'

'Loading and unloading involves heavy items, often requiring the use of a trolley.'

'Ok I get it, it's not for regular shopping. Please, I won't do it again.'

'Just thought I would let you know, for your information.'

I don't know whether I was angry or relieved when I sped away. Christine's mood had picked up by the time I arrived home.

'Matt and Bianca have texted. They should be here by about five.' She shouted down as I unpacked the bags.

Stu 3

'That bloody road. You can't pass anything. Why don't you get a decent motorway down here?' Matt blasted through the door, embracing Christine who cooed, and giving me a slap on the shoulder. Bianca followed him in. 'That smells good. The usual is it Stu?'

Matt had been a friend studying history with me through my undergraduate years. He was now in the commercial world and had met Bianca, a publishing executive, a few years ago.

We sat around the table. I spooned out big dollops of the gooey mess into bowls and passed it across.

'I love the burnt cheesy potato on top, Matt,' Bianca said.

'In that case I'll give you a double helping.'

The wine was going down well.

'Missing London yet?' Matt enquired, between mouthfuls.

I and Christine glanced at one another.

'Oh. Have I said something I shouldn't have?' Matt nudged Bianca.

'No, it's ok Matt. It's just that we were discussing how we feel about being down here earlier today,' Christine said.

'I do miss London, or at least walking around the city.' I said. 'I love being in amongst those massive stone edifices, decorated with echoes of empire and the people who ran it, built with all that plundered loot and the profits of slavery. Now the world brings its loose money to us voluntarily, and so we now have a layer above, stretching into the sky of concrete, steel and glass. But what's most wonderful about it is that the footprint of the earlier settlement, I mean the Roman, Saxon and mediaeval town, is still there and visible. Even the names of the streets give it away. Think of Fishmongers, Cheapside and Poultry.'

'Poultry,' Matt repeated. 'I have always thought it a contradiction in terms that billions of pounds could be sitting on Poultry.'

'You're thinking of paltry, you idiot,' Bianca exclaimed.

'I don't care. I still don't want a chicken managing my retirement fund!' They all laughed.

'You talk so well about it, and with such passion, Stu, I always thought you should have stuck to academia,' Bianca said kindly.

I thought about how I should respond. That door was firmly closed behind me now.

'I do enjoy teaching. We get school parties coming through the museum, and they all want to hear something about the Battle of Hastings. I like to shake it up for them. All they know is that it was Anglo Saxons versus Normans. The English against the French. I like to tell them that in fact Harold may have identified more with being Danish than Anglo-Saxon. Ok, there was probably some Saxon royal blood in his lineage, but his mother was Danish royalty, and his parents' marriage may have been arranged by the Danish king Cnut. It's telling that he and his siblings had given names that were Danish, not Saxon. And of course, William would have been very much aware of his own Norse ancestry. He was Rollo's great great grandson after all. So really the Battle of Hastings could be seen as a fight between two Viking dynasties, over the precious jewel of a prize that England was back then. The foot soldiers in the battle were English and French respectively, but the leaders and nobles had a high percentage of Scandinavian blood. It just emphasises how the Viking sea-warriors had won the wars of the previous couple of hundred years and dominated the land-based monarchs.'

'Wow, Stu. You really like to turn things on their heads.' Matt silently clapped his hands.

'Well, I think there is a bit too much respect for orthodoxies.'

'Maybe you are well suited to being in Hastings. It does seem to be a place for mavericks after all,' Bianca said.

'Do you remember when you came down for pirates day last year?' Christine said.

'Now there were proper pirates there. None of your banker types in fancy dress. These were people who owned the costume, black eyepatch, tricorn hat and breaches and dress coat. In fact, I think some of them wore it year-round. Proper pirates. I think they were channelling something,' Bianca said.

'Yo ho ho and a bottle of rum. That's what they were channelling,' Matt added.

'No, the real pirates are the ones on mobility scooters. They bear the wounds of past battles. Skull and crossed crutches on the back, and the stump of an amputation pointing the way. Can you imagine how scary a fleet of them would be coming down the prom, tacking against the wind?' I said.

'Going "Oooh Aaarh" on their horns,' offered Bianca.

'Yeah, they'd have just done a raid on the benefit's office,' Matt chuckled. 'On another note, Stu, I was looking at your eyes as you were telling us about the Battle of Hastings. There was a certain messianic gaze going on. You haven't been looking at that stuff on the dark web again?'

'What do you mean?'

'You know. All that conspiracy theory stuff about the battle not being at Battle and so on.'

'It's not on the dark web, and it's not conspiracy theories. There are quite well constructed arguments by some pretty good amateur historians.'

'Well, can I give you some advice? If you are planning to write a book about Hastings, don't put Hastings in the title. It's cursed. Publishers won't touch it. In fact, probably best not to mention Hastings in the text either. Bianca will back me up, won't you darling.'

'It must be all the witches round here. You told us last time we came that St Leonards had the highest concentration of witches in England. I think we saw one going into next door on the way in,' Bianca said.

'It was that Aleister Crowley that started it, what with his black masses here in the 1940's,' Matt added.

'Matt's right about the publishers. I can't think of a book that has sold well about Hastings, even though it's one of the most fascinating places in England,' Bianca said.

'Well, I hadn't even thought about writing about it. But it does sound like a bit of a challenge now. Might consider it,' I said.

'Anyway, I think you're very lucky to live here. Hastings attracts the most talented artists, writers and musicians, like moths to a candle flame in a hurricane lamp. You can see them all beating against the glass, their beautiful furry bodies with spectacularly patterned and colourful wings. But once they are in there they just can't escape.'

'Can we change the subject?' Christine looked distressed.

Stu 4

The dishes put on the side, we got ready for going out. I helped Christine get her winter coat on.

'Look at us. What a bunch of London types. You can spot us a mile away,' said Matt.

'You know what they call us here? DFLs. Down-From-London's. I got into a classic DFL scrape today. I haven't told you this yet. They didn't have any aubergines at the supermarket, so I went crawling around the streets looking for fresh fruit and veg from an ordinary shop. Found one, and parked up in a loading bay. On my way back from the shop, there was a parking attendant by my car. He said, "This is for loading and unloading only, sir." His eyes flicked down to my aubergine poking out of the bag at waist level, then back up to my face. "Are you loading or unloading, sir?" How much more DFL can you get than that!'

'Come on you two. We better hurry or we'll miss the parade,' implored Christine.

I don't know exactly how I ended up in the shop doorway. We were walking line-a-breast down the High Street along with a lot of other people searching for a good vantage point to watch the procession of bonfire societies. I turned round to see how far away the leading group in the parade was, but my view was obscured by a line of special constables, shepherding the crowd in front of them, of which I was a part. The sound of drums and firecrackers was intensifying, funnelled up the narrow street with its half-timbered buildings on one side and shops on the other.

'Clear the road now please,' a constable bellowed just behind my head. For some reason I went left, unaware that Christine, Matt and Bianca had gone right, along with all other sensible people in the crowd. I found a nice little spot in an antiques shop doorway, recessed from the narrow pavement and only a couple of feet from the kerb. I thought, this will be great. I'll be almost within touching distance of the folk in the parade. On the other side of the road, I saw the back of Christine's coat as she climbed up the half dozen stone steps onto the raised walkway. Ahead of her were Matt and Bianca. Bianca waved vigorously from the place she had secured, her face excited as the procession was approaching. She grabbed Christine's arm and pointed down in my direction. Christine locked onto me, and I smiled back and raised my arm in mock salute. I watched as people jostled by the railing up there, trying to get the best position. Behind them, the curtains were open in the Georgian bay windows, and rooms glowed from shaded lights inside, silhouetting witchy cut out shapes placed next to the glass. I looked up and down and I was the only person left on this side of the road. OK. It's either make a dash for it and try to compete with the others to get a view, or else relax and revel in my special status. I was aware of lots of pairs of eyes on me from the crowd arrayed just ten yards opposite. I turned nonchalantly and inspected the dimly lit items for sale in the window of the now closed shop. Look, there's a ceramic phrenology head, and behind, a reproduction diver's helmet. I turned back to my spectators. Christine was looking a little concerned. The sound of drums was growing and the acrid smell of burning torches wafted down the road.

The first standard bearer was in line with me now. Three flaming torches were angled from his magnificent banner which he held proudly aloft. A gust of wind flattened the flames for a second, but they recovered, far too well fuelled on the kerosene-soaked rags to be blown out. Following the standard was a line of drummers. They started up just parallel to me, rapping out a staccato tattoo on their snare drums, keeping in time to their marching speed. The sound bounced back at me from the row of houses opposite, giving a me visceral call to arms in the pit of my stomach. Feathered black top hats completed their black 17th century costumes. A woman in the group was dressed in a wide bustled gown, decorated with a hundred tiny LED lights that flashed on and off, cycling through the primary colours. This was exciting, I was almost in the parade myself. Society after society passed, each representing a Sussex village, and each with their own distinctive tradition of costume. Here was a column of Roman legionaries following their centurion. Next a chain gang of convicts, then followed an order of monks led by their abbot. The flaming torches were borne by the flanking marchers, and I had to swing my head back on several occasions to avoid getting singed. An ominous rumble like a deep death rattle: metal wheels and loose axles on the cobbled street approached from the right as the column advanced left. Dragged by chains, the half oil drums made a rising screech of a noise. They were the hearses to carry the dead and dying torches. I watched them go by, entranced by the sound and the glowing embers contained within.

My head was still turned when I felt a tap on my shoulder. I looked round and there was a face, just six inches from mine. Not an ordinary face. This one was covered in makeup, a big red nose and exaggerated eyes, arched halfway up its forehead. Its tongue came out and, with a spread palm on each side of its head, it let out the most extraordinary scream.

My hands came up involuntarily on each side of my head, and I found myself screaming back, joining this clown in a strange harmony, against my will. A second later he was gone, and I turned my head to follow as he scooted up the road to catch up with the procession. What was that? Then a white flash rose from my feet, an ear-splitting percussion, and a blast wave hit my face as I looked down. And then silence. I felt my legs buckle. The flash had saturated my retinae, all I could see was white. The silence was replaced by a thin thread of noise, it's pitch just sitting below the upper threshold of normal hearing. The thread grew in volume until it felt as though I was being overwhelmed. Patches of vision started to return and, as I rose from a crouch, I became aware of the concerned faces of Christine and Bianca approaching me. The crowd had been let back onto the road and was moving slowly to follow the parade.

If I looked towards Christine's nose, I could see her mouth moving below in my peripheral vision. Her central face was still obscured by a cloud of yellow. I turned to Bianca, and her mouth was moving too. It looked as though they were saying something to each other. Behind them, Matt was laughing, but a silent laugh. It looked a bit sinister. He dipped and tucked his shoulder under my arm to give me support and, with Christine on my other side, we advanced with the crowd up the street. Matt was booming now, and it broke through my impaired hearing.

'Make way! Make way! Is there a casualty clearing station nearby? This one's got shell shock.'

At the turn of the street, where it joined the seafront, a St John's ambulance was parked. Its rear doors were open, and I could see into the brightly lit interior, its shelves neatly organised for all eventualities. Matt broke away and went to speak to one of the crew who was standing just outside. I still couldn't hear what Christine and Bianca were saying. Matt returned, and with exaggerated lip movements, and high volume, he enunciated.

'I was just asking them if they had an emergency hearing aid.'

Bianca punched him in the side, not best pleased, by the look on her face. He turned to her and pretended to look hurt, as though it had been a reasonable thing to ask for under the circumstances.

Christine held on to my arm and propelled me forward, keeping in pace with the others. The parade ahead had reached the giant bonfire that had been constructed on the Stade. Its core of stacked pallets was faced with timbers and planks, and it was topped by an effigy of a famous politician in cartoon form. The societies formed up around its base, the torch bearers circling around it. On a given signal they threw their torches onto the wooden structure, and within a minute the flames had taken hold. The wind whipped a stream of embers spiralling from the side of the pyre, the heart of which now glowed yellow and orange.

My hearing was starting to return, the thread of white noise still prominent but I could hear Bianca say.

'Look! That's the first one going up.'

A bright dot ascended just off the vertical against the black night sky, trailing a wobbly rising tail until it was high above our heads. Then there was a report as it exploded, and a beautiful red peony expanded to fill the field of vision. The battery of mortars got going, each salute followed by a report to produce green chrysanthemum, then golden willow with its draping branches descending to surround us in colour, some with falling leaves, others with crackle effect, then brocade, then silver fish scattering in all directions under their own propulsion.

The barrage gathered pace, one shell following the last, so each successive exploding flower had a pistil inside that expanded and took over the spectacle as the first faded. The people with their heads tilted back were transported by this cosmic beauty and went with it as the climax approached. My chest was struck by a heavy report that heralded an enormous red, green and yellow willow, the limbs growing rapidly from the core, then hanging and flittering as they slowly descended, the fade delayed beyond what seemed at all possible.

A collective "Wow" rose from the spectators, followed by an impassioned round of applause. Whoops and whistles of appreciation sounded from every corner; the collective neural chemistry of the people treated to a balm of rare quality.

Then Matt said. 'We'd better get this casualty home.'

Stu 5

I turned off the road and parked up on the verge. Opposite was a row of houses, each plot once occupied by a fisherman's cottage, which in succession were being replaced by modernist square cubes as record producers and rich lawyers saw the value of a beachside home. The top floors had a perfect, unobstructed sea view. The ground floors, sitting below sea level, nestled behind the very necessary defensive wall that, it is hoped, will keep the waves out for decades to come. This quiet shore was becoming my safe place, a place of peace to explore when the tide was out.

The car journey had given me a chance to reflect on the previous day's events. I had loved the parade and the fireworks, but my ears were still ringing from the explosion. At breakfast Bianca showed me the video on her phone that she had recorded from the raised pavement opposite to where I was standing.

'Look, don't the torches look wonderful reflected in the shop windows?' she said. The sound of drumming came through the tinny speaker, as the marchers went by. Then there was a sharp high-pitched crack.

'Take it back a bit, love.' Matt was leaning in over her shoulder. 'I think you'll be able to see that clown dropping the banger.'

Bianca dragged the video back ten seconds. I wasn't proud to see myself nose to nose with the clown, mirroring his actions. As he ran off you could see him flick, with some force, from his left hand, an object onto the ground. Then the explosion. I felt a bit sick as I saw myself crumple slightly.

'Stu, I'll send it to you,' Bianca said.

'You should take it to the police,' Matt added. 'He could have killed you if you had a heart condition.'

I thought for a second. 'I know, but here is how I reckon it would go. "Very well sir, we'll pick up six clowns from the street and have an identity parade. Take your time, sir. Which one of these naughty men pulled a face at you and then made a loud noise?" They would laugh me out of the station.'

'Well, if you've still got tinnitus in a year, you might regret not having reported it at the time,' Christine said.

'Look you two. We're going to head back now. It's been a lovely and eventful weekend. Hastings never disappoints.'

Christine was content to see them go, after the obligatory double kisses. She had several hours marking to look forward to, her regular Sunday chore. It gave me a chance to have some time to myself and clear my head, under cover of leaving her undisturbed.

The tide was out a long way. Wonderful. I part strode, part slid down the shingle, in a hurry to get to the glistening shoreline. The yellow sun was dancing on the gentle wave tops in the distance and reflecting from whole slabs of wet sand in between. To get to the water's edge I first had to navigate the perilous sunken forest. Seven thousand years ago, when the land extended much further out into the English Channel, this beach would have been covered by trees. The trunks are still there, now lying flat, preserved in the anaerobic conditions like a dense criss cross game of pick-up sticks. And growing on the worm-hole pitted trunks is a bright green weed, completely frictionless when wet. The sole of a boot will just slide when applied to the surface, and many a time I have landed on my butt. So, despite my haste, I took great care to place my feet carefully, choosing the firm mud between the trunks wherever possible.

Where the forest ended, and before the flat sand started, there lay a miniature landscape. Rivers of sea waters, left after the receding tide, made their way through gorge and ravine, over cliffs and waterfalls, with each tide carved anew. I felt like a god observing this perfection in feet and inches from six feet above. It looked so real, as a drone might see from five thousand feet.

Once on the firm sand, I strode westwards, enjoying the sun on my face. I looked back at the impressions my boots left, trailing behind me. A group of juvenile seagulls took to the air, wings flapping into the gentle breeze. Like a vanguard some plovers kept ten yards ahead of me, darting into the wash of each wave as it brought fresh tiny shrimp to eat. The cliffs rose to my right. Soft and friable, they are vulnerable to collapse, especially after rain. That which is a headache to the homeowners atop the cliff, at risk of losing some stretch of garden or worse, brings a bounty to fossil hunters, each fall having the potential to break open a treasury of wonder that had been sealed for tens of millions of years. I paused and looked at the cliffs. The low angle of the sun showed them at their best. Thin layers of burnt umber interspersed with every shade of ochre and the occasional dark brown and grey, were all piled up in the horizontal strata. Contrasting light and shade together with the stillness of the air produced a crisp clarity of view. The cliffs reflected as a perfect inversion in the mirrored surface of the rockpools that lay between me and their base. I was entranced.

Picking my way over the boulders of past rockfalls I reached the shingle that lay under the cliff. Warnings abound of the dangers of getting too close, but I was feeling carefree and careless. How romantic it would be to be killed by a falling iguanodon's thigh bone. The dot of my human time to be subsumed by the vastness of geological time. What nobler an end than to experience subhumation under a pile of ninety-million-year-old rock. To become part of this earth might add an ounce of significance to my existence.

I scoured around, looking for evidence on the planes of fracture revealed as the boulders below my feet had dislodged from their ordered place in the strata above. Each plane had represented the end of a layer of deposition; the turn of season as the flood receded in one year, millions of years ago. The flora was tropical then, and the fauna mainly dinosaur. On previous visits I had found many imprints of dinosaur feet, or rather their filled impressions, the next season's deposition of material taking the shape of the hole left by the dinosaur's foot that had been baked into the surface the previous year.

Candidates presented themselves as I hopped from one boulder to the next. There were streaks and curls and meshes that may well have been the fossils of plant stems and ferns. Then, aided by the high contrast of the low sunlight, it caught my eye. A swelling on the rock. One, two, maybe three digits, it was hard to tell precisely given the erosion which each high tide had brought to dull the edges of my find of the day. It represented one step made aeons ago, an event that took barely a second in time then, but which I could see now, the interval so long after, that it was impossible to conceive of it in human terms. It truly was a wonder.

I felt refreshed. My trips here always had to culminate with a discovery to make me feel truly satisfied. I could leave now cleansed. The problems of the weekend, and of Christine's unhappiness left behind for a while. What significance could they have when you think in terms of millions of years?

Stu 6

I sat by my coffee at the breakfast bar. The sound of the explosion had left a high-pitched whistle that I couldn't shake from my brain.

Christine had just left for school. After I had returned from my sojourn at the beach the previous afternoon, she had decided it would be a good time to "have a talk".

'I think we have to do something Stuart.' She never called me that, unless my full attention was required. 'You're just drifting in that job, and I'm working day and night to keep this school afloat. I don't owe them anything. What do you think about a move back to London? Before we get stuck here, trapped "like moths in a hurricane lamp" as Bianca called it.'

All I could think of were the practical reasons that would make it difficult. 'Well, we couldn't afford anything like this to live in. And our quality of life, what we can do for recreation, is much better here.'

She wasn't persuaded. 'Life isn't just about what's practical. It's about being emotionally fulfilled as well. I'm going to start looking for jobs. Maybe you should too.'

I did my usual tour of the exhibition rooms of the museum, and then checked in with Colin at the till in the reception room which doubled as ticket purchase desk and gift shop.

'All right, mate? Good weekend?'

'Yeah. We went to the bonfire, but some clown let off a banger next to me, so my head's still ringing. And when I say some clown, it actually was a clown.'

Colin laughed. 'You get some wild ones in those processions. I always keep well back.'

'I'm going to take it easy today,' I replied. 'I'll be in the office.'

The computer took a while to load. I sat back in the black leatherette chair and looked out of the window. There were some council gardeners working on the shrubbery just across the gravel approach to the museum, making it look nice and "civic". Once the screen had fired up, I checked the emails first. Nothing new over the weekend. My mind kept returning to Christine, and her suggestion I should be looking for another job. I just didn't feel the impetus in the same way she did. I rather liked it down here. If I start looking for jobs advertised in London, it's going to ruin my day. So, I drifted into an hour of random searches.

Hastings clowns...a series of images came up. Fifty pounds an hour for children's parties. None of them looked like my clown. Scary, but not that scary.

How long does tinnitus last... Jesus, I wish I hadn't searched for that. *It generally gets worse and can be a major precursor to depression and even suicide.*

Let's keep it clean. The internet can be a dangerous place.

Saxon hoards...that's better. Porn for history nerds. Look at those lovely piles of silver coins and crumpled gold beakers. And look at that beautiful gold filigree inset with red garnets. That's incredible craftsmanship. Imagine metal detecting and then finding that on the end of your spade.

Latest Saxon finds...Pottery...pottery...sword hilt. Ah, sword hilt that looks interesting.

Link to *Suomi Museum: latest finds and acquisitions.*

Mmm. That'll be in Finland. Saxon? In Finland? It seemed to take ages to load.

219

A Saxon style sword hilt (blade broken off) found recently on a small island off Helsinki. A red stone is set in the pommel, and part of a religious inscription is preserved in the metal ring surrounding the stone.

I hovered over the image with the cursor. The magnified area kept flashing on and off. Eventually it steadied.

...*GODWINS*... The letters are in Latin script. That's odd. They were still writing in runic script in Northern Europe around that time. But it does look Saxon. Look at the shallow curve on that short guard. Unusual to have a pommel that's decorated though. Hang on. *GODWINS*... Godwinson! Harold Godwinson! The family name of King Harold. It couldn't be. It's just too weird. Found in Finland?

My heart thumped and I started to sweat. I had to stand up. I walked over to the window. The gardeners were packing up their tools to move on to another job. I went into the narrow galley kitchen and put the kettle on. A mug of tea, that's what's required. Maybe with two sugars. They say that's good for shock.

Back at the computer I peered at the screen to have a closer look and check my eyes weren't deceiving me. No, definitely a Saxon sword, probably English.

The Suomi Museum. Where's the contact page? Ah. Send message.

"Hello. My name is Dr Stuart Richardson, and I am the curator of the Museum of Hastings in England. You have a Saxon sword hilt on your new finds page. I think I may be able to help you identify it. It is absolutely imperative that you do not clean it. PLEASE DO NOT CLEAN IT!"

Time to take a little walk. I tried to keep calm and did another circuit of the exhibition rooms. Not many people in. I casually looked at the various items through the glass. I

220

smiled at a lady on her own. She looked back nervously. I must have been exuding agitation rather than the tranquillity I was trying to fake.

'Colin, I'm just going to get a breath of fresh air.'

'Ok, boss.' He didn't look up from his book as I headed for the door.

The border was newly dug. Lovely black soil. They've done a good job. Probably put some bulbs in for the spring. I could see the wall behind as well now. It's normally covered by the laurel foliage, but that was all cut back. Beautiful yellow sandstone blocks.

Right. I've given them enough time to respond. Let's go and see if there is a reply.

In the office I peered at the screen. No response yet. Back to the Suomi Museum website. Staff. I scrolled down the list. Aava Heikkinen curator. And it had a telephone number. Good. I wonder what the board will think of me making international calls.

It went to an ansafone. 'My name is Dr Richardson, from England, and I am ringing about the Saxon sword. Please, please do not clean it. Ring me back as soon as you get this message.'

OK, that felt clumsy. I suppose it carried the important information though.

Give him or her a while to respond. I searched the Jetsy website. Flights to Helsinki don't look to cost too much. As long as you don't take any luggage. How soon could I fly? I might need to get there quickly if they don't get the message. Week after next. Oh shit.

What next? Contact the chair of the governing body. If I'm going to travel, I need an allowance. I am sure they could dip into one of the accounts they have for donations.

'Hi, it's Stu Richardson here from the museum? Sorry to disturb, but I have just seen on the internet what could be an incredibly important relic, a sword that could have belonged to Saxon nobility, and might have relevance to the Battle of Hastings. Anyway, it's in Finland... Yes, Finland... Finland... I don't know what it's doing in Finland. They've only just found it there... No, it wasn't in a back storeroom. They found it on an island... Yes, I agree, it does sound very improbable... Anyway, I think I might need to book a flight to Helsinki, and I was wondering if the museum might cover my costs... Why do I need to go? It's very important they don't clean it. If there are any traces of soil on it, it could give us some accurate information as to where it had been deposited, and also date...Yes, I could just tell them over the phone not to clean it, but they are not responding to my messages yet. Can I send you the link to the website? It might help if you can actually see it... OK, we'll talk later. Bye.'

The light flashed on the phone. I picked it up.

'Aava Heikkinen here. Can I speak to Dr Richardson please?' Her English was perfect.

'Hello, it's Stuart Richardson. Thank you for ringing back. You have a very exciting find on your website.'

'Yes, I got your message. And in answer to your request not to clean it, we are not stupid. We have some of the most sophisticated laboratories in the world for dating and the geo-archaeologists at the university are attached to our museum.'

I had to think. How could I compete with a capital city museum? They obviously would think I was incredibly parochial.

'Well, I hope I could contribute with an opinion on the sword? My PhD thesis was on Anglo-Saxon nobility so I hope I have some background that could be useful. How convinced are you that it is a religious inscription on the pommel?'

'It says "God wins", so it is suggestive of a warrior's imploration for victory.'

'Can I offer an alternative explanation. It could be part of the surname "Godwinson", The inherited name of King Harold, son of Godwin.'

'Ah, yes that is very intriguing. Would that be the Harold who was slain at the Battle of Hastings?'

'The very same.'

Stu 7

I managed to get my first leg over the barbed wire, but the second was proving trickier. Moving it backwards and forwards I was able to unhitch my trouser leg from the thorn and swing my boot over to contact the ground again. This was the back way to Senlac Hill, the site of the Battle of Hastings. Cut across the footpath and turn right. Quite straight forward really. The main entrance was up by the abbey and access was controlled by Heritage-4-All, or heritage for all who can afford £40 for a family ticket, as I liked to think. It had been a long time since I had last stood on the battlefield, so it felt like an imperative that I re-experience it now that a possible tangible connection had been discovered.

The two days since that first conversation with Aava, the curator in Helsinki, had been a bit fraught. On reflection my excitement at the discovery was a little over the top. It got dampened as the complexity of various issues became apparent. My chairman of the Governors, once he had seen the link I had sent him, had also become rather excited.

'Stuart, we've got to get hold of this for our collection. It's gold dust. Think what it could do for our profile. I would be happy to approve your expenses to go over there and bring it back to its rightful home.'

I rang Aava to tell her I was about to book a flight, really just checking she would be there on those dates.

'Stuart, if you are thinking you might be able to return to England with it, I am afraid it will take some time to get approval.'

224

'Ah, I suppose you'd have to check with your governance committee.'

'Definitely but think about it. Why shouldn't we keep it here? It's a fine example of English Saxon work that would add something to our collection. How many items do you have in your museum from other parts of the world?'

My mind flashed to at least a hundred, some of them incredibly precious and rare. We now have an indigenous engagement protocol at the museum, respecting access to objects that may be of cultural or religious significance. However, we hadn't gone so far as to suggest, if delegations visit, that they can take items home with them. The argument always is, think of the educational value to the world if these objects are available in nations far away from their home. It triggers interest, and is like a sort of reverse cultural imperialism. The fact that they were often obtained by nefarious means tends to get brushed under the carpet. She had got me.

I rang the chairman again.

'We can't give up just like that, Stuart. Isn't there some leverage we can exert? Won't geoarchaeology analysis require soil specimens from around here as a comparator? We could withhold those until we can reach agreement. I'll write a letter to my counterpart at the Suomi Museum.'

'I have an idea. Maybe we could just ask to take it on loan, and get the analysis done here. You know, these loans can extend towards the long term sometimes.'

'Not a bad idea, Stuart. Shall we see if they will agree to that?'

The wait was on. I booked a ticket, let Aava know, and hoped that her governing body would rush through a decision before I arrived there. I felt itchy to get going. It seemed like the right thing to do was to take a day off and burn that nervous energy in the great outdoors and explore the beautiful countryside of East Sussex.

I climbed the shallow incline in the direction of the abbey. Scattered trees and the odd hedge lay between me and the pale yellow sandstone of the abbey buildings. Some lay in ruins; others were restored to house a fine school. It was a cool, hazy day. Summer was now long gone, and the leaves were starting to turn from green to yellow. The summit wasn't too far away. Tradition had it that the abbey was founded on the site where King Harold fell, slain by the Norman victors. I heightened my senses, sniffing for the smell of battle. Nothing came. I strained to hear the clang of sword against sword, the swish of an axe head slicing the air, the whinny of a rearing horse. But it was silent. There was no atmosphere of battle. The space felt wrong. It was too wide. If Harold had set up his shield wall at the top of the hill, he would have had no chance of defending it against attackers coming up the hill. He could have been outflanked on either side. Would he have been so naive? It seems unlikely, as he already had experience of command, having pulled off a stunning victory in the north of England only weeks before. I turned and looked down the hill. It faced southwest in the direction of Pevensey, obscured from view by some small rises. Doubts that had swirled in my head for some time started to crystallise. Pevensey, the supposed landing site of the Norman fleet. Why there? It would have been dominated by the massive Saxon shore fort of Anderida, first built by the Romans. Why risk landing an invasion fleet next to a fort that could house a garrison of defenders? And why would William choose to land at Pevensey if his strategic intention was to set up his encampment on the peninsula that Hastings was then, so hard to reach from Pevensey, hemmed in by the bay on one side and a series of great tidal estuaries on the other. There was over ten miles of sea and a tidal inlet to navigate between the two. Not easy for men and horses on the march. I decided to move on.

Drizzle was falling by the time I had covered the three miles east to Sedlescombe, and I continued beyond the village to the lane that led to Hurst Hill. My walk had taken me across the isthmus that would have separated the land of the tribe of Hastingas from the rest of England a thousand years ago. When Harold had arrived to confront the Normans who had occupied this territory, surely the subsequent battle must have occurred somewhere in this geographical choke point, and the Normans would have had to have broken through here from their Hastings encampment to invade the country further north. I crossed the River Brede close to Sedlescombe and entered the territory where the Roman road from Rochester would have spilled the weary men of King Harold after their long march from the north. Hurst Hill had been proposed as a possible alternative battle site in an internet treatise by a brilliant amateur historian. He arrived at it by deduction as the most likely site in terms of physical structure and its geographical location.

Grey laden skies provided an enhancing backdrop to the bright colours appearing now in mid-autumn. Yellow discs of silver birch leaves, like gold coins tipped from a purse, shone in the low light, and red and burnt orange was starting to populate the diminishing canopy above my head. A low bank of gold defined each side of the wet black tarmac, funnelling me up the narrow lane. The incline was moderate rather than steep, then it levelled off onto a smallish plateau, with sides that descended into gullies on either side, a stream at the bottom of each. This was a place where you could set up a defensive shield wall, the area narrow enough to resist an assault from the flank.

I eased the rucksack from my back and took a swig of water. Looking across the head of the Brede valley, the opposite bank was close enough for Harold to have been able to see figures and movement in a Norman camp if it had been set up there. I tried to see the area devoid of trees and summon the spirits of the battle. The tinnitus in my head broke up, the thread of high-pitched whistle modulating slightly allowing the entry of other sounds. I don't know whether it was fatigue from my walk, but did I hear a tumult, the roar of men's voices raised in a desperate gory effort? I thought so. I sat against a tree and shut my eyes. First it was there, and then it slipped away. Elusive when I tried to pin it down, I couldn't anchor it in my consciousness. The more I tried the less it would come. The sound of the tinnitus rose again, and this time wouldn't be disturbed.

I walked on down the Brede valley, through woods and past the traces of two millennia of iron workings. The area had been exploited for its mineral reserve first by Celt, then Roman and later Tudor. In amongst the trees there were large hollows, some thirty or forty yards across, where the iron ore had been scooped out. Streams ran red, the colour of rust. Patches of woodland floor, where the light penetrated, were carpeted in bracken, its flaccid tips changing from green to yellow and increasingly assuming the copper hues of autumn. I stopped on the path. A movement caught my eye to the left ahead. A doe, just ten yards in front of me, leapt silently across the path. It was a high leap, as though she was averse to applying her hooves to the ground upon which man had trod. Her cushioned landing raised not even a rustle in the leaves, and she was off. But then there was another, and another, from left to right, each repeating the first's leap, until seven or eight had crossed. And there was not a sound. Without any auditory confirmation of such a sight, it took me a few seconds to register. Was it real or imagined? It was certainly magical, and it was real. I felt so lucky to have witnessed it.

A gap in the trees allowed me to survey the Brede valley, its course going eastwards to meet the sea near Winchelsea. It was broad, and, a thousand years ago the bottom would have been filled with water. Ships could navigate even as far as Sedlescombe in Roman times. It would have been the route to service the iron workings, and to take valuable timber out of the Wealden forest to the port at the end, and onwards. That port, at the time of the battle, was probably known as the port of Hastings, and lay where Winchelsea lies today. The land of the lower Brede valley had belonged to the Abbey of Fécamp since 1015. It was already in Norman hands.

Why would William not have used this connection to make this his landing place and his base for his invasion of England? It would have been friendly territory, controlled by allies, and would have allowed him to gain a foothold and organise his men without the threat of harassment or opposition. It had even been proposed that the land opposite Winchelsea, on the north bank of the Brede estuary, a thousand years ago could have been known as Peuenisel, or Pevenesellum, or another variant spelling of Pevensey. It just fits better than the received history. Both the geography and the politics of the time point to the Brede valley playing a significant part in the invasion of England by the Normans in 1066.

I mulled this over with a pint in front of me at the pub in Brede village, footsore and in need of rescue. I could see that Christine had seen my text. I hoped she may be able to come and pick me up on the way back from school. It wasn't long before I felt a nudge on my shoulder.

'Hello, darling. Good walk?'

'Wonderful. It's incredibly beautiful, and it gave me a chance to think about the battle and its site. I think I may be going over to the dark side.'

'Oh dear. Not more complications,' she smiled.

'Why don't we eat here? The menu looks great.'

We ordered two Sussex smokies, while I recounted my day, and she hers.

'I love the haddock with the gooey cheese and potato. It's a triumph.'

Satisfied, we emerged into the dusk and Christine gave me a lift to the car I had abandoned some hours before in Battle.

'You know Stu, I think you've been happier the last few days than at any time since we moved to Hastings. All you needed was a project.'

It was the first time we had felt in harmony for a long time.

Stu 8

'Pint of Harveys and a gin and tonic please.'

'That'll be nine forty, thank you.'

The barmaid peered flatly through two black cakes of makeup that circled her eyes. I wasn't sure if she was a year-round goth, or whether she had made a special effort for tonight. It had been Christine's idea to come out on Halloween.

'Stu, it's the one night of the year when Hastings actually makes sense. It's so naturally ghoulish here, it looks as though the people haven't had to make any effort at all.'

Christine herself had made a lot of effort. She looked magnificent. She was topped with an ash blonde wig, piled high, and her face white with a black beauty spot by the right corner of her mouth. Beneath her winter coat there was a scarlet ball gown.

'I never thought I'd get to wear this again.'

The colour was perfect and matched the theatrical blood streaming from a wide gash she had crafted across the width of her throat. We both agreed she had channelled Marie Antoinette to a tee.

We took our drinks out onto the street. There was a low mist that made spectral rings around the light coming from the Victorian streetlamps. I was pleased with my cassock. Christine had spotted the djellaba robe in the souk in Marrakech, a nice thick brown woollen one suitable for cold nights in the desert.

'You've got to have this,' she had said as we agreed on a price. It had hung on the back of the bedroom door for five

231

years. Now was its first outing. A length of velvet curtain retaining rope round the waist, and I was transformed into a mediaeval monk, especially convincing with the hood up.

'Er, I have got you this to finish the costume,' she had said hesitantly, unsure of my reaction. It was a plastic fox's face with two eye holes to see through and a gap under the jaw if you wanted to push the snout up.

'Ha, I love it! This is proper Reynard the Fox!' My mind went back to the tales of the mediaeval fox monk, who valiantly fought his way through Europe.

'I can't wait to get out there!'

We stood sipping our drinks at the edge of the narrow pedestrianised road, hemmed in by cafes and closed shop fronts. A crowd of eccentrically clad revellers had gathered, under a twenty-foot effigy of a witch, crafted in Salem style. Her head was out of focus in the low cloud, but she wore a simple white bonnet and a black puritan dress. The perspective made her pink papier mache hands seem enormous. She stood on a wheeled carriage, to be manoeuvred as the evening progressed.

A lady approached from the left, pushing a buggy. She was clad entirely in black, a Victorian frock complete with bustle, leather lace up boots, and a black net veil gathered in from the broad rim of her black hat. I wondered whether it may have concealed a pram-face as she got closer but feared something more sinister. She pulled up just next to us at the edge of the crowd. Her toddler in the buggy was taking long draws on his bottle which he held in his right hand, high to the side of his head so he had a clear view. He looked like an experienced bottle feeder, one who could do it with attitude. I looked again. He's not a thirty-five-year-old skinhead midget, is he? No, probably three or four years old, but a little old for the bottle. His eyes fixed on me. Ah, he's going to say something like 'Oooh, fox.' Instead, he raised his pudgy left hand, forefinger extended. He looked at me intently. The tip of his finger flicked back, and he mouthed the word 'Bang!' Ok, I get it. 'Foxy dead.' I pretended to crumple slightly, but he had already turned his gaze away.

I looked around. To my right, who would have guessed it, there was a woman with the same fox mask. She had a short grey puffer jacket on, and a mane of russet red hair poked out of the hood to frame the mask. I looked down. Just beneath the waist of the jacket at the back, and above her rounded buttocks, emerged the shaft of a tail at an angle just above the horizontal, which then curved down and around to a red fur bush. Her hand came down and flicked it. The tip moved up towards me. Sexy vixen, I thought. It's amazing what putting a mask on can do for your libido.

The first tones sounded from beyond the crowd. Deep brass chords, prolonged and interrupted, so slow there was doubt as to whether the next would start. Then the theme emerged. It was the slowest, most menacing interpretation of the Specials song "Ghost Town" I had ever heard. The descending harmonies plumbed a depth that reached the limits of human perception. The pace barely picked up, but I could see between the watchers, a front man, white faced and black eyed, suit clad limbs in extended stiffness, moving in an offbeat rhythm. He raised his megaphone and with an electronically distorted voice emitted the phrase 'We're living in a Ghost Town.'

With the tolling of a single handbell, the procession started. The pallbearers were immaculately turned out in there in their black frock coats and white blouson shirts, puffing out at neck and wrist. Their top hats swung in unison as they bore the coffin down the street to the next pub. They were preceded by cardinals and bishops, and followed by the great witch effigy, pulled along like a giant child's toy. We trailed behind, enjoying the whole spectacle.

'This is incredible,' Christine said. I turned towards her to reply, but the figure in front had stopped so I bumped into his back. I retreated slightly as he lifted his bent head and turned towards me slowly. He was holding something in his hand.

'I would suggest you don't disturb me so early, young man.' His face was full turned to me now. That was some makeup. Or was it truly that the flesh on his face was gone to reveal the bony stump of a nose, empty orbits and a full set of teeth unadorned by lip and cheek? A chill descended through my body. It couldn't be makeup. I was close and this was no illusion. In his hand was a metal scythe. The light glinted off its edge.

I fell back stunned. Christine was smiling over me. The figure had carried on his way and could not now be distinguished from the rest of the crowd in the funeral cortege.

'What's the matter, Stu?'

'Didn't you just see that?'

'What, that old man you bumped into?'

'He had the face of the Grim Reaper.'

'Er, Stu, I don't think you are holding your drink like you used to. There was nothing out of the ordinary about him. I got as good a look as you.'

I got up and shook my head. Yes, maybe I had imagined it. The atmosphere was such that it would be easy to be transported to somewhere a bit wild. The procession was disappearing up the street, and I was in no mood to chase after it.

'Let's take a break and enjoy the setting.' We sat on a wall and soaked in the low light from the lamps, diffused by the mist, playing on timbered eves and closed shop fronts. I started to gather myself. I had had a shock. I raised my mask so I could see out from under the fox's jaws.

'You're looking a little pale, Stu. Take your time.'

The tinnitus had stepped up a level and was rising to screaming pitch. I banged my hand over my ear, but it made no difference. The sound of the procession had receded into the distance, but from the same direction there was a shrill ringing, the sound of a bicycle bell. It was getting closer. Rounding the bend, a bizarre sight came into view. The bicycle was fully lit all round its frame, handlebars and rear flexible mast, with multicoloured LEDs that flashed on and off. Red, green, blue and yellow lines of lights rushed around, flowing like hyperactive electrons around a circuit board. It was almost too bright to look at. The lights strung through the spokes were arranged eccentrically so that as the wheels turned it gave the illusion they were going up and down and expanding then contracting. And astride this two-wheeled pantechnicon, leaning back in a "sit up and beg" riding position, was a man in a onesie with big polka dots, a neck ruff and red patches on both cheeks and nose. His white face was framed by a curly orange wig.

He accelerated, and when level with us turned his head to face me, released the handlebars and with his hands cupped by his ears, stuck his tongue out at me.

'That's my clown!' I flew up to standing and started to run after him. I lifted the hem of my robe to keep it out of the way of my pumping legs. I was making progress towards him; I thought I'll have him in a second. But he had deliberately slowed down, and teasingly wiggled the back wheel while he coyly turned around to watch me. He pushed hard on the pedals, and the gap widened. I was getting short of breath as he made a left turn into a twittern. He had ten yards advantage on me, and when I entered the alleyway, he was nowhere to be seen. There should at least have been some residual glow of the lights reflected off the weatherboarded walls if he had taken the corner ahead. It was silent and dark. I explored the narrow passage, no gates or doors. It took a left and there were some steps, quite a lot of steps, turning this way then that, progressing up the hill. The paving stones levelled off and I leant against the horizontal boards to regain my breath. It smelt dank, with undernotes of piss. I looked up and could see a narrow slit of black sky between the buildings on either side. Behind the left side of my head a small window had been cut in the wooden wall. It had an oval metal frame with rivets rather like a porthole. An orange glow came from it, creating a shadow of me that folded up from the ground and onto the opposite wall. I turned to look through it, and as quick as a flash a hand drew the curtain on the inside. The light level in the passage dropped instantly and my shadow was no more.

I found my way back to the street by continuing along the passage until it opened on one side to become a raised walkway. Christine was sitting below on a wall, chatting comfortably with a stranger. I carried on the walkway and down the steps to regain street level. Christine turned to me and then back to the stranger as if to say, 'I'm ok now', and the stranger carried on their way. She started to giggle as I approached, and before long was convulsed by laughter.

'That,' she took a breath, leaning forward and then up again, 'was probably the funniest thing I have ever seen.' Her sides were shaking. 'Your legs going round and round as though they were on a wheel... I wish I had filmed it.' Her voice rising in pitch, struggling to keep control. 'Did you catch him?'

'No, he just sort of disappeared up an alleyway.'

'Oh, shame. I'd loved to have seen the fight. "Fox savages clown in seaside brawl."'

I started to giggle now. 'Well, you're not looking too serious yourself, Marie Antionette.'

'Well at least I got my head sewn back on. Yours is looking a bit beyond the point of repair.'

We looked at the poor fox-face in my hand. He had taken a beating when I was rushing through the passages.

'My poor, foxy, warrior monk,' she said in an exaggeratedly coquettish European accent, reaching out to me and clasping my head sideways on to her decolletage, her grand imperial bosom. 'Let's get you home. I feel the need to test exactly how strong that vow of chastity of yours really is.'

Stu 9

A gentle hum and the train accelerated away from the stop. There was barely any vibration as we reached cruising speed, the scattered birch trees and blocks of residential housing racing by. The light was low, and the clouds looked as though they may release their snowy burden soon. I settled back, happy and excited to be in Helsinki. It's amazing how we, in the 21st century, have such control over place, I mused. Ok we don't have control over time, that passes at a regular pace whatever we do. But now, for the price of just a single westerner's day's work, we can be anywhere in the world within hours. So different to previous generations, when travel took enormous amounts of time, effort and money. However, it must be remembered, it does require a passport, and a visa to get where you are going, so large chunks of the world's population are excluded. They have to do it the old-fashioned way. And although we can't control time, we can influence the future. I wondered what cost my air journey may have years down the line. A marginal contribution to sea level rise, a life impoverished by the loss of workable land. A life lost to a new and unprecedented season of flooding.

The train came to a halt at the central station. Descending to the platform I felt a sharp chill in the air, more extreme than I had ever experienced in England. I was pleased to be wearing my bright red ski jacket. I moved with the other passengers with their pull along cases, towards the ticket hall. I had my small rucksack, all that was required for a two-night trip. The ticket hall was busy, people milling, anxious to find their correct train, not to be late and miss it. I strode through, looking forward to exiting, and to be able to look back at the station's frontage.

I positioned myself in the plaza in front of the station, making sure to avoid the tramlines. Enormous granite men, two on each side of the entrance, adhering to the front of the building, or rather the front of the building adhered to them. They echoed ancient Egyptian caryatids. The square upper body muscles blocked out in stone suggested incredible strength. And at waist level each held a sphere of light, an orb of black metal lines enclosing opaque white glass. In this November daylight, they glowed. Hey, traveller, take this light on your journey. You will need it as the line takes you north, through hundreds of miles of deep dark forest, in temperatures almost incompatible with human existence, where the spirits and demons rule.

I sighed with awe. I had been so looking forward to seeing these sculptures, created right at the end of art nouveau, and before art deco had got going. What a wonder. They didn't disappoint.

I fired up my phone and the map app. Aava has been very efficient. She had suggested a hotel not too far from the museum, which was reasonably priced for Finland, so that was to be my first stop.

I climbed the museum steps and pushed through the swing door. The hotel room had been adequate, and enabled a quick wash, but I was excited to get out back into the city. Entering the ticket area of the museum I waited for the receptionist to notice me.

'My name is Dr Richardson, I think Dr Heikkinen should be expecting me.'

239

'Wait here.' The receptionist picked up the phone and buzzed through to a back office.

A dark-haired bespectacled woman poked her head through a side door.

'Dr Richardson? Hello, come through here and follow me please.' She seemed rather formal, stiff even. I followed her down a narrow corridor of the the type I was all too familiar with, common to museums across the world. The open doors to the offices displayed a degree of clutter not allowed in the gallery spaces. We carried on and entered a laboratory with a couple of high stools arranged before the work bench.

'Sit, please. I trust your journey went well?'

'Yes, very smoothly thank you. The hotel is great,' I lied, but felt I needed to inject a bit of energy into the conversation. 'Thank you for suggesting it.'

'You are welcome. I would like first to discuss the arrangements that the museum committee has decided regarding the artefact.'

OK I thought, she doesn't mess around. Straight down to business. My heart started thumping. I hoped the journey hadn't been a waste of time.

'Given the potential cultural significance of the item, it has been decided to release it to you as the representative of the Museum of Hastings, and we trust you will take responsibility for its analysis by a reputable laboratory in England.' This could be better than I had expected. Not just a loan but I think she is suggesting they are actually gifting it.

'We would like to have a formal handover tomorrow. If you are in agreement, this could be done on the island where it was found. I hope you wouldn't mind, but a film crew will be there too. It is a special moment for both our institutions, so it should be recorded.'

'That sounds wonderful. Yes, it's a good idea. It will be good publicity for both of us. Thank you.' I felt relieved. It's going to happen.

'Shall we have a look at it then?' She smiled for the first time and we both relaxed a little, the formalities completed. She reached under the bench and brought up a plastic box.

There it nestled; the swaddling folded back. It was very much as I had expected from the photo on the website. The metal of the blade stump was loose and friable, inclined to break off with any jolt or knock. The guard was still intact and showed a characteristic Saxon shallow curve.

The grip was varied in its preservation. The metal wire winding around and around the tang to give it bulk was exposed in places, but there were areas where the upper layers were still there, of horn and maybe fragments of leather. And now our eyes came to the pommel. I had not seen one like it before. It did have the shape typical of Saxon swords, like a flattened oval with the edge next to the grip taking a straight line. But at the end, making it unique, was inserted a large red stone, smooth and oval-shaped to match the shape of the pommel itself. Adjacent to the stone there was a strip of yellow metal, now edging it by just one third of its circumference, the rest of the circuit having been lost. I felt convinced it was gold. And in the metal, placed there probably by a craftsman using a fine chisel to stamp the impression of the letters, it said "godwins".

'Lovely, isn't it?'

I felt stunned and it took a while for me to find some words.

'Yes, it's remarkable,' I said weakly.

'I think there will be enough material in and under the guard to work with for the laboratory analysis. As you can see, we was very careful not to disturb it at all. We don't want the dirt shaking out, do we?' She smiled again.

'I'm sorry, I'm a bit overwhelmed. If this does suggest it belonged to Harold Godwinson, it will be one of the most significant artefacts ever discovered in the story of England's development as a nation.'

'It's such a shame that there isn't any more of the inscription to see. That would have nailed it,' she said.

'The lettering is so fine, and created on such a small scale,' I said.

She leaned in, peering at the pommel. 'I think they done it with maybe a round tipped chisel so they could rock it according to the angle.'

I leant back. Her English was so good, but with her Finnish accent there were strange colloquialisms that jarred. I couldn't quite place them. It seemed odd.

'You speak excellent English. Where did you learn it?' I asked.

'Well, we all learn English at school. Nearly every Finn speaks good English. But I also spent a summer at a language school in Hastings when I was a teenager.'

Of course, the Sussex "we done it" and "we was there". How odd not to have mentioned her connection to Hastings, I thought. She said it as a throwaway line, really of not much significance. I wanted to pursue it further.

'That's interesting, tell me more.'

'There's not much to tell. Every kid goes to a language summer school. I am still in touch with my host family though. They were really kind. A lady called Marion Withers, and her two foster sons. She used to say she was very, very old, but in fact she looked quite young. We used to joke that her middle name must be "Never".

'Ah, I get it. Marion Never Withers.'

'Anyway, because she didn't have any children of her own, and she had been a midwife before, she called us "her babies".

'That's nice.'

'I had a chat with her after you called me. It reminded me to get in touch.'

'Mmm...'

She gathered herself up. Idle chat I suspect is something she's not very familiar with.

'I am going to have to work through this evening preparing for tomorrow. It means unfortunately I am not going to be able to use the ticket I bought for a classical concert this evening. You would be very welcome to take it. It would be a shame if it goes to waste. It is at the "rock" church. The hall is carved out of granite in the hillside. I think you will like it.'

Stu 10

Christine's face appeared on the screen.

'Hey. You got there ok?'

'Yes, it's fabulous here.'

'I'm so jealous.' She stuck her lower lip out. It seemed enormous so close to the camera.

'I've got some really good news. It looks as though they are going to gift us the sword hilt. I've seen it and it lives up to expectations. There should be enough residual material to be able to do an analysis.'

'That's great. So, you think you will be able to bring it home?'

'Yes, I think she has done the documentation for a special export licence.'

'It sounds as though you managed all your business in the first hour. Well done. What are your plans for the rest of the day?'

'Well, she's given me a ticket for a classical concert. It's a bit odd. She only had one and she said she had to prepare some work tonight. It's not exactly traditional hosting, is it? Oh, I forgot to say there's an official handover tomorrow on the island where it was found. They're going to film it. Should be good publicity.'

'Oh, great. What's the concert programme?'

'I've just looked it up. Let me just check. It starts with Mussorgsky's Night on a Bare Mountain. Although they called it a "bald mountain". Then Smetana's Moldau.'

'Wow. That's some pretty intense stuff. It's all brooding storms if I remember rightly. I thought Finns weren't meant to be expressive.'

'Your brilliant. What a mind you have. I knew you would know the pieces.' I gave her a big smile.

'Don't forget to bring me back a piece of that designer glass. What's his name? Alvar Aalto, I think.'

'Will do. Love you.'

'Byeee.'

My boots crunched on the thin layer of newly fallen snow as I stepped out of the hotel. It had started earlier when I returned from the museum, just as the light of the day was fading. It was nice dry snow. Not like the wet snow we occasionally get at home. My map app was set to guide me to the concert hall.

In fifty yards take a left turn.

The streetlamps looked so pretty as the snowflakes, coloured yellow in the artificial light, danced beneath and slowly descended to the ground. The left turn took me to a major shopping street. There was the odd car and a few pedestrians around, but you couldn't describe it as busy. I paused to look in some of the windows. Here was a children's clothes shop, with orange pumpkins and flying witches, the Halloween display going on a little past its sell by date. Ah, a craft shop. They're always good in these Northern European cities. It must be the long winter nights that need occupying. Now, what I really need is an upmarket tourist shop. That could be one across the road. Pedestrian crossing. Not much traffic. Is it one of those countries where you get arrested if you cross while the indicator is red? Oh, fuck it, life isn't long enough. Let's go. I trotted across and looked in the shop window. That's what I need. Look, they have a glass display. I went inside.

'You are interested in our designer glass?' The shop assistant approached from behind while I inspected the brightly lit mirrored shelves. 'Er, yes I am just looking at the moment.' The assistant hovered. There were some really nice pieces with a crinkly side, quite irregular in shape. All different sizes, some clear, some opaque white, some translucent sea green.

'Those are a classic design by Alvar Aalto. As you can see the sides look like a wave that is building, building, and as you turn it around, it is about to break.' She held it up and rotated it for me to see. 'It's a little Finnish joke. His surname, Aalto, means wave.'

'Oh, that's wonderful, my wife asked me specifically to bring one home. Now which one do you think?'

'Well, as it is a wave, how about the one in sea green?'

'Yes, I'll take it.'

I felt smug as I strode along, taking care with the carrier bag and its precious cargo, shielding it from hitting lampposts and pavement furniture. It had been so easy. The sword hilt was sorted and now a perfect gift for Christine all within a few hours of arriving.

In 300 feet, take the right fork.

Ok, this doesn't look quite right. I know this app. Sometimes it takes you off piste. The narrow passage cut at an angle between two shop fronts. I looked at the map on the screen. It did look as though it could slice a considerable section from the walk, a short cut, the hypotenuse to a triangle. I looked at the time on the phone. Browsing had put me back, and the concert was due to start in half an hour, so I had to take it. The alley was poorly lit, any light coming from the street end, and in fact it looked like a dead end just a few yards ahead. I tentatively made my way up, the shadow from my body intensifying the darkness. Ah, I know, let's put the phone torch on. Suddenly everything was illuminated. The brick sides of the alley rose four or five storeys, with the odd window high up but nothing near the ground. There would have been no point putting one there. The alley took a sharp turn to the right just ahead, where I previously thought it may have ended. I quickened my pace, confident now of my route. It joined on to another street after a further fifty yards, and with a left turn there I felt relieved. Not too far now.

It seemed to be a residential area. The tall dull red brick buildings lined the streets. I bet the apartments in there are quite grand.

Turn right and your destination will be straight ahead.

The rock church was not quite what I was expecting. The street made a wide fork, the brick apartment blocks lining each side and curving round to embrace a bare granite natural dome. It was like a giant boulder placed in the middle of the city. Or rather the city had been built around it.

The entrance, constructed of steel and glass, looked like the entrance to a bunker. I pushed the door and entered. The warmth hit me and unwrapping my scarf and undoing my coat became essential. The atrium was low ceilinged and had a table running along the left-hand side. A young woman smiled a greeting at me.

'I have a ticket for the concert.' Proffering it in her direction.

'That's fine, as you can see, we have racks over there for your hat and coats.'

People were starting to mill about, and chat. It looked like a meeting place for old friends. They were hanging their things on coat hangers and just suspending them randomly on the rails. It looked like a trust situation. That's probably the Finnish way.

I made my way to the seating. It was arranged in arced rows, on the level. I found a spot three rows in from the back. I nodded and smiled at a couple with their children, two seats away.

For a church, there wasn't really much sign of religiosity. A discrete silver cross marked what I guessed was the altar, set behind the seats and music stands that awaited the arrival of the orchestra.

The ceiling was of bare grey stone. It was not high, probably twenty or thirty feet from the floor. The natural contours allowed shadows to form in its hollows and cracks. I looked up and tried to conjure patterns and shapes, but no images would form.

The seating was filling up now, and the chatter intensified. A tension, common to the minute or two before any performance, was palpable in the air. Then the murmuring fell and a silence, apart from the odd cough and chair scrape, accompanied the entrance of the orchestra. The musicians made their way in two columns, down the aisles from behind the audience, to meet at the low stage in front of us. The noise picked up again as they adjusted the angle of their chairs, arranged their sheets of music and started tuning up.

The conductor held his pose in front of the orchestra. Silence and stillness. And then it started. His arms waved, in what I am sure was a controlled and measured fashion from the perspective of the musicians, but from behind it could be seen as the movements of a drowning man. This was no gentle introduction. We were right in the middle of the storm from the first bar. A frantic tumult of brass, string and drum bore down on me. Without the dilution that a high vaulted ceiling would have offered, the sound bounced from the unyielding granite just a few feet above my head in this claustrophobic space. I felt sick in the pit of my stomach. The glass vase, resting against my lower leg, started to vibrate. It had found a resonant frequency. I hoped it wouldn't shatter. I tilted my head up to look at the ceiling. Now there was movement. The cracks and crevices merged and separated, and I could see flecks of spray, sheets of spume moving this way and that, white crests forming on waves of grey and green that seemed to grow from nowhere. The music cracked and rent, like timbers splitting. Wave upon wave formed, grew and then broke. I looked forward again at the conductor. His frantic movements were subsiding now, as though defeated, giving in to the inevitable fate of a man submerged.

I too was exhausted. I had never felt so directly involved in a piece of music such as this before. The pause before the next piece allowed me to gather myself. I settled my breathing, and it began. This was a more melodic composition, reflective of a pastoral scene perhaps. It was comforting after the storm we had just endured. I let myself go with the repetition of the few chords that built gently in pitch. I started to scan the members of the orchestra. The violinists were moving in unison, focussed on their sheet music and occasionally glancing up to the conductor. The brass section was taking a well-earned break after the first piece. They were sitting back, and gazing around, not required at that time. The percussionists at the back were lined up and focussed. One, a young female, dangled her triangle in front of her face. The beater was poised, held

249

lightly in her right hand, ready to strike. I am sure she looked at me. It was only for a second, but I feel convinced it had happened. Her stare then settled back on the conductor. The tension in her face grew, it was getting close. There was no room for error. It had to be precisely on the beat. The conductor gave a tiny flick of his baton, from inside to out, throwing the signal to her, which she caught without falter. The beater struck. The high frequency wave hit me. It was the same frequency as my tinnitus, which from slumber leapt at this tasty titbit, flung into its mouth, like a sea lion in a zoo catching a sardine. Yum. It took off, energised by being fed, and obscured all other sound. I put my hands over my ears, but that only magnified it in my head. I rested my head down, my eyes shut, chin on my chest. I must sit this out. And indeed, over the following minutes, it did subside, and the gentle harmonies took over again.

Stu 11

My plate looked a picture. So I took one. Shiny slices of brown coated, pink fleshed, hot smoked salmon next to silvery marinated herring, nestling in a perfect curve made from the slices of a boiled egg dressed in mayonnaise with a sprinkling of paprika, and a crimson dollop of glistening bilberry jam on the side. It was my second plate.

Who would've thought jam goes so well with fish?

I could see Christine had seen it. I resumed shovelling at my breakfast, keeping an eye on the phone, waiting for her reply.

Looks delish. How was the concert?

Amazing. I don't think I have ever felt so involved with the music before.

That's great. I've got to get ready for school now. You have a great day. XX

Smiley face. Heart. Heart. Heart. XXX.

I had slept surprisingly well, given how disturbed I had felt on getting back from the concert. I told myself, you've got to get a grip. Since discovering the sword hilt on the internet, the excitement seems to have sent me a little crazy. It's as though my sensitivity dial had been turned up to eleven. And what is it people get when they're developing psychosis? Isn't it something like "ideas of reference"? The newsreader on the TV sending out messages just for them? How could a 'ting' from a triangle be just for me? I'd never thought I would be vulnerable to that sort of thing, but clearly this is new territory. No more funny thoughts. Let's just focus on the day ahead.

The map app guided me down to the harbour. Aava had said to rendezvous at 10am. This is going to be fun. I looked around for signs of a film crew. The breeze was getting up, but the snow from yesterday was melting. I spotted Aava by the ferry ticket kiosk and waved. With her was a tall man, wrapped up in a massive puffer jacket, and next to him a smaller man with a large rucksack and carrying a tripod.

'Let me introduce the museum director, Eino. Eino, this is Dr Richardson from England.' Eino reached over with a serious expression and a proffered hand. His eyes fixed on mine with a gaze that seemed a little too prolonged.

'Call me Stu,' I said and smiled trying to relax as I shook his hand. He just carried on looking and didn't say anything.

'And this is Aarne, the museum photographer. He is going to be videoing the handover so we can attach it to a press release later.' Aarne raised a hand in acknowledgement. 'Now we must wait until the two youngsters who found it to get here. I've bought tickets for them, so I hope they get here before we have to depart.'

Eino and Aarne didn't seem very chatty. I had imagined something a little more glamorous in the way of a film crew with reporters and masses of equipment, but clearly they were working to a budget. Eino started stamping his feet as he did a small circuit on the quayside.

A young blonde woman with a blue streak in her hair came running from the direction of the city centre, dragging by the hand a young black man, his coat trailing in the wind. She was puffed out by the time she reached Aava. Aava looked at her fiercely and there was an exchange in Finnish.

'Dr Richardson, this is Isla and Mohammad. They discovered the sword hilt between two rocks on the island.'

Isla looked at me, with a twinkle in her eye. Not typically Finnish. She looked a bit mischievous. Mohammad looked pleasant enough, but seemed distracted, looking around and scanning the other passengers who were now boarding.

We found seats facing one another. Isla seemed a bit edgy, as though uncertain how to start a conversation.

'You had better tell me the story. I'd love to hear it,' I suggested.

'Well, we were on a beach cleaning expedition with the Suomi fellowship, and Mo and I had fallen back from the rest of the group, and we sat down on a rock, and Mo somehow felt something hard under his foot. So, he reached down and lifted this bit of metal.'

'Did you know what it was straight away?'

'Well, it certainly looked like a sword handle, so I suppose, yes. Are you from England?'

'Yes, I work at a museum near the place where the sword may have come from. How did you meet Mo?'

'Oh, he arrived in Helsinki as a refugee. We were both on the fellowship programme. You must excuse him today.' I glanced at Mo who smiled weakly back. 'He was expecting a bit more of a film crew, like the last time we came here. Plus, he doesn't like boats very much.'

'I also was thinking there would be a bit more to it.' We had found common ground. 'What happened the last time you were here?'

Isla leant forward and became more animated. 'Oh, it was brilliant. We went out on a private motorboat, they had a proper director and cameraman, and they made us act out the finding of the sword while the reporter spoke in front of us.'

'And they had a drone.' It was the first time Mo had spoken to me.

'He's obsessed with that drone. Have you seen the news report?' Isla ran her finger down her phone screen, scrolling through her saved items.

'Here it is.' She reached over to turn the screen so I could see. The rocking of the boat meant it was hard to keep in focus. The opening shot was the two of them walking hand in hand along the beach, then it cut to a news reporter. 'You can see us in the background. It took ages for Mo to find the replica buried in the sand. Look, there he is holding it up. It was so funny. The reporter just had to keep talking until he did it.' She was chuckling at the memory.

'They made us walk up and down three times on the beach to get the drone shot right.' Mo added, starting to come alive to the conversation.

'Do you think they are going to make us do all that again?' Isla asked.

'I'm not sure, but I think it might be a bit more serious. A sort of official hand over.'

Aarne arranged us positioning Aava to the left of the rock, me to the right and between us but set back a bit, but not to obscure the rock, were Mo and Isla. He rushed back to his digital SLR camera to check the framing. Aava had a sheaf of paper in her hand which she was checking. So that was what she was working on last night. Aarne dropped his arm as a signal for Aava to start. Aava cleared her throat and held her script at chest level.

'Today we welcome Dr Richardson from the Museum of Hastings in England. He is here to receive, on behalf of the English people, an ancient relic that may have extreme cultural significance for them if it is proven, by laboratory analysis, to be connected to the Battle of Hastings in some way, or at least to have been in possession of one of the Anglo-Saxon nobility at the time. It is the remains of a decayed sword hilt, of Saxon character and with part of an inscription on it which could connect it as I have just described. It was found just by this rock by these two young people only a few weeks ago.' She nodded to Isla and Mo, who in turn nodded to the camera. 'When it came into our possession, an image of it was placed on the new finds and acquisitions page of our website. Within days I had a phone call from Dr Richardson, pleading,' she looked to camera for emphasis and repeated, 'pleading for the repatriation of the relic to England.

'This was not an easy decision for the museum to take. We had long discussions as to the possible consequences of it returning to England. It would have been very easy for us to say no, and to keep it for our collection as a representative of a distant culture, albeit one just on the other side of the continent of Europe. But, in the spirit of good relations and to repair damage there has been to the status of the United Kingdom in the eyes of her European neighbours by recent political events, the decision was made to indulge Dr Richardson's request. And that is why we are here today.' Aava paused. I stiffened expecting to go to the handover itself. But Aava wasn't finished. 'We hope, and indeed expect, that the repatriation of this artefact will set an example to other museums,' she looked at me, 'who maybe in receipt of similar requests from indigenous peoples all round the world who have been separated from items of cultural and religious significance during the era of colonisation. We expect that the Museum of Hastings will be the first to honour this duty. It is surely their moral obligation to comply.'

Aava folded her papers and passed them to Eino who exchanged them for the plastic box containing the sword hilt. All I was thinking at the time was "Oh Christ, Oh Christ, I'm going to be expected to respond to that." The panic meant that no words would form in my head.

Aarne arranged Aava and me an arm's length apart. Once he was back at the camera, he gave Aava a nod as a cue. She very deliberately reached out with the box, its clear top panel facing the lens so the artefact within could be seen, for me to take it. The handshake that followed was slow and long. I turned and faced the camera and smiled with my mouth, but not my eyes. What the hell am I going to say? Why hadn't I prepared anything?

Aava peeled off and was in conversation with Eino. Maybe I could plead with them not to release the video. The world would never know what had just been said. What can I do now to make it "unpublishable"? Strip naked and run into the sea?

Aava returned. She wants to talk to me.

'Would you mind if we shot the handover again?'

Yes please, I thought. Anything for more time.

'We think, from the point of view of the optics, that the handover would be better if Mohammad gave it to you. It was he, after all, who found it.' She nodded to Mo to come over. 'Mohammad, would you mind, for the sake of the cameras, presenting the box to Dr Richardson?'

Mo looked a little confused. He had the box placed in both hands in front of him. I stood before him, the camera over my left shoulder so the artefact could be seen through the lid. Mo wouldn't make eye contact with me. His head dropped and he went into a shallow bow as he lifted the box towards me. I took it with both hands and made a brief bow back. He retreated, head still bowed, taking slow backward steps.

Oh shit, I thought. What flashed into my head were those line drawings you could see in Victorian boys' adventure books, of natives bringing tribute to their colonial masters. This is looking even worse.

Aava and I were repositioned so I could make the acceptance speech. How do I keep it from sounding churlish?

'Thank you, Dr Heikkinen. I am sure, as the representative of all the English people, that I would have their full backing in thanking you for your exceptionally generous gift of the sword hilt so it can go back to its rightful home.' Oh God, Oh God. 'I feel certain that on analysis it will be proven to be what my first instincts were that it was. Namely the possession of King Harold who died on the battlefield at Hastings.' I took a gulp and despite the cold wind, I could feel my face flush. 'This ceremony has brought home to me the significance of items to people who may be very geographically distant from where they are now.' Good. Hopefully that is sufficiently obtuse that no one will be able to unravel it. 'We should all endeavour to bring harmony to the world, and respect their historic rights to possess items that are of significance to them. Thank you again.' Did I go too far?

Stu 12

I nearly missed my connection at Paddington. The trot along the platform meant I was puffed out when I sat down at a window seat in a near empty carriage. I arranged my bags: my trusty rucksack for an overnight stay, and of course the precious cargo of the sword hilt in its plastic box plus two containers of soil, sealed and labelled, enclosed together in a small pull along suitcase. I settled back, ready to enjoy the journey through the Buckinghamshire and Oxfordshire countryside.

The few days since I had returned from Finland had been busy. Dr Amy Pettigrew, of the Department of Earth Sciences at the University of Oxford had taken my call after I had emailed her the details of the find. She sounded enthusiastic.

'Yes, if you can deliver it up here, I think we would be able to do an analysis for you. You would have to leave it with us overnight. And of course, we will need reference samples of soil from the areas you think may be possible sites of its original deposition.'

The soil sample from Senlac Hill I obtained surreptitiously. A quick vault over the fence with container and trowel at dusk, and then a brisk exit back to the car. For the Brede valley sample, I contacted the landowner. He was incredibly welcoming and arranged to meet me in the valley.

'We've been waiting a long time for some academic interest in this place,' he said. 'Those that live around here, and who have some interest in the history, are convinced that the strategic significance of this valley has been underrated by historians. If you look just up there, on the ridge opposite, at Court Lodge, Edward III and Queen Philippa watched the Battle of Winchelsea in 1350. I believe we routed the French. Of course, it was a sea battle. All this was underwater then. Virtually every mile going upriver from the estuary there are the remains of moated houses, or other types of stronghold, dotted on each bank of the valley. Those wouldn't have been built unless they were needed for the defence of the realm, or necessary to secure the goods that came through here. And it wasn't as though it just became important all of a sudden. As I am sure you know it was a possession of the Normans fifty years before the invasion. Deduce what you like from that.' He smiled, twinkling his eyes at me.

We set about collecting a sample of the black soil. He had brought a spade. I cut a section from the big lump he presented to me and placed it in the container. He made a gesture as though to wish it Godspeed and return with fair tidings from afar.

The bus from the station dropped me right outside the college. I looked up and rising above the tall blank curtain wall, there was a neoclassical sculpture of a female figure that stood underneath a dome. Ah, that must be Queen Philippa, the founder of the college. I had been pleased to find, after a quick search, a connection between the source of the soil specimen, and Dr Pettigrew's college, where she had kindly invited me to stay. The gate below the sculpture was stoppered by two enormous wooden doors. In the right hand one a small rectangle of a swing door had been cut. I ascended the stone steps and pushed my way in.

'Dr Pettigrew has booked a guest room for me I believe,' I shouted through the hatch of the porter's lodge.

'Ah you must be Dr Richardson, I'll just get the envelope with the key in it.'

'Would that be Queen Philippa above the gate?' I enquired hesitantly.

The porter looked at me. 'You're not the first to ask that.' He kept a professional demeanour despite the tedium of repetition. 'No, that is Queen Caroline, the wife of George II. You'll discover they're always doing queer things like that around here. I think you can find Queen Philippa round the corner by the library.'

He handed me the envelope. 'Now you need to go through the small arch into back quad, turn right and you'll find it in the second staircase along.'

I dragged the pull-along up the path that divided the quad into two. The harmonious rhythm of pillar, arch and window, inspired by Nicholas Hawksmoor, bounced me along from either side.

There were two keys in the envelope, because there were two doors to the room. The first key unlocked the outer door, which swung open to reveal a second door just six inches in. Ah, I see. If you keep the outer door closed, you are not inviting visitors. "Showing your wood" I believe it is called. The double entendre hit me, and I had an internal schoolboy giggle for a moment.

The room was cuboid in nature. It had tall windows along one wall, and good old fashioned iron radiators attached to another. The whole of one corner was eaten into by a yellowing plastic capsule. Further exploration showed it to contain shower, toilet and basin, all sealed to prevent the escape of water into the room. This must be their solution to the problem of creating ensuites in an old building. You don't want guests having to go down to the rows of baths in the basement, still there but now in cubicles, for the use of undergraduates.

I looked through the window. Opposite, at an angle, was an ancient stone-built church, and between, the heads of cyclists bobbed, their bodies and machines obscured below sill level as they took the short cut along the lane.

'Oh my, look at this.' Amy Pettigrew took it very carefully from the box, anxious not to knock any loose material. An aficionado of ancient dirt, she was a leading expert on the analysis of samples to provide a date and location for found objects.

'We're going to have to take this down in very fine layers and label each one carefully.' she spoke in a low voice while she slowly turned it. 'So, it has been on an eastern Baltic beach most recently. We can identify the uppermost as that. I think there should be reference samples for it I can access remotely. What may be deeper ingrained we are not quite sure. Obviously, it might have been acquired on a stop somewhere on route between England and the Baltic. Ideally, we can get a match with one of your two samples next. If there is anything lower than that, that would be a bonus. It could be a sign of an earlier place it had been deposited or may even have been acquired at the place of manufacture.'

'So which techniques are you going to use?'

'Well, to establish when it was put in the ground, I doubt there will be enough organic material for carbon dating. I would suggest we use optical stimulated luminescence. You can do that even on a single grain of sand, and I reckon there should be some specks of inorganic material deep down we could use. To get a match for the locations there are several tools in the armoury. Firstly, there is particle size analysis.

261

Each sample of soil carries a range of particle sizes, the precise distribution of which, in a graph format, can give a unique signature to a particular location. Then there is microfossil analysis. Am I right in thinking the Brede valley sample is likely to be a fluvial deposit?' I nodded. 'So, it should be rich in microfossils. Again, the distribution and type will be unique to a specific place. Finally, there is trace element geochemistry. Every district has a distinct pattern of concentration of trace elements, so that could be an additional thing to look at.' She looked at the black flaking shards that made up the stump of the blade. 'It would be really nice to do some metallurgy on the blade to identify the proportions of trace elements there also. That could tell us where it was forged. Maybe save that for a later date?' she smiled. 'Cup of tea?'

Stu 13

I took a shower in the plastic capsule and got dressed for high table. Amy had said to meet her outside the buttery at 19.45, so I was well ahead of time. The sound of ethereal voices was drifting in either through the door or through the window. I went to the window and looked out. A yellow streetlamp, encased in a four cornered metal box, cast an eerie side light on the coarse stone wall of the church opposite. The cyclists' helmets had ceased to bob, and the whole ensemble of church and lane looked distinctly devoid of people. I decided to head out into college to track down the voices.

It didn't take long. The chapel was set between back quad and front quad, and at its entrance my ears could savour delicious rising harmonies as the choir practised its repertoire of sacred music. It was a heavenly sound. I was at the intersection of the dark, cold air of the outside, made visible by the condensation of my breath as it escaped my body, and the warm, light interior of the chapel, with its colour and high vault, the sound as seductive as the Sirens drawing ancient sailors onto rocks. How, in times past, this must have been such a lure, a comfort, a protection when the world was full of danger and mystery. Then I thought of the technology I had been discussing earlier with Amy at the Department of Earth Sciences. Oxford at the cutting edge, forging forwards to leave no mystery unexamined. It felt like a conundrum that the two universes can exist in one place. Both have their beauty.

I moved on to the buttery entrance. Amy was waiting there.

'I am afraid, I hope you don't mind, but you have to wear a gown. It's formal hall tonight.' She reached to a clothes rail behind. 'We have spares here. This one looks ok.'

I reached my arms in through the sleeves and out again and became draped in black. We waited a few minutes while a few fellows gathered.

'Ok. Come this way.'

We formed a small procession into the hall. There was a loud scraping of chair legs, pushed back in unison, as the students stood for our entrance. The men were mainly dressed in dinner suits, the women in trendy evening dresses, all with a little shorty black gown over the top. I felt multiple eyes following me, but resisted the urge to look back. It didn't seem right to gloat at my unexpectedly elevated status. We ascended two small steps on the dais at the far end of the hall and Amy directed me to stand behind a chair.

'Benedictus, benedicat.' With a loud clatter the quiet was broken as everyone sat down and the sound of chatter filled the hall. I looked around. Mainly 17th and 18th century portraits formed a sort of tide mark halfway up the wood panelling that circuited the room.

'What a load of tosh.' The man opposite me, who had just said grace, was grumbling to himself. 'I wouldn't care if the provost came and did this hocus pocus once in a while. She's good at that sort of thing. But it always seems to fall to me as the presiding fellow.'

I smiled at him. He smiled back and continued, leaning in with a confidential air. 'Just look at them behind you. With their smart suits and shiny pink faces. When I was their age, I was throwing Molotov cocktails and tearing down walls. All that the kids these days seem interested in is respecting tradition and seeing who they can impress for a job in the city.'

'I had better introduce you,' Amy said. 'Harry Samuels, Regius Professor of History, this is Dr Stuart Richardson who has travelled up here today. He's the curator of the Museum of Hastings.'

'The Regius bit is just so I can be semi-retired and have a bit of fun while some whippersnapper does all the hard work of running the department. Hastings, eh? Bit of history around there, what?'

'I have brought up a relic for Amy, Dr Pettigrew here, to do some analysis on. I hope we might be able to get a date and location for its deposition.'

'Well surely you know where it was deposited. Where was it found?'

'On an island off Helsinki.'

'Some sort of Finnish fetish object? They were pagan until fairly recently.'

'No, that's where it gets a bit interesting. It's a Saxon sword hilt. And it has an inscription on it with the lettering spelling "Godwins".'

'Ah, now I get the Hastings connection. You're thinking it's Harold Godwinson's sword.' The professor was two steps ahead. 'Well, that would be mighty interesting, but also incredibly improbable.'

'If Amy can establish a date and location for it, maybe we could convince some people.'

'Amy, I gather carbon dating is going out of fashion a bit now. What's the latest technology? It's some sort of luminescence isn't it.' He raised his fork and took a mouthful of the hors d'oeuvre.

'Yes, it's optical stimulated luminescence. Quartz as a mineral has a natural tendency to luminesce when exposed to light. When it is buried the stored energy that causes the luminescence decays at a regular rate. So, measure the change and you get a reading for the length of time it has been out of the light. And we can do it even on a single tiny grain, invisible to the naked eye.'

'That's absolutely fascinating. This is why I come to high table. It's where science and the humanities can meet. You can learn so much.'

The plates were replaced in front of us.

'Oh God, not guinea fowl again. There can't be one still alive within a hundred miles of Oxford,' he said.

I ventured a little more. 'I am hoping the location data might also be interesting. I have brought up two soil samples from different sites, to see if that yields something about the location of the Battle of Hastings.'

'We know where it happened. Senlac Hill,' he chewed glumly.

I cleared my throat. 'The problem is nothing has been found, in the physical sense, by which I mean the objects left after a battle, to confirm that as the site. There have been a lot of archaeological surveys, but all fruitless. I was wondering whether it might make sense, and I wouldn't be the first here, to re-examine the geo-political contexts of the invasion, and try and deduce where an alternative site for the battle could be. That's why I have brought samples of soil both from Senlac Hill and the Brede valley, which I think could be a credible alternative.'

'I can't say I've heard of the latter but aren't you ignoring something. There is substantial documentary evidence that the abbey was founded on the site where Harold fell, in fact if I remember correctly four or five documents in the century following, one by the monks of the abbey themselves.'

'I hope you don't mind me saying this but... "They would say that, wouldn't they?" It clearly would be to their advantage to promote the view that the battle occurred on their ground. In fact, it would make a nonsense of their foundation if they hadn't said it. And the other sources may well have taken the monk's word for it also. They were all on the same side after all.'

'But if we ignore the documentary evidence, where are we? It's all we've got.'

'Well, the science now is at a level where it could challenge the received opinion. What people wrote then was hardly objective news reporting. It was all about protecting your interests.'

'Ok. So, say the scientific techniques confirm that your sword hilt was found in the... the Brede valley, was it? I take it there is or was a river there? It in no way confirms that's where the battle happened. You know as well as I do there was a long tradition of breaking fallen warriors' swords and dumping them in rivers at sacred sites.'

'I agree, it would not be a confirmation, but it would at least open the argument for debate.'

'I'm enjoying this,' he said gleefully. 'I know we have just had pudding, but shall we continue this upstairs with dessert?'

They all rose. "Benedicto benedicatur", and they were off.

The senior common room overlooked the hall from a gallery high up. A metal railing stopped the fellows from dropping upon the undergraduates who were now getting a little rowdy. Dessert consisted of petit fours, cheese, fruit and

267

chocolate. Amy passed me a cup of coffee from a neatly laid table with a beautiful white tablecloth on it. The room was one of comfort and studied elegance without being cluttered. Table lamps cast a low warm light over leather backed armchairs. Folded newspapers lay on low tables.

The professor was solicitous. 'Could I interest you in a glass of port? Or, if you'd prefer, our wine steward has brought up an exceptionally fine Tokay. It's been in the cellar thirty or forty years now.'

I sat in a wingback chair cradling a glass of the honey-coloured wine. The professor sat at an angle to me.

'I'm fascinated by how readily you are prepared to unhitch yourself from the evidence that exists for the site of the battle.'

'I'm hoping to replace it with some true scientific objective evidence.'

'But as we discussed in hall, that would not necessarily give any indication of the site of the battle, only where the sword may have ended up after. Let's just have a think about where we are in history now. We are probably going to face, over the next few decades, the greatest threat to rationality there has been since the enlightenment began three hundred years ago. There is a proliferation of wild ideas on the internet, many of which get traction in people's minds with absolutely no evidence at all, and that is starting to swamp the body of thought-through, evidence-based knowledge. One could see us all drowning in a sea of filth. Don't you think, as an academic, you have a duty to uphold whatever evidence there may be?'

'Well, I am trying to re-evaluate the existing evidence and maybe see it through the lens of how people thought at the time, and the way the institutions they represented behaved in a political sense to protect their own interests. I think they had no interest in an objective truth.'

'It could be said that we all have an agenda. After all, we can only answer a question that we know how to ask. But I am fearful, and we must fight. I don't want this to be the end of days for the age of reason.'

Stu 14

What do museum curators do when they have a bit of time on their hands? They check out the opposition, that's what. Although this contest would probably be like the third round of the FA cup, a second-tier team in the conference pitted against the premier league. Amy had said the sword hilt should be ready to pick up by mid-afternoon, so I had the best part of the day to visit some of the most interesting museums in the country. I plotted my route on the map app before setting out.

The lane by the side of the college was narrow and bounded by stone walls on either side. It seemed that pedestrians did not take priority. As I was halfway up and passing under the window of the guest room in which I had stayed, a posse of cycling students came round the corner ahead of me at full pelt. I froze, stuck in the middle of the lane as they skilfully avoided contact, precision marksmen of the front wheel. I advanced tentatively and as I approached the bend, I kept close to the wall on the inside, calculating that they couldn't strike me there. I stuck my head out around the right-angled corner. All clear. No chance of another cycling horror show I thought.

The lane widened slightly and passed the provost's lodge on the left, then after a meander, past the home of Edmond Halley, astronomer and comet discoverer. It ended with my passage under the Bridge of Sighs, on this occasion without getting my feet wet. The enclosed cloister of an elevated walkway, a reproduction of the Venetian original, spanned not a canal and gondoliers, but cobbles and wheeled students, scarves wind-stretched behind them, late for lectures.

A right turn brought me up to my first stop. The Pitt Rivers Museum. An ethnological classic. Where's the entrance? Oh, I see you have to go through the Natural History Museum to get to it. I resisted lingering too long by the megalosaurus skeleton. That wasn't my mission today. But I did take the time to look up and absorb the atmosphere of the light and airy atrium, giving over, through arched balustrades, to the upper rooms where the great debate of 1860 had occurred. The Bishop of Oxford versus Thomas Huxley, a supporter of Charles Darwin. The bishop mocked his opponent with the ludicrous thought that Darwin's grandmother could have been an ape. However, rationality won the day... eventually.

Down some steps at the back, and the light level faded. It was hard to make out the pattern of cabinets arranged crossways, stacked to the top with objects. The ceiling was low, and the room felt claustrophobic. My tinnitus stepped up a notch as I started to weave between the displays. The artefacts were intriguing, most with their original yellowing labels, tied on with string and written in ink by hand when they had been first deposited in the museum after disembarkation from the furthest reaches of the nineteenth century world. The overall effect was one of an overstocked Parisian flea market that hadn't sold anything for a hundred years.

There were South Sea headdresses, Japanese netsuke, African instruments, South American beadwork. The variety and proliferation of objects was at the same time amazing and frustrating. The low light level made it necessary to peer in through the glass to get a view, which even then could be interfered with by the angle of the next object. And the labels were impossible to read. I so wanted to engage, but the sound in my head rose from the steady high-pitched thread towards a screech that could not be ignored. I gazed at a beautiful green jade Tiki, a tiny homunculus, its babyish head tilted to one side, its oversized shell inlaid eyes pleading for a return to its Māori home. In my head it screamed.

I fled from the museum, trying not to attract attention. I paused on the green outside. The fresh damp air of the November day restored me, and before long I felt able to move on. Thirteen great stone heads faced me when I retraced my steps to the junction. They rested high, each on a pillar, herm-like, and regularly spaced above the railing that protected the Sheldonian theatre. Thirteen philosophers, acting like security guards for the sanctum where degrees are conferred, and behind that, the repository for all knowledge acquired in the English-speaking world, the Bodleian library. Ten feet up a great stone face, bearded, looked imperiously over my head. In my peripheral vision, I sensed his colleague on the next column leaning towards me, his eyes fixed on me. I switched my gaze. No, that one was looking straight ahead also, staring at a horizon he could not see. Back to the first head. I focussed as well as I could on my periphery. There... the heads on both sides were leaning forward and looking at me. I could almost feel their cold breath, their faces stern, judgmental. What could they see of me, the state I was in? I turned and walked along Broad Street. The final pillar had its head back, laughing, a rictus set in stone two hundred years ago waiting for me, this day, this very second, to walk beneath him.

I took the steps up to the door of the History of Science museum. The first hall had cabinets of astrolabes and

272

microscopes, the tools of the enlightenment, the foundations of the scientific world we now enjoy. But I felt an inexorable draw to a lower room, windowless and dark, which housed the vessels and retorts of earlier alchemic experiments. Against the end wall, preserved since his visit in 1931, leant a blackboard filled with the annotated equations of Albert Einstein. No one could take it upon themselves to erase the workings of the great man, so easy to have done with the sweep of a duster. I stood in front of it, soaking in the majesty of his distillation in mathematics of the universe as it exists. An itch in my right hand, an unknown force, alerted me to the possibility of changing a plus to a minus, or the reversing of a "greater than" symbol to a "lesser than". Would it result in the whole universe being irredeemably changed? I retreated, not trusting the power to control myself.

I carried on my planned route along Broad Street, then a shimmy on St Giles to the entrance of the Ashmolean. In the foyer a poster read "Spellbound: magic, ritual and witchcraft." Sounds interesting. I worked my way through the well-lit gallery spaces, exhibits illuminated by LEDs, like in a fine retail jeweller, enclosed in glass, recessed at irregular intervals in the spotless white walls. Then I entered a darker place, a place of witch marks on beams, and interred protective objects, single shoes or ragged dolls, retrieved from wall cavities at the restoration of ancient buildings. I recollected the mummified remains of a dead cat nailed above the bar in a Hastings pub, found at the time of building works. My tinnitus purred. A steady hum, primed to take off. My eye caught a dark cabinet illuminated from above. It contained the crystal of John Dee, adviser to Elizabeth I. A pretty thing on a chain, I imagined them gazing together into

273

its depths, guessing at what was to be. And then, below the crystal, I spotted his scrying mirror, the true tool for divination. Slightly larger than the size of a ladies' handbag compact used for adjusting lipstick and makeup, this one had a surface of black glass. I stood before it, the noise in my head accelerating. I tried to resist its draw, averting my eyes to the sides, but its power was overwhelming. My gaze was pulled towards it, and, within the circle of its margins, I saw a face. Not my own face, but the face of a woman. It was there only for a second before it wrinkled, cracked and then crumbled to dust.

Stu 15

I loved the crunch of shingle under my feet, and today it was extra special. Two pairs. Christine had taken the afternoon off from school, a rare event in itself, but to accompany me on a trip to the beach made it exceptional and noteworthy. We held hands as we slipped part way down the pebble bank and trotted the few steps to the shelter of the nearest breakwater. We settled down, torso and legs touching, out of the wind. Patches of sunlight came and went far out to sea, and then a golden orb broke through between two clouds, a fan of sunbeams striking the distant wave tops. The water pulled back. A strong, noisy draw as it dragged the stones of the beach with it. It rose slowly into a gather, that grew and grew to a vertical wall, the top breaking up into white foamy spume before folding forwards to crash as it hit the foreshore. A beautiful, round cycle of metronomic precision, each complex part of the movement repeated ad infinitum. It held us hypnotised.

'I love my vase,' Christine said, snuggling into me. 'You can really see the wave in it.'

She had screeched with joy when she unwrapped it on my return from Helsinki.

'Thank you for coming with me today. It really means the world to me.' I felt content. My mission to Oxford was completed successfully. The sword hilt was in the safe back at the museum. Amy had done a tremendous job of removing the dirt. It now looked like a relic ready for display. She had even stabilised the metal blade with resin to prevent further

275

flaking. Now it was just a matter of waiting for the results of the analysis.

'It's been really good seeing you energised the last few weeks Stu. I really can't remember when you have been quite like this before.' I couldn't either. 'How do you feel about it?'

I thought for a minute. 'It's been good. It's made me realise how bored I had been at the museum. As you said, I needed a project.'

'I am so pleased you've been better. But wouldn't you say you have been having some disturbing thoughts as well? I was thinking of when you saw the Grim Reaper at Halloween. You've never behaved like that before. And chasing the clown? It's not really like your previous self.'

I hadn't told her everything strange that had occurred since then, but I wondered if by some sixth sense she knew about them.

'Stu, I hope you won't be angry. It's only because I am really concerned about you. I have booked an appointment for you at the doctors for this afternoon. I am really worried that, with your change in personality, and the tinnitus as well, that you,' she hesitated, before, with a sob, saying, 'you might have a brain tumour or something.'

The waiting room was full. As the receptionist had explained, Dr Khan had had an emergency earlier, so everything was a bit pushed back. I looked around. Old lady, old lady, hoody, baby. Christine was scrolling through her messages as she had been doing ever since we sat down half an hour ago. The door opened a crack and Dr Khan's nose poked through. With a slight twitch of it he beckoned old lady number one through. Must be a regular I thought. Required only the subtlest of calls. I drifted into a reverie. How am I going to explain to him all that's happened in just a few sentences? The doctor's time is limited. His attention span might not be sufficient.

'Stuart Richardson?' I got the full face of Dr Khan, waiting by the door. He had a broad, kind face, probably still in his thirties, and he smiled as I got up. Christine gathered her things to join me. I followed him into his consulting room.

'Hello, I'm Dr Khan. How can I help you today?'

I hesitated. Christine stepped in.

'Actually, I rang for the appointment. Stuart was exposed to a loud bang about three weeks ago now and he has had ringing in his ears since, but around the same time his personality began to change, so I was thinking, maybe the tinnitus was just a coincidence?'

Dr Khan was looking at his computer screen. 'Just to clarify, it's Dr Richardson, is it?' He turned to smile at me.

'Yes.'

'I probably need to know if you are a medical doctor.'

'Oh no, no. I have a PhD in history. Doesn't qualify me for much actually.'

'Oh, I am sure that's not true. Can you tell me what happened?'

'Well, I was at the fireworks parade, and some clown let off a banger right next to me. My hearing really hasn't been the same since.'

Christine stepped in. 'It's as though he is sensitive to everything. Not like he used to be. He's much more positive. And when we were out at Halloween, he thought he saw the Grim Reaper, and then he ran after a clown on a bicycle. He used to be a bit reserved if anything.'

'Ok, I know the costumes are pretty good now. Would you say your alcohol consumption has changed?'

'Not really.'

'And are you sleeping ok?'

'Yes, like a log.'

'And, I hope you don't mind me asking, has your sex life changed?'

'Better than ever.'

'Can I take a look at you?'

Dr Khan got his otoscope and had a good look at both ear drums. 'No sign of a perforation. Now please follow the light with your eyes.' He made a sort of cross in front of me. I couldn't help inwardly reciting: spectacles, testicles, wallet and watch.

'I would just like to take a closer look at the back of your eyes.' Dr Khan went over to the light switch, and we were immersed in darkness.

My phone vibrated. I looked down. It was a message from the museum chairman. Give me a call as soon as you can.

'Sorry about that,' I said.

Dr Khan was marked in the room by a bright light which sent out rays to make it appear stellate, and it danced around as he approached.

'Just look straight ahead,' he instructed in a flat voice while he came in from the side. I could hear his suppressed breathing. 'And now the other eye.'

What does the chairman want? He never contacts me.

'Well, looking at your optic discs, that's where the nerve comes into the back of your eyes, I can't see any changes to suggest you have any increase in pressure in your brain. I know you were worried about a brain tumour...'

'That was me actually,' Christine interrupted.

'...ah, yes, sorry, the receptionist told me. Possibly a more common cause for your symptoms could be stress? How have things been lately?'

'Well, there has been a lot happening at the museum, and I have been having to do more travelling than normal.'

'Can I make a suggestion? Can I see you again in three weeks, and see what's happening with your symptoms then? We can decide at that point if we need to be looking at more investigation. There may be a chance the tinnitus will have settled by then. But I have to say that once you've got it, it can last a long time.'

Christine looked less than pleased as we left the surgery.

'Can we just hang on a minute before we move away. The chairman of the museum committee wants to talk to me.'

I pressed call back on my phone.

'Hello, it's Stuart Richardson here.'

'Stuart, thanks for getting back to me. I had a call from the Daily Messenger this afternoon asking for me to comment on a video that apparently is circulating on the news wires.'

'Oh.'

'I hadn't seen it, so he sent me a link. It looks like some sort of fucking hostage video involving you.'

My mind went immediately to an image of me in the desert, clad in an orange jumpsuit, kneeling with a knife to my throat.

'Can we meet in the office at the museum tomorrow at 9am? I think we need to have a chat.'

Stu 16

It was already dark when I heard the crunch of car tyres arriving on the gravel outside. Christine and I were waiting in the hall. We faced each other.

'Good luck. I love you.' She slipped something into my hand. 'It's a little laughing buddha. I've cast a spell on it so it will always protect you.' She reached over to kiss me.

The driver was holding the rear door open as I descended the stone steps.

'Hi, I'm Bob. Hopefully we'll have a clear run.'

Sitting alone on the back seat gave me a chance to reflect on the events of the day.

The chairman was sitting in my seat in the office when I had arrived at nine.

'I think I am going to have to set this up as my command centre. The story is really going to take off today I reckon.' He swivelled back and forth in the chair while I went out to the corridor to pick up a grey plastic one and then sat next to him. I don't think I had seen him from the side before. Tight, crinkly, salt and pepper hair, surprisingly thick. Heavy framed black spectacles sat halfway down his nose as he leant forward with head tilted back slightly to view the screen. A video was downloading on the computer.

'Let's just take a look at what you said.'

We watched the video in silence. The director had made a good job of splicing the segments together. It was almost seamless. Aava looked very calm, competent and assertive as she made her speech. Then came the handover.

'Who the fuck's that?'

'That's Mohammad. He's the refugee who discovered it on the island. Rather sweet, don't you think that they let him hand it over?'

'Mmm. Looks a bit odd,' the chairman said grumpily. Then we came to my acceptance statement. It didn't look good. I looked scared.

'Would you like to tell me exactly what you were trying to say?'

'I suppose I was trying to weave a route through by being gracious in accepting the artefact, while not committing too much to the business of repatriation, which seemed to be her agenda. She hadn't given me any warning of what she was going to say.'

'It comes across as though you were trying to be evasive. And you did sort of commit to returning items. Do you know what effect that would have on our museum? It would bloody well empty it. And the knock-on effect for all the other museums in this country and abroad? You've really set the cat amongst the pigeons.'

'Well as you know we do have an indigenous engagement policy. And it does state that any reasonable request for repatriation of artefacts would be considered by the board.'

'Yes, emphasis on the word "considered". We can consider it for as long as we like. Could be a decade or two. We're not going to give them back just like that.'

I was feeling quite chastened now. He turned to me. He could see my cheeks had reddened.

'Let's have a think about the story we want to present,' he said, trying to change tack.

'It's incredibly exciting. I'm sure the story in itself will be much more powerful than this bit of ephemera on the side.

For the first time we have an actual physical artefact that could be connected to the Battle of Hastings. With scientific analysis it could give us a clue as to the site of the battle. Either at Senlac Hill or in the Brede valley.'

'I don't know why you're obsessed with this Brede valley thing. But I think we could play it to give the results an air of suspense. One of my neighbours is friends with that judge on the Saturday night dancing show, what's it called... Dancing with my cat, or something? Anyway, Hermione Newbiegone might be willing to add a bit of glamour to our news conference. I thought we could get her to open an envelope with the results to make the announcement. Do you think this scientist could send them to us in paper form? Unfortunately, the only day she is free is this coming Friday.'

After I had sent several poorly worded texts which she had failed to answer, I managed to track Amy down at her lab.

'You would like me to send the results on paper, to arrive by this Friday?' she said, in a disbelieving tone.

'Yes, it was my museum chairman's idea. He thinks it would add suspense to the news conference we are planning for then.'

'Ok, the timing is possible, we're making good progress. But I can't say I have sent anything by snail mail for years. We normally email everything in a zip folder for this sort of situation.'

'I'm sorry. It is a bit unusual. But he is insistent. He's already had a bit of a go at me this morning. I don't want to antagonise him further. So, please...'

'Ok. I'll get it sent by recorded delivery.'

*

The chairman remained on station all day. Several enquiries came in from various news organisations. Then early afternoon a call came from a researcher at Newsnight.

'We're just trying to put together tonight's show and we would like to do a piece on this very interesting discovery of the sword hilt in Finland. I gather your museum has been involved in trying to retrieve it?'

'Yes, the museum curator has just been on a visit to Helsinki, and was fortunate enough to return with the artefact, so it is now in our possession here in Hastings.'

'Oh, that is very interesting. We have seen a couple of videos that have been posted in Finland. One is in Finnish and seems to be a news report with two youngsters who, from the look of it made the discovery. The second is in English, but we couldn't quite work out what the outcome was. Was that your curator in the second one?'

'Probably.'

'And what is his name?'

'That could have been Dr Stuart Richardson. He's here if you would like to talk to him? ...Stuart!' The chairman bellowed with his hand over the phone. Then sotto voce, 'I've got Newsnight on the line. Do you want to talk to them?'

'Hello, is that Dr Richardson?'

'Hi, thank you for showing interest. This really could be the most important development in what we know of the Battle of Hastings. There never has been physical evidence that we have been able to relate to it. No material suggestive of a battle has been found at the assumed site next to Battle Abbey itself. All we have are reports written decades after and which may have been influenced by what was politically expedient for the authors. That I suppose could cast doubt on whether the battle itself occurred there or whether another site may be in the running for the battle. Specimens of soil from deep in the crevices of the artefact are at this moment being analysed at a laboratory in Oxford and compared to soil samples from near the Abbey, and from the Brede valley which has been postulated as an alternative site.'

'Sorry, can I just take you back a bit. What is it about the sword hilt that makes you think it could have been in the battle?'

'That's my fault. I didn't explain. On the end of the hilt there is an inscription, just part of a word, which says "godwins". I think this could be suggestive that the sword belonged to Harold Godwinson, otherwise known as King Harold.'

'That really is astounding.' The researcher sounded genuinely taken aback. 'We would like to run it as the piece at the end of the programme, you know after we've done the politics, we like to have something a bit more cultural. Could you make it up to London if we sent a car?'

'This will give you a chance to redeem yourself, Stuart. Just make sure you keep it on track. They'll have forgotten about all that repatriation stuff if you dazzle them with the history and science.' The chairman was encouraging.

I went home to get ready. Christine looked worried.

'Are you sure you want to do this Stuart. I know you have been showing signs of strain, I don't want this sending you over the top. You must agree you have had some funny thoughts lately.'

'Well, the doctor didn't seem too concerned, did he? I think this will be good for me. We've got to get it out there, it's such an important find, and this is an opportunity I can't miss.'

'I don't think the doctor got the full extent of what has been going on. You weren't exactly forthcoming.'

'Well, we can see what he says in three weeks' time.'

The car drew up outside Broadcasting House. Bob came round to open the door.

'If you just go up to the reception desk, they'll be expecting you.'

A young production assistant was already waiting for me.

'Hi, Dr Richardson? I'll take you up to your dressing room.'

I followed down a longish corridor. Now there's a name I recognise, I thought. Loose pinned to a door was a piece of white A4. Typed in giant sized bold, it read "Prof Archibald Slater".

'Here's yours.'

The next door down also had a piece of A4. It read "Dr Stuart Richardson".

Stu 17

I sat alone in the dressing room, looking in the mirror. Archibald Slater, talking head extraordinaire, presenter of the series "What have the Normans ever done for us?" and the external examiner at the viva for my PhD five years ago. He was terrifying.

'So, Mr Richardson,' The "mister" was said in a way that was particularly extended, dripping with contempt, 'where exactly is the evidence you have for that assertion?'

'Well, if you look at my references number 34 and 55, I think you will find…'

Slater interrupted, 'I have to say it is very thin indeed. Overall, your evidence base is shaky to say the least.'

My home examiner had stepped in. 'Shall we move on, Professor Slater? Now, Stuart…'

I should have guessed he would be my interlocutor for tonight. He and the Newsnight presenter Nigel Craxham had a famous friendship, forged on the grouse moors of the Earl of Hexborough. "What ho. Another interviewee blown to smithereens," as feathers fall on their heads.

What do I do now? I have hung my coat up. That clown would know what to do. He was a wizard with makeup. Might be a good distraction tactic. Appear with a big red nose. No one would know what to say.

There was a knock at the door. 'Dr Richardson, thirty minutes to go. Would you like to come through to make up?'

The assistant producer settled me in my seat in the studio.

'After the opening music, Nigel is going to say a little about your segment at the end of the programme, and at the same time we will do close-up shots of first you, and then Professor Slater. Look straight into the camera. Best not to smile, it just makes you look silly.'

I felt silly already. I had declined the lipstick in makeup but had gone for a bit of powder.

'Ooo, you do look a bit pale. Let's get some life going in those cheeks. First time on telly?'

'Er, yes…'

'I can always tell. That Prof Slater seems to be here every other week. He always favours a bit of rouge.'

The familiar theme tune sounded in the studio. I could hear a distant 'three, two, one...Nigel' from the gallery.

'Good evening and welcome. Tonight, we will ask: "Have we been getting it wrong about the Battle of Hastings all these years?" We have with us Dr Stuart Richardson, curator of the Museum of Hastings, who has recently brought back a sword hilt from Finland which he asserts could have belonged to King Harold…' The red light on the camera facing me lit up. I sucked my cheeks in and gave it my best "blue steel" stare. '...and debating with him, Professor Archibald Slater of Cranleigh University, expert on early mediaeval history.' Slater sort of gurned into his camera. It struck me how much he looked like an overexcited poodle. That long snout with round horn-rimmed spectacles sitting atop, and a mane of spongy white tight permed hair. 'But first, does it really matter what colour wallpaper the Prime Minister has? Over to our Westminster correspondent outside ten Downing Street.'

The studio relaxed. A few minutes just to gather before the next live segment. Craxham and Slater had leaned into one another and seemed to be sharing a joke. That's quite some dialogue going between them, I thought. Slater broke off to look towards me. Was that a smile? He wasn't smiling with his eyes. He went back to Craxham and said something. They both laughed.

God, those lights are bright. And hot. Why did I wear a sweater? I'm perspiring like crazy.

I felt a nudge from behind.

'Do you mind if we mike you up? Oh, you are looking a bit shiny...makeup!'

I felt hands inside my sweater, pushing leads through.

'Can I take this thing off?'

'Afraid we can't do that. You've had your opening shots. Continuity and all that? We'd get murdered.'

I shut my eyes, trying to rehearse my arguments. Yes, there is a possible alternative site for the battle. Possible or probable? There are three techniques being used on the soil from the sword hilt. How much should I explain? They'll need some explanation otherwise they won't understand that the science could tell us where it was buried. How long will I have? Now when it comes to questions about repatriation of artefacts, go with the balance argument. Educational value in the host country versus rights of indigenous people.

The political piece was winding up.

'Just when we think we know everything there is to know about the most pivotal moment in English history, something new turns up. Here is a report from our Helsinki correspondent.' I heard "Roll VT" from the gallery. I could see the package on the monitors in front of us placed between the cameras. It was quite distracting seeing Slater out of the corner of my eye, his head darting around like a dog pulling at his leash. Ah, there's the shot of Isla and Mo holding up a reproduction sword hilt. Now they've cut to Aava reading her speech from a vast sheaf of notes. Oh God, Oh God, there's me...

The VT ended.

Craxham put his finger to his earpiece. 'We have some breaking news...'

The feed changed to the Helsinki correspondent, live, talking to camera, against an inky black sky over a snowy cityscape.

'This afternoon, whilst checking out this story, a source within the Helsinki police department passed me some information that casts a rather different light on things. Apparently, the sword hilt in question was retrieved in a raid on a drugs gang before being passed to the Suomi Museum. It throws into doubt its authenticity, and I suppose everything that follows on from that...'

'Professor Slater, what do you make of this?'

'Well, I have always doubted the provenance of this object. It really is quite ridiculous that an item from the Battle of Hastings could end up on an island in Finland. Now we know it was in the hands of traffickers, I suppose it all makes sense. And of course, a migrant being involved, with all the sorts of contacts he may have had, well...'

'Dr Richardson, surely you can't deny it's been trafficked? Jesus Christ, after all, it's over a thousand miles from where it should have been!' Craxham leaned back with his hands across his belly, and a self-satisfied look as though he had just made a killer statement.

'Well, there certainly was a lot of traffic running between England and the Baltic in the late Middle Ages with the Hanseatic league trade, so I suppose it could have got there on one of those ships...'

'Professor Slater?'

'I have to say that's just pie in the sky. The thing is clearly a fake anyway. People just didn't put their names on swords. It's like suggesting they sewed a label into their school jumpers!'

Craxham leaned towards me, his eyes penetrating. 'Dr Richardson, you're a bit of a fantasist, aren't you?'

I gulped. 'Well, there's the Wareham sword, which was found in a river. It has etched on its grip "Aethling...owned me" so there is a precedent for Saxon warriors to have marks of ownership on their swords...'

The title music was starting to roll. The floor manager was windmilling.

'Sorry gentlemen, we'll have to end it there. Tomorrow we'll be asking...'

Stu 18

Christine stroked my hair and kissed me on the forehead before leaving for work.

'You were brilliant. You really fought your corner.' She whispered into my ear. I tried to go back to sleep. The conversation in the green room after the show kept coming back. I couldn't shake it.

Slater and Craxham were together, each clutching a glass.

'Bad luck old chap.' Craxham said as he turned to me. 'You can't win them all. Whisky?'

'I'm sure I've met you somewhere before.' Slater was peering at me. 'Now where was it?'

I got out of bed. The rain was hitting the window. A gale was blowing in from the southwest. Aava's line at the Suomi Museum went to ansafone.

'Aava, it's Stuart Richardson here. I need your help urgently. I did a TV interview last night. If you search for Newsnight with yesterday's date you should find it. It should be self-explanatory. Ring me back when you've seen it.'

I looked again at the weather. It seemed that the only sensible thing to do was to go out into it.

I was not far from the seafront when Aava rang back. I took shelter in a doorway to take the call. Sheets of rain close to horizontal swept past.

'Stuart, can you hear me? There seems to be a lot of interference on the line.'

'It's my end, Aava. I'm outside and it's raining heavily.'

291

'Ok. Got you Stuart. Who was that man?'

'His name is Archibald Slater, and he is a popular TV presenter here.'

'Well Stuart, some of the information in the report is correct. I apologise for not warning you beforehand, but it isn't that relevant. We did receive the sword hilt from the police. They said they retrieved it from a minor drug dealer, and they were confident it hadn't been in his possession for more than an hour or two. They didn't think any crime had been committed around it. It may have been exchanged for a small supply of weed, but not enough to justify criminal proceedings. So basically, it is clean, and we have every reason to trust the story of Mohammad and Isla finding it on the island.'

'I can tell you think it all stacks up, but it's going to take something for the British media to let go of a story like that. They love a controversy.'

'I could try and get something in writing from the police here. Would that help?'

'Yes, anything Aava, anything.'

I crossed to the promenade. The waves were rolling in. Spray flew from their tops and cream coloured foam blew in light aerated chunks up the beach. Let's hope no one saw the interview, I thought. What are the viewing figures for Newsnight? And we were in the graveyard slot.

The rain was getting harder. I dashed down the steps to the entrance of Bottle Alley, a sort of tunnel under the promenade that would keep me dry for the half mile to the pier. On my left, the wall was decorated with shards of broken glass, multicoloured, the product of thousands of mid-20th century drunken evenings, now literally set in stone. To my right, apart from the regular concrete pillars, it was open to the beach. And that is where the roar of the sea came in.

Each crashing sea wave threw a sound wave, dissipating when in the open, but when trapped in the concrete space, it resonated and was changed, made square and amplified, amplified by the artifice of man the builder. With each booming detonation, the sound, somehow metalled by the walls, set vibrating the rectilinear column of air, behind me as well as in front. I chose to walk in the middle, through the puddles and scattered pebbles of the last high tide, my head raised like a cursor, tracking the centre line as defined by two diagonals, top corner to bottom corner opposite, of the square approaching in front and receding behind. I counted ten steps before the crash repeated, to be followed by the rasping sound of the draw back, shingle pulled inexorably down the beach, and then a silence. It felt like being in a kettle drum, waiting for the next fall of the beater. The regular repetition was hypnotic. The effect was to cleanse my mind, washing it with a stimulus so powerful it allowed no other thought in.

In one such silent, expectant, interval, I heard the ring of a bicycle bell behind me. Before I knew it, the cyclist was in front, hood up and pedalling hard. He let out a two-tone whistle, rising at the end. It sounded like a wolf whistle. Is that for me? No, lolloping up from behind, a black Labrador appeared, following the cyclist. How very Hastings, I thought. Not only taking your dog out for exercise on a bike, but also doing it in the dry when there is a storm raging.

I was sorry when my passage through Bottle Alley came to an end. My tinnitus, which had been masked by such high-volume sound, returned, but somehow seemed sweeter than before. It didn't feel like the bitter threat it once had been. A calmness overcame me.

The rain was abating when I set foot on the wooden boards of the pier. A prize winner of minimalist design, it was a restoration, or rather a recreation after a devastating fire ten years before. A small swelling, with a cafe inside, was all that now marked the site of the grand Victorian hall that once had dominated the seaward third. No attempt had been made to ape the glory and tainted glamour of pier life as it once had been. What had been created was a field of ghosts, fifty feet above the waves.

I read at the silvered plaques, now beginning to tarnish. *Jimi Hendrix played in this ballroom in 1967.* A very public announcement. Screwed to the railing around the edge, were much more personal announcements. *Our beloved parents John and Edna first met at a dance here in 1955 and quickstepped their way through the next fifty years together.* The nostalgia was almost too much to take.

I walked to the end. You could see the rise and fall of the swell beneath through the gaps between the planks. Beyond the end, redundant rusting support girders continued before petering out, no longer required, outside the margins of the new structure. The waves crashed around them, wobbling some. I turned and looked back to the promenade, two or three hundred yards away. At the eastward end, in the distance, the waves struck the harbour arm, launching plumes of white spray into the sky. To the west lay my route home.

My mobile chimed. A text from Amy in Oxford. *Slight hiccup Stuart. The dating won't be ready by Friday, but the location data is ready to send. You should get it tomorrow.* Oh, no. Another thing to go wrong for the news conference. It dawned on me that the chairman hadn't tried to contact me today. Maybe he's generously allowing me to rest after a late night. Or else he can't bring himself yet to address the horror of the interview.

When I returned home, soaked but refreshed, there was an envelope on the mat that had been pushed through the door. I opened it, and inside was a white card, with gold embossed lettering forming an arch at the top. *Hastings Witchery-Pokery*. Beneath, in spidery handwriting, it said:

Dear Dr Richardson, we would be honoured with your presence if you would attend a psychic reading of the newly acquired sword hilt. Please meet below the clock house in the park at 19.45.

Regards. M.W.

Stu 19

Christine had her head down. The pile of books to her left steadily diminished as the pile on her right accumulated. I had cooked her a stir-fry before she settled down to her evening's marking. I felt the card in my pocket.

'Christine, I think I'll go out for a walk. I've been in all day,' I lied.

She looked up and gave me a questioning stare. Then her gaze fell back to the exercise book before her.

I opened the door and slipped into the night. It was still damp, but the wind had dropped and the moon was up over the sea. I could make out the clock house just on the other side of the park. Its top floor was perched on the far road, like someone's chin looking over a wall. The remaining three floors dripped into the park below, now in deep shadow.

The path down was steep and from the borders rose the earthy scents of leaf decay, refreshed by the day's rain. Moon shadows cut across the way, making it difficult at times to be sure of my footing. I took care to skirt the pond at the bottom, the low metal fence being a trip hazard, and casually made my way to stand next to the masonry of the ground floor of the clock house. I looked around. This was the realm of undercover cops and drug dealers. I examined my cover story. "Oh, I'm just waiting to meet some witchy friends, officer." "Aren't you the one who came into the station to report a clown for being too noisy?"

I felt a hand gently touch my elbow.

'Dr Richardson, it's so nice you came.' The voice was silky, and comforting. Rather like a nurse preparing a patient for a difficult procedure.

'Glad to be here,' I replied, already spellbound, and feeling strangely compliant.

'We don't have to go too far, and there are two of us here to guide your way.' I couldn't see his face. His hood was drawn forward, it's opening filled with black shadow. His colleague, who was shifting slightly uneasily from foot to foot, was also dressed in a hoodie, and likewise his face was obscured.

'Now just as a routine measure, would you mind if we slipped this over your head?' He held a black cloth bag in front of my face. With not a thought to challenge the request I nodded my assent. It smelled of chalk dust, and was that a hint of snooker ball? It was quite loosely woven, and I guessed in daylight I would have been able to see through it, but at night, no hope.

'We are just going to turn you to the left, is that ok?' I felt a hand on both arms now as they manoeuvred me anticlockwise for three rotations. That'd be widdershins then, I thought. My trip to the magic exhibition in Oxford was not wasted.

We climbed up the steep path, a reassuring hand on each of my elbows, and I felt secure in their care. I guessed we had exited the park and were walking up the pavement. The street was silent, apart from the wet release of our soles on the tarmac. Across the road now. They slowed and warned me of the kerb. Up some steps and I heard a key enter a lock and turn.

'Mum, we're home.' The soft voice gently raised, directed up the hall.

I was guided into what I guessed was the front room. It had an overwhelming smell of wet dog.

'I think we can take this off now.' He lifted the bag from my head. Still hoodies up. 'We'll just go and help Mum make the tea. You'll be ok for a minute?'

I nodded. The room was lit a dull orange by a table lamp to my left, the thin filament bulb barely pushing much light through the heavy cloth of the shade with its tasselled fringe. Curled up on a sofa to my right was a vaguely familiar black Labrador, its head down resting on its paws, but its eyes were alert, watching me.

Behind me were two more chairs, like mine upright, with white antimacassars over back and arms. Opposite me was a table, and behind that a dresser, with little china ornaments lined up on its shelves. My eyes went back to the table lamp. Its ivory-coloured porcelain base took the form of a Roman urn, and just next to it stood a framed photo of a young woman. I felt sure I recognised her. Dark hair. Serious glasses. It's a younger version of Aava. She was wearing a T-shirt, and was half facing the camera, looking in holiday mode. Aava had mentioned a host family in Hastings. This must be them. What a coincidence.

The tea entered in procession form. The boys were at the rear, one holding the tray and, at the front was a rather tall elegant middle-aged lady, in a knitted pale green twin set, her spectacles with pale frames rising at the sides matched perfectly with her subtly tinted finely coiffed hair. She seemed, at first impression, as though she could have been a recently retired librarian. That was, until she opened her mouth.

'Off! Shadow! Off! Yer gurt dallop!' The dog slunk off the sofa and slipped out of the room. 'I can't abide dogs me'self. They come in all clodgy, and need cleaning up after 'em. Do you like dogs, Dr Richardson? I'm more of a cat person, me.'

She didn't wait for my reply before continuing. 'I only have it because of the boys, they insisted on having one. They're foster boys, by the way, not me own. A right couple of chop-backs, they are.'

I wasn't sure how to respond. The boys had now sat down behind me.

'I saw you looking at the picture of Aava. She's such a lovely girl. She always sends me something at Christmas. These pearls came last year.' She fingered her necklace. 'And of course, she rang me after they had found the sword hilt.'

She poured the tea into a fine white china cup and reached over to pass it to me. 'I'm sorry, how rude of me. My name is Marion. I haven't asked how you are. You must be beasted after that long journey into the shires.'

I thought, Oxfordshire? 'Er, yes, but I'm getting over it now.'

'And how be the ringing in yer 'ead?'

'I think I'm coping with it much better now.'

'I'm so sorry about that, but I think you'll admit you and your wife have been much 'appier since it started. Russell does favour the pyrotechnic when deliverin' a spell. I've told him many a time to tone it down a bit. Russell, say sorry to the gentleman. And take that silly hood off!' I turned as Russell pulled back his hood. He looked at me and meekly raised his hands to his ears, cupping them as he gave a thin smile and mouthed the word "sorry".

'And of course, you know Colin from the museum.' I turned further, and, after removing his hood, Colin glanced at me briefly, his eyes dropping. He looked a bit embarrassed.

299

'How is the museum? I haven't been able to go in there for years. All that clamouring and rattling through the glass. Those spirits really want to go home. You really oughta let 'em go, dursn't ya?' She gave me a pointed stare.

'Now I suppose we better get on with it.' She lifted two other framed photos from down by her side and arranged them next to Aava. One was of me, probably taken at the museum when I first joined. The other was of Isla and Mo. It could have been a still from the news report.

'It's better when we are peeling off the layers that we have some sort of presence from the people who have possessed it. That's why we are so grateful to have you here, as you are the most recent to own it. I'm sure you will be interested to find out who it belonged to in the first place.' She said, looking at me intently.

'Ok, let's get started.' She settled in a chair on the other side of the table, and shook her head slightly, as though concentrating, trying to focus on another place. Her left hand moved under the table, and with her eyes still closed, much to my surprise, she lifted the sword hilt onto the top.

'I…I assumed you were going to do it virtually. It is a psychic reading after all…,' I blurted out. Colin, Colin, I thought.

Marion opened her eyes. 'Oh no, that wouldn't do. How are we going to peel off the layers if it isn't here?'

She held it before her and rotated it slowly. 'It's very salty, isn't it?' she said.

I wondered whether her powers of divination extended to chemical analysis, or whether she had had a crafty lick earlier.

'It's come up rather nice, hasn't it? Considering it was in the gawm for so long. "God wins", what do you think that

300

means? We can't let it go unanswered, can we?' She flashed a smile at me.

'Now, I think you'll be easy to take off. You have a very distinct aura.' She shut her eyes and shook slightly.

'Aava will be no challenge. I know her so well.' Her forehead creased, and it was done.

'These two,' she said looking at the photo of Isla and Mo, 'I'm not so sure about. He's a poor soul, this one, isn't he?' She shut her eyes again. 'The girl has a familiar scent. Almost as though she were one of me own.' She shuddered. 'I have released it now. It's been easy so far because no one had it for long. This is where it gets harder. It was lost for a long time and went into a deep sleep. I hope you'll forgive me, but I must descend into a more intense state.'

She rested her head down next to the sword hilt and seemed to be unconscious. The dog whimpered from outside the door. Then she lifted her head suddenly.

'There is a terrible knot to unpick. I'll be jiggered if there's not a way in. It's those Baltic spirits somewhen back. They come out of that vast forest covering half of Russia. There's no stopping them. They're just out of control.' She rested her head back down. A frown came on her face and a terrible shaking. Her voice rose from a low drawl, at first indistinct, then clearer.

'Jack, Jack I knew it was you. I saw you hiding something in the sprod of that tree. The waves, then I heard you crying for me. Jack, my baby, my baby! I oughtna let you go!' She was hysterical with tears streaming down her face.

I didn't know where to look. I turned to the boys, but they were no better than me. Then, from the front door there came a loud cracking sound. At the window behind my head, an intermittent magnesium blue light cast through the thin

301

curtains to illuminate the room. From the hall there were desperate, strained shouts of "armed police!". The door to the front room flew open and two men tumbled in, helmeted and armoured and with short automatic rifles raised and roving, a torch beam from each dazzling us as it caught our eyes in turn. I and the boys raised our arms, almost reflexively. Marion was too stunned to react, half in this world, half in another.

'Stand up!' We stood. 'Turn around and keep your hands visible.' We turned. 'Hold your hands out behind you.' We were 'cuffed. I saw an officer handcuffing Marion. She didn't look as though she knew where she was.

One by one we were led outside, an officer clinging tight to each upper arm. There were police cars blocking the road on either side. I saw Christine's face through the back window of one of them, flashing blue.

'Lie face down on the road!'

I knelt down. It was hard with my arms behind my back.

'Come on! Kiss the dance floor!' An officer gave me a gentle knee in the back, and I fell forward. Next to me Marion hit the cold wet tarmac hard. Her glasses skewed off and, after an instant of recognition, I watched as her face wrinkled, crumbled and then turned to dust.

'I'm sorry Stu. What could I do? I followed you into the park, worried I was going to find you hanging from a tree. You've been so odd lately, and with the TV interview I thought you were going to do something. You never go out at night like that. When I saw them putting the bag over your head, how was I to know you weren't being kidnapped? I had to ring the police.' Christine was sobbing. I watched through the police car window as the paramedics strapped the lifeless corpse of Marion to a stretcher and carefully placed her in the back of an ambulance. They had tried resuscitating her, but I knew she was dead from the moment she hit the ground.

'Well sir, we had better get you home. You've had an eventful evening by all reports.'

Stu 20

Matt and Bianca had come down for the press conference.

'Wow, you're a fucking PR genius, Stu. Complete car crash of a TV interview, and next day you get yourself kidnapped by witches, then rescued by the SAS. If that isn't throwing a dead cat on the table, I don't know what is.'

'Shut up, Matt. Can't you see he's in a delicate state,' Christine said. I tried to smile; it came out wanly. 'Anyway, the media don't know about any of this, and the police have promised not to reveal anything yet, so keep schtum!'

They had wanted to walk with me to the museum, but I preferred to go alone. Coming round the corner it was a bit of a surprise to see half a dozen white vans parked on the gravel, their big satellite dishes aligned pointing to the sky.

The chairman was waiting in the office. 'Ah, the wanderer returns!' Seeing my expression, he lowered his tone slightly. 'Christine rang me. Said you'd been involved in a police incident. Bloody brave of you. How did you know Colin had stolen it? I always thought he was a bit of a rum chap. Shame about his mother though. I gather she had a heart attack when the police arrived. You would, wouldn't you? Shall I say a few words? He is still technically an employee after all.'

'I moved my lips, but before I could get anything out, he carried on. 'Come and meet Miss Newbiegone. She's in the hall.'

I followed him through the door to the hall that was set up for the press conference. Spotlights dazzled me.

'Hermione!' the chairman uttered in a loud whisper, but she was not to be distracted, posing for three photographers who were jockeying with one another to get the best angle. With one hand on the narrow upright presentation cabinet placed centrally in the room, she half turned to look over her shoulder into a lens. She wore a tight fitting red sequined gown with an angled black fringe that revealed her right thigh, elegantly lifted around the corner of the cabinet. The camera shutters clicked.

'Just bring your head down a bit, love. We need to get it in the shot with a close-up of the sword,' a photographer instructed.

'She's obviously a bit busy now. Let's go and sit up by the table,' the chairman said. We went up to a low dais and took our places. 'It was good of the police to return it so promptly this morning,' he continued. 'Bloody difficult setting it up in that cabinet though on my own. Ah, here she is.'

Hermione Newbiegone worked her way past the chairs along the back of the dais. As she passed, the chairman said 'Hermione, meet Dr Richardson, our curator. He's the reason we've got the sword here.'

I half rose and reached my hand out. She looked rather different to her appearances on TV, the makeup a little more subtle, but easily recognisable was her beautifully coloured mid brown hair which fell around her shoulders in cultivated curls, her trademark.

'Hello.' She gave me the briefest of smiles and took her place next to the chairman.

I turned back to the hall. The seats were starting to fill up. I spotted Christine, Matt and Bianca at the back. Behind them was a row of TV and film cameras set up on tripods. On the front two rows were seated an assortment of reporters, one or two I recognised from the news stations. Their eyes were fixed on their phone screens.

'I reckon we can kick off, don't you?' the chairman said in a low aside to me. He adjusted his microphone, cleared his throat and faced the audience.

'Thank you for coming today, to this unveiling of a truly historic relic, recently acquired by the museum.' The noise in the room quieted. 'Before we start though, I would just like us all to pause for a moment's silence, as one of our dear colleagues at the museum here lost their mother in a police operation nearby last night.' He lowered his head. I thought, why did he have to mention the police? A low murmur rippled around the hall as journalist to hungry journalist compared notes. Why hadn't they heard about it? Nothing normally slips past them.

He lifted his head again. 'I am sure Dr Richardson, our curator here, can give you more details of the significance of this find, not only to our museum, but also to the nation as a whole. Over to you Dr Richardson.'

Oh, no. Another unprepared speech on its way.

'The discovery of a Saxon sword hilt on an island in Finland seems an improbable beginning to a tale that will add such significance to the story of the Norman Conquest of England. Artefacts from that time are rare, and rarer still are any objects that can give us clues as to the true story of the Battle of Hastings. In fact, up until this point they have been virtually non-existent. Okay there has been documentary evidence, bits of writing after the event, and of course the Bayeux tapestry, but they were made at a time when there was no thought of presenting an objective truth, rather they were produced in a way to advance the interests of the writers, or the powerful men of the time who were their sponsors.' This is going rather well I thought. I hope they understand that bit.

'We received the sword hilt in an uncleaned state. That was essential to its usefulness. Each layer of dirt contains traces of the place in which it had lain. The top layer will be Finnish. Our hope is that the deeper layers will reveal where the object was deposited after it had been lost in battle. This sophisticated analysis has been performed at a laboratory in Oxford, where the dirt has been compared to two locales in this area. The first is the traditional site for the battle at Senlac Hill, immediately by the place where Battle Abbey was founded. The second is in the Brede valley, a few miles from the Abbey, but presenting a more credible geographical location for the battle to have occurred there. None of us in this room know the answer yet. So over to Miss Newbiegone to reveal the result.'

The chairman scrabbled around the table in front of him and passed an envelope to Hermione. She stood slowly, accompanied by the synthesised shutter flap sound of multiple cameras. A smile to one side then a smile to the other. She received the proffered letter opener from the chairman and slipped it into the envelope. Out came a sheaf of papers. Her face dropped for a microsecond, then the professional smile was regained. She flipped through the pages, working towards the back. 'One moment please.' She turned and leant towards the chairman, shooting him a piercing look.

'Hang on a second, Hermione. I'll just find the relevant bit.' The chairman also flicked through the pages, then pointed to the final paragraph and handed it back to her. 'Why didn't you just put the answer on a card in an envelope,' he whispered out of the corner of his mouth to me while still looking forward.

'Because I was being kidnapped, and Colin is in police custody, that's why,' I answered, similarly sideways.

'And the winner is…' Hermione, regaining her composure, and, flashing a smile at the audience, read from the page held high in front of her. '… with an amalgamated weighting… and P point zero one… two standard deviations from the mean… with 52%... it is… the Brede valley!'

Someone clapped at the back, slowly and deliberately. Thank you, Matt. I joined in with a little more verve and soon it took off round the room. I feared they didn't really know what they were applauding, but did that matter?

'I think we can take a few questions now.' The chairman said to the audience. A reporter on the front row put her hand up.

'If it's 52% Brede, does that mean it's 48% Senlac?'

'Not necessarily. It's not a zero-sum equation. Next, you over there.' The chairman pointed.

'Will you have to give it back if it's proven to be stolen property?'

'The Finnish police have reassured us that it isn't stolen property, despite it being retrieved during a police raid.'

'When will you return all the other stolen property in your museum?'

'We have documents proving the provenance of every artefact we have in the museum. I think that's a debate for another time.'

'When are we going to see the refugee who found it. Is he in the country?'

'I believe a visa application has been lodged with the Home Office. They have said it will be processed in the normal way.' Out of the side of his mouth, directed to me, sotto voce. 'In that case probably never.'

It was a masterly performance by the chairman. We lined up. He and Hermione on one side, and myself on the other, the sword hilt in the middle, as the photographers took their final photos.

Stu 21

A cold northerly wind blew up from the valley. The sun lit the few remaining red and gold five-fingered leaves, survivors of a gale, still clinging to the lower limbs of the maple tree in the churchyard. The coarse stones of the church seemed hyper-defined in the low November light, alternating dark shadow with bright peaks on the vertical surface. I looked up to the clock. Its black hands indicated two minutes to eleven. A point in time, drawn forever forwards. The time behind accumulates while the time ahead diminishes.

I had driven to the airport to pick up Aava. With her was Isla. Her first trip to England. She was weeping in the car.

'It's just not fair. Why couldn't Mo come? He was the one who found it.'

Aava wrapped an arm round to comfort her. 'I'm sure he will make it in due course. All he needs is his visa approval. It can't be too complicated.'

I had enjoyed showing them around the museum. Aava, with her stern gaze, inspected the cabinets with their diverse exhibits. Then we came to the sword hilt, in its own special place, lit from above by an array of concealed LEDs.

'Wow, I never thought it would look like that,' Isla exclaimed. 'You've polished the metal, and the stone is so red and shiny now.'

It really did look a picture. The poster boy that I hoped would bring hordes of visitors to the museum.

*

We shivered as the hearse drew up. Christine, tall and elegant in black to my left and on my right, in their Finnish winter coats, stood Aava and Isla. Behind the hearse a police van opened its doors, and out stepped a custody officer, closely followed by Russell, attached wrist and ankle by a chain. Colin followed, himself linked to another officer. They blinked in the bright light. I could see they weren't property clothed for the cold weather.

A single bell tolled from the church tower as the pallbearers, in their black frock coats, eased the wicker coffin from the rear of the hearse. Balancing it on their shoulders, they carried it the few steps to the lych gate to rest for a minute under the simple pitched roof. Then they hoisted it up again, and with a steady rhythm, swinging slightly from side to side, they picked a route through the gravestones to a freshly dug spot at the outer reaches of the churchyard overlooking the valley. We followed, serenaded by the clink of chain from Russell and Colin. No church service, they had instructed the vicar. She wouldn't have liked that. Not her style at all.

Green cloth covered the sides of the grave. We stood back as Marion was slowly lowered into the ground. I looked over to the far side of the valley. A multitude of crows took to the air from the newly skeletal trees, a swirling mass of black dots rising into the sky.

Isla was weeping again next to Aava. Aava squeezed her hand.

'She would have loved to have met you. You would have been very special to her. I think you have a very important connection.'

311

My mind drifted as we stood in silence. Amy had rung earlier to tell me the dating had come through. The optical luminescence for the Finnish layer had confirmed a date for deposition of between 1450 and 1500. The analysis of the deeper layers was less clearcut. It was a blurry reading she had said, but it couldn't be ruled out that it had been first buried in the 11th century. But 1450 to 1500. That was quite something. My theory, developed on the hoof under pressure from Archibald Slater that night in the TV studio, that it had been taken to the Baltic on a Hanseatic trading ship, now had some credence. I recollected our conversation in the green room...

'... I know, I recognise you now. You were that postgrad I viva'd some years ago, weren't you? Pretty flimsy thesis. I remember thinking then you were the sort that, if the evidence didn't quite stack up, you'd make up some sort of story to fill in the gaps.'

Well Professor Slater, maybe I am. But isn't that history?

Epilogue

The dinghy took a wide turn at the buoy and released its spinnaker. The sail flapped for a moment and then billowed as the wind caught it, accelerating the boat on its new course. The round shape made me think of how Christine's belly will swell in the coming months, propelling us towards a new future. She had been so happy at the ultrasound, clutching my hand and beaming with anticipation at the announcement that we were expecting a boy.

I put the binoculars down and settled back at my desk by the window that looked over the sea. The museum had been generous with time off, time to recover, time to try to make sense of the events surrounding the discovery and presentation of the sword hilt. Much to the chairman's delight, the media attention had led to an increase in footfall, but this was now beginning to tail off. Sales of metal detectors in the area had rocketed as ambitious treasure hunters took to the hills, hoping to discover the true site of the battle of Hastings. The countryside buzzed.

The police inspector had seemed disappointed when I declined to press charges for kidnap. He had difficulty understanding that I was willing to have a bag put over my head and be led by two men whose identity at that time I did not know. How could I explain that a clown at the parade had cast a spell on me as instructed by a witch born in the Middle Ages? The clown Russell had been released, but Colin could not escape the theft of the sword hilt from the museum safe. He was placed on bail to be in court at a later date.

The image of Marion's dying face haunted my sleepless nights. Had I really seen it in Oxford in John Dee's scrying mirror days before her actual death? I lost confidence in my memory. I felt certain I had seen it, but then, if I had, wasn't I subscribing to the irrationality of a magical world? The circularity was tantalising, and not in a good way. It felt like torture. And then there was her reference to Jack, her baby, the earliest possessor of the hilt, before we were interrupted by the police. Could it be he was the clue to its discovery in the Baltic? From her statement it would seem he had run away with it.

After the funeral, I sat opposite Aava at a cafe near the cemetery. Christine chatted to Isla next to us. I was desperate for Aava to give me some insight into the events of the evening at Marion's house. We sat in silence for a minute. Then I recounted how I had been taken there and Marion's psychic analysis of the sword hilt. Aava listened, showing no expression. Her eyes blinked through her heavy framed glasses.

'You don't seem surprised, Aava,' I said.

'It sounds exactly like the sort of thing that Marion would do.'

'So, you knew she was involved in witchcraft?'

'Yes. She told me she was over five hundred years old.'

'What do you think about her saying that Jack was her baby? You told me at the museum in Helsinki she was childless.'

'Well, maybe she had to give him away. She told me her husband died when she was very young, and it couldn't have been easy to manage. It may not have been uncommon for neighbours who had lost children themselves to look after the young of single mothers. It's quite possible she maintained some sort of relationship with him as, from what you have told me, she knew he had gone away.'

My head was spinning. Was I really talking about an eyewitness recollection of something that occurred centuries ago, with a seemingly very rational fellow museum curator?

'I'm confused, Aava. Do you really believe all that Marion said?'

'In Finland, almost all the country is forest, and for six months of the year it is dark. You don't have to go far before you have lost contact with the modern world. Even the sanest person must accommodate the forces to which one is subject when separated from those comforts. It's not difficult to appreciate the spirit world and lead a rational academic life as well.'

Christine interrupted. 'Hey, you two. Isla just told me she's part English!'

'Well, only 1% on DNA testing,' Isla interjected. She looked at Aava. 'We were hoping to come here to get a DNA sample from Marion to see if it matched, but it was too late.' Her voice tailed off, her expression dropping.

I looked at Aava, questioningly. She realised this needed some explanation.

'If Jack had taken the sword to Finland, and had been shipwrecked, he may have survived, and his genes could have entered the local population. It's not impossible that Isla is descended from him. Given the small amount of English DNA in Isla it must have been a long time ago, and there wasn't a lot of traffic at that time between England and Helsinki. Tallinn across the gulf was the major centre then, when it was known as Reval. It would have taken a storm to bring them to Finland.'

315

Jack's story was taking shape in my mind. The elements began to slot together.

Isla and Aava had a flight back to Finland that evening. On the journey to the airport, we talked about Mo. His status was now assured, and Isla was looking forward to seeing him again.

'Of course, he wasn't really interested in the sword hilt,' Aava said. 'He had far more important things to worry about.'

I sat looking out of the window, waiting for inspiration. The dinghy race was coming to a close. I had to write something that would make a mark. Something to answer the critics who thought it impossible that a relic from the Battle of Hastings could have been discovered on an island over a thousand miles away. Unbeknownst to me, on that very morning, and at that time, the low drone sounding in the headphones of a sole metal detectorist, sweeping the green turf of a hillside not so far away, took off from a steady irritation to a high-pitched unbearable screech.

The opening sentence came to me.

"A rope tightened and then creaked as the breeze filled the sail."

Mark Freeman studied at Cambridge and Oxford Universities. He has recently completed a career as a GP in St Leonards-on-Sea. When not carving words, he can be found carving wood. Visit him at his Facebook page "Mark Freeman woodcarving".

Next from Mark Freeman on Wordcarving books

2069

A dystopian future fiction novel

Harriet, a young female doctor navigates the ethical challenges in a world of government led euthanasia programmes and genetic engineering for enhancement in an economically and biologically divided society. She flits between the underclass, populated by the generationally poor plus the scarred victims of biomechanical misadventure (her mother is one), and the super-rich with their ambition to leave the planet.

The squirrel lifted its paws and looked back at Jemima Burns through the window. She called him Arthur. He was on his circuit of branch, fence top, then washing line. She had a particularly good view now then leaves had fallen. His paws gripped the branch of the silver birch again, and he was off.

Arthur. So nice to see him again. How long is it now since he passed away? Must be ten years at least.

'Can I take the tray away now, Mima?' Roni nudged her on the shoulder. She looked at what was left of her lunch. Quite a lot really. The gravy looked lumpy, and the custard was cold, so she didn't want to have another go at it.

'We can save it for later if you like?' Roni. Such a nice young man. Very kind and gentle. You wouldn't think he had travelled round half the world to come and work here.

'When I get back, we can watch the film together.' Oh, that sounds good. I've got a date for the cinema. Haven't been to one of those for a very long time.

Roni rolled the screen over the sticky carpet, so it stood just in front of Jemima's chair. It was almost as big as a cinema screen to her.

'What's the film today, Roni?'

'It's called "The ultimate retirement package." We watched it last month if you remember.' Jemima didn't, but she was interested in who might be in it.

The Department of Health and Age Management, or HAM for short, had issued an instruction to all residential homes earlier that year to show the film to each resident on a monthly basis. They check the returns carefully, so Roni reminded himself to take an image of Jemima in front of the screen to send in.

'Oh, I like him. He does the afternoon quiz show. Do you like him, Roni?' The opening titles were rolling. Roni was looking intently at another resident across the lounge who looked as though she might topple out of her chair.

We're going to show you, the emphasis was on the last word, *how you can increase your wealth, and help society at the same time.* The part time quiz show host was pointing directly at the camera.

'He's got such a lovely smile. You could almost believe every word he is saying.'

The film went to a washed-out sepia colour. A man was on the floor of his house clutching his chest and rolled over and vomited.

Do you want to die alone? In pain? With nobody's hand to hold.

Jemima's bony fingers wrapped tightly around two fingers of Roni's left hand. The film changed to a shot of a graveyard, pallbearers carrying a coffin, a single mourner at a graveside.

And be put in the ground, with no one to grieve for you? That's wrong, there was one person, she thought.

Well with the ultimate retirement package, you can have a fun wake before you pass away. Why let all the others have a great time? The screen filled with colour. Balloons hung from the ceiling of what looked like a posh cafe. Young people were milling about excitedly, and in the centre of a low stage there was a man, beaming from ear to ear as his children and grandchildren came and hugged, and others were standing in line to put their arms around him. Champagne was flowing and there was a large celebration cake in pride of place on a table. *Feel right at the heart of your family, on such a momentous occasion.*

'They really look as though they're having fun, Roni.' The party was rocking now with the kids on the dance floor. Then the music quieted. The crowd looked up to a big screen suspended above the stage. It showed an ECG trace, a deep bass tone beating initially regularly, then wobblingly irregular, then it recovered slightly, and then it went to a flat line, with a piercing monotone.

Good-bye gramps! Someone shouts from the dance floor. *For he's a jolly good fellow! For he's a jolly good fellow!* The song takes hold. Then, with a chorus of *Ker-ching* sounds, red, blue and yellow lights flash at the hips of the onlooking family members, through their party outfits. An excited buzz rises again in the room.

'I remember when we had coins that could actually make that noise.' said Jemima. Roni was looking out of the window.

The quiz show man was looking serious. *If you sign up for the ultimate retirement package, your family benefits, society benefits, and for the next three months only, the Department of Health and Age Management will throw in an extra 25% on top of your legacy. That's an extra quarter on top of your saved capital. Think what that could do for your family.* His face lit up again. *But hurry, the offer ends first of April. Stop burning money like there's no tomorrow. Make your family proud of you. Attend your own funeral. Don't miss the fun. Do it the modern way!*

Roni's attention was back in the room. 'What did you think of that, Mima?'

3

'Well, there seemed to be one or two things he got wrong.' She considered. 'But the man's family seemed pleased.'

'You have a think about it, Mima, and let me know. The annex is only next door.'

Jemima's friend Miriam had gone to the annex the previous month. She had said "it's only like eating jelly for pudding." But of course, she hadn't been back to tell her what it was really like. It did look like a good party though. And Alex and his husband David would probably be able to build that extension they've been talking about. I don't know where we would get all the party goers though. She looked around the lounge. Miriam didn't want a big fuss, but I quite like the idea of the party. Celebrating my life and all that. I suppose the staff would come.

'You can have a chat with nice Dr Harriet next time she comes.' Roni added. 'I know you like her.'

2

Dr Harriet Sparkes was looking at her feet. The floor was just starting to move. Clouds of yellow, green and red blew around beneath her, and then started to coalesce, picking up the rhythm of the pounding beat as bright pulses, defined shapes, gathered then dispersed. She could see her friend Claudia's toes poking through her gold lace ups, and Gina's were encased in multicoloured shroom leather. All six feet were taking small, synchronised steps. Harriet felt the floor respond, a perfect response in timing and intensity, nurturing the rhythm, resisting when necessary, giving when needed. It made her feel like the best dancer in the world.

Harriet tilted her head back. The sound was rising up to the vaulted ceiling, filling the air gaps between the buttresses, their stones reflecting back the colours sent up from the floor. Whoever the genius was who thought of buying up the nation's churches as JelliShake venues, well, they must have made a lot of money for their corporation, she thought. This is just brilliant. Silent for so long, and now filled with sound again. Not very monastic though.

Saturday night was the one opportunity to see her friends. They had grown up together in the village, but Claudia and Gina were pretty well confined to screens all the week. She was lucky as a doctor. She had the freedom of a gubernator to take her to patients if they needed face to face. She needed the "Goobie" more often than you might think.

The pace of the music was picking up, accelerating, rising in pitch and then stopped suddenly. The girls looked at each other, faces excited in anticipation, knowing what was about to happen. A big bass drop, and they started moving again to the new rhythm. She breathed in the scent of sweat and perfume and felt herself moving as one with the mass of bodies, bathing in the pond of primitivism.

Another bass drop, the music was getting louder, the colours more intense. Impulses from the floor led her feet, rippling from side to side with a low vibration almost barely perceptible at first, then sending waves up her legs. Her friends' faces flashed in front of her, lit from below, their ecstatic grins building. The frequency of the vibration rose. Gina was the first to go, her eyes shut, as trillions of her cultivated microbe gut lodgers released their load, each one measured in picograms, but collectively a substantial dose carried from abdomen to brain, a massive endorphin rush.

Her head down, her hair swept from side to side. Harriet watched as Claudia went next, and then she gave in herself, the frequency now matching perfectly the trigger for her biome's release.

Bodies were scattered over the floor, some sitting stunned, others curled up, yet more just lying watching the lights play on the ceiling. JelliShake gave way to JelliRoll, the floor moving up and down in low waves as chill out music played. A collective calm settled in the church.

Printed in Great Britain
by Amazon

84507871R00192